THE
ARTSTARS

BLUE LIGHT BOOKS

ANNE ELLIOTT

THE
ARTSTARS

STORIES

INDIANA UNIVERSITY PRESS
INDIANA REVIEW

BLUE LIGHT BOOKS

This book is a publication of

Indiana University Press
Office of Scholarly Publishing
Herman B Wells Library 350
1320 East 10th Street
Bloomington, Indiana 47405 USA

iupress.indiana.edu

Indiana Review

© 2019 by Anne Elliott

Manufactured in the United States of America

Cataloging information is available from the
Library of Congress.

ISBN 978-0-253-04436-5 (paperback)
ISBN 978-0-253-04437-2 (ebook)

1 2 3 4 5   24 23 22 21 20 19

Versions of these stories have been published
in the following journals: "Light Streaming
from a Horse's Ass" in *Fifth Wednesday
Journal*, "Three Lessons in Firesurfing" and
"Aquaria" in *Hobart*, "War" in *FRiGG*, "Pink"
in *Witness*, and "The Beginning of the End of
the Beginning" as a Ploughshares Solo.

Selection from "A Dark Summer Day" by
Denise Levertov, from *Collected Poems of
Denise Levertov*, copyright ©2013 by Denise
Levertov and the Estate of Denise Levertov
reprinted by permission of New Directions
Publishing Corp.

Selection from *The Triggering Town: Lectures
and Essays on Poetry and Writing* by Richard
Hugo, copyright ©1979 reprinted by permission of W. W. Norton & Company, Inc.

For Leslie:
artist, wild child, mama bird, angel

I want some funny jazz band
            to wake me,
tell me life's been dreaming me.
I want something like love, but made
            all of string or pebbles,
            oboe of torn air
to tear me to my senses.

   Denise Levertov, "A Dark Summer Day"

All art is failure.

   Richard Hugo, "Statements of Faith"

The most complicated and difficult part
of it was only just beginning.

   Anton Chekhov, "The Lady with the Dog"
   Constance Garnett, translator

CONTENTS

ACKNOWLEDGMENTS

I'VE BEEN A WORKSHOP-ADDICTED EMERGING FICTION WRITER FOR about twenty-five years, so the helpers are too numerous to name. I'll stick to mentioning those who touched the stories in this collection.

The institutions: Virginia Center for the Creative Arts (where the tea is indeed refreshing); Vermont Studio Center; Zoetrope Virtual Studio; Drunken! Careening! Writers!; 92nd Street Y; the Center for Fiction; Tin House Workshops; Table 4 Writer's Foundation. Thanks for the support of time, quiet, funding, wisdom, and community.

The editors: Vern Miller at *Fifth Wednesday Journal*, Aaron Burch at *Hobart*, Ellen Parker at *FRiGG*, David Michael Armstrong at *Witness*, and Ladette Randolph at *Ploughshares*. Thanks for giving these stories their first audience and helping me make them better. And to Essence London at *Indiana Review* and Ashley Runyon at Indiana University Press—thanks for taking on this collection with encouraging enthusiasm. You have made the debut process fun.

The early critical readers and angels, professional and otherwise: Virginia Vitzthum, Maria Luisa Tucker, Janice Erlbaum, Cheryl Burke (damn, I miss you, girl), Emilie McDonald, Kelli Dunham, Gennette Zimmer Detwiler, Clem Paulsen, Sonia Pilcer, Kathleen Warnock, Gloria Holwerda-Williams, Marina Zaytsev, Lisa Light, Kerry D'Agostino, and my many awesome Zoetrope friends and reviewers. Thanks for reading so carefully.

The family: My late mom, Jane Elliott, who always encouraged me to be an artist but also learn a trade. (Who knew it would become a theme?) Jim Elliott

and Anne Avery; Tom, Melanie, and MJ Elliott; all the Barrs and Averys—
your unconditional love is palpable and keeps me going. My sweetheart, James
Barr—thanks for the patience, love, and silliness and for putting up with my
mess. Keep rocking out in the basement.

Most of all, thanks to the beautiful, complicated, doggedly productive artists in my life who inspire these characters. I hope you see this collection as my
love letter to you and your work. The world may not know you, but you are true
stars to me.

THE
ARTSTARS

Light Streaming from a Horse's Ass

THE FIRST TIME YOU SEE THE HORSE IS IN THE PARKING LOT. HE'S propped on his side in the back of a pickup. He looks so real you wonder if there is a taxidermist in your building, because it wouldn't surprise you. It really wouldn't, since under you lives a trapeze artist with practice gear rigged to her ceiling—your floor—and to the east of you is a bunch of guys who spin metal cones all day, and above you is a man who photographs lightning hitting skyscrapers across the river, then sells the prints to the buildings themselves. So many odd businesses here at 1205 Manhattan Avenue—the crossroads, where Brooklyn brushes up to Queens, where Newtown Creek flushes into the East River—that stuffing dead horses seems almost normal.

You have no money. You have no heat. This is normal too.

In the downstairs hallway are mail receptacles, no two alike. A bushel basket. A cutoff spackle bucket. A galvanized country mailbox, with red flip flag, bolted to the wall. Yours is a metal salad bowl with your name painted in glittery enamel: *Maddie Tucker, Inc.* The *Inc.* was an afterthought. Everyone has it. But the mail itself, which you sort communally, betrays the truth: you live here. It's not legal. Mastercard bills, lingerie catalogs, voter materials, student loan statements: the kind of mail you hope the fire inspector won't see.

You have drills, too, you and the guy next door, who you sublet from. He's a performance artist. Trustafarian. He subdivided his space and rents out the half with no heat. He refused to sign the sublease unless you were prepared to *go into hiding*. But you like this idea, the cloak and dagger of it, keep your underwear in a locking file cabinet and your jeans in a custom closet on wheels that spins around and looks just like an art crate. And the ladder to your bed loft retracts

1

on a pulley, and a board slides over the sink to cover the dirty dishes. In thirty seconds—you've timed it—your space looks perfectly industrial.

You're a photographer, for now anyway. You studied it in school, even won an award. Not that the award helps pay the bills. So you photograph actors. You find it amusing. They are plentiful. They are easy. Just ask two questions, and they'll talk about themselves for an hour. You meet them in Central Park, place them in the dappled glow under a tree, just enough sun to lighten their eyes and give a sparkle to their dental work. Have them smile at that dog over there. On rainy days, it's even easier: you take the train to their crappy apartment in Astoria or Hell's Kitchen. Clamp full-spectrum floodlights to the Ikea bookshelf or the shower curtain rod. Encourage them to talk. To laugh about evil casting directors and being too old for their current pictures. Stacks of their previous headshots sit on the desk, ready to toss. You feel sorry for them. They can't afford this picture any more than you can afford not to take it.

It's three hundred bucks for a bunch of proofs and two master prints. Two photo sessions a week, three if you're on a roll, some seasons drier than others, like now, in the weeks before Christmas, when actors spend their money on parties and presents. Rent is two weeks late. You can afford to say no to nothing. And so you're at the tiny Queens apartment of your last client of the year—late twenties, male, blond hair, Dudley Do-Right look—seventeen degrees outside, so Central Park is impossible—taking his photo in front of a dirty kitchen window (nice light, thanks to the dirt), and he sees you take an unintentional glance at the fruitcake on the table right as your stomach lets rip an enormous empty rumble. The actor, who you've already mentally nicknamed Dudley, does something no actor has ever done before:

"I know it's none of my business, but are you OK?"

His concern, straight through the lens, bounces off the mirror, to your right eye. You click the shutter. That will be a good one—a little mystery, casting directors love mystery—and Dudley's hand reaches into the rectangle and lowers your camera to the table. "Hey, Maddie. I asked you a question."

You sink onto the kitchen chair, and it explodes from your mouth in a blur: you've eaten nothing but rice for four days, rice with sugar that is, because you have no heat and the sugar wards off hypothermia, and you cook it on a hot plate standing next to a space heater with gloves and a hat on; you are out of photo paper, and you have no idea how you will get his headshot printed, maybe borrow from your upstairs neighbor the lightning guy; and your family expects you for Christmas, but you have nothing but homemade presents, which are, frankly, getting old. Dudley, he listens. Then he releases a slow laugh as he stands up, walks over to the fridge, pulls out a Swiss Colony gift pack with Tillamook

The Artstars

cheddar, summer sausage, water crackers. Then a Harry and David gift pack with individually wrapped pears. A bottle of white wine, half-finished. An entire roasted chicken, untouched. Finally, two melamine dinner plates. "Dig in."

You're speechless. He laughs again, and you notice his canine teeth are pointy in a beautiful, very un-Dudley way, and he takes the camera from your hands, then hands you a knife and fork. You have no choice.

You find yourself laughing with your mouth full, and the wine goes to your head. Dudley asks questions, a lot of them. What is your real work like? What is your favorite photo subject? What do you love about portraiture? What do you dream about at night?

"I've been dreaming of horses, lately," you say.

"A horse, what does that represent?"

"Are you a psychologist?"

"If you were an animal, would you be a horse?"

"Maybe. What about you?"

"An eagle. I wish I could fly. What do you wish for?"

"I don't wish."

"No, I don't imagine you do." He reaches across the table and wipes a cracker crumb from your cheek. "Maybe you should."

You go home with a full belly, two rolls of Dudley, and a fifty-dollar advance to pay for paper. And a whole fruitcake, which the actor was going to throw out anyway. It is dark. And there he is, the horse, standing on the loading dock like he's waiting for you. His black mane flows over one eye, catching the gold glow of the streetlight. He's wearing a halter, too, as if he could spring into life and walk wherever you lead. You scramble onto the concrete dock to get a closer look. You're alone with the horse. You pet his nose. The fur feels real, and it is real, stretched over something rigid and dead. Poor guy. You pet his cold neck, look into his enormous chestnut-glass eye, then work your way toward his tail. Strange. The tail is gone—only a hole where it used to be, a hole into a dark void.

You only have one roll of film left, but this cannot be ignored. You drop your backpack, shield your camera with your body. Reload as fast as you can—damn, glove lint getting inside—try to blow it out. You start shooting the horse's face, out of habit, hold up your white hat to reflect streetlight into the glass eye. The wind catches his mane and your hair, icy and damp, straight to your skull. You put the hat back on, get your footing on the concrete ledge, then begin reframing intimate bits of the horse: artificial teeth around a dewy plastic tongue, the triangle of negative space under the neck, the oddly incomplete rump.

A clang behind you makes you jump. The roller door rises, then fluorescent light blasts from the loading bay onto you and your horse, and a man's figure emerges in silhouette. He has a long graying beard and a pointy knit hat. You recognize him—from the parking lot, the street, the hallway, the freight elevator. "Hey," you say.

"You like my pet?" The man steps onto the dock and pats the beast on the shoulder.

"I do. Are you a taxidermist?"

"No, no. I wish." You think of Dudley: *What do you wish for?* "I build stage sets. Out in Jersey. My shop was throwing him out because he's busted." In the new light, you can see what he means. Parts of the fur are worn away, bald spots over some kind of plastic.

"His tail is missing."

"Yeah, but I love him just the same." He strokes the mane, around the eye, cocking his head at his beloved. "I wish my wife felt the same way. I brought this guy upstairs, and the dog wouldn't stop barking at him. Then my wife said she was creeped out and told me to get rid of him. I've been carting him around in my truck, but they said it's going to snow tonight. I guess I'll just leave him in here." He indicates the half-empty loading bay, a shared space, hardly secure. "Hey, you wanna see something cool?"

"Sure." You wonder what could be cooler than this.

He takes a Maglite from his belt and shines it right into one of the glass eyes. "Go look in his butt. In the hole. Go look."

You obey—put your eye right up to where the tail should be, like a viewfinder. And the amber glow from the glass eye fills the pale inside; you can see everything in negative, the yellow fiberglass cave of his neck, the four dark tunnels where legs begin, the muscular shoulders, the gently curved back. The world inside a horse's skin. "Wow." You look for a full minute, then back away. The man is beaming, proud of his discovery.

"Hey, maybe you could help me move him in."

"No problem." You grab hold of the angled back legs, then have a thought. "Hey, aren't you worried about leaving him in here? He'll get paint on him or something."

"You have a better idea?"

So this is how you take in a boarder who happens to be a dead horse. You leave him in the big empty part of your space, next to the windows. You let him face out, give his glass eyes a view of the United Nations and Empire State. You flop onto the ratty sofa and just look at the horse looking out the window. He seems happy.

You go into your darkroom and seal the door shut, then load the two rolls of Dudley into a canister. You turn the light back on and stick a thermometer into the chemicals. No need to worry about overdeveloping—you can see your breath. Start the timer, agitate the tank, agitate your body to keep warm. You hold the wet negatives up to the light. Dudley's face is dark, his teeth darker, the shadows of his hair bright and curly. You give in to the shivering, finally, hang the strips to dry, and crawl up the ladder into bed.

Sleeping is the one easy thing to do in an unheated industrial space. You've invested in an electric mattress pad, extra toasty near the toes. Two comforters—one down, one acrylic—plus your hat, and remarkably, breathing the cool air is refreshing. Like camping.

You wake to the sound of the metal spinners to the east, whirring machinery, Spanish voices. You sit up and plug in the extension cord near your head. It's connected to the space heater and coffee machine down in the kitchen area. Last winter you were not smart enough to think of this trick. You've learned. You lie and wait, tuck the comforters around your chin, try to muster the courage to get up.

The coffee maker groans its last groan, and you're out of excuses. Under the covers, you put on three pairs of socks, two pairs of long johns, army pants, a tank tee, a crew neck tee, a long-sleeved thermal, two sweaters, and fingerless gloves. You adjust your hat, turn off the electric mattress pad, and climb down the ladder.

The horse is still looking out the window, where you left him. The morning sun has entered his eyes and mouth now, and his whole body is glowing through the bald patches. The hole where his tail should be is beaming, too, like a lamp. You pad over to him, stroke his mane. "Good morning, Sunshine." He doesn't answer, but you expected this. Outside, snow has drifted against the windows in gentle vales. The sky is clear.

You have a few exposures left in your camera from last night. You start from across the room, on a tripod, to capture the beam of light shooting from his butt into the dusty air, the crisp shadows of his body on the plank floor. A few more portraits of his face, which seems to be smiling as he looks out at the snow. Then, you turn his body slightly and aim the lens right in the tail hole. Inside, the valley of his neck looks like drifted snow. You click the shutter. It is your last frame. You pull the camera off the tripod and rewind.

You need more film. And paper too—you have a paying job to complete. You hear music through the ceiling: Coltrane. Fritz, the lightning guy, is awake. You decide, instead of schlepping into Manhattan, to try to convince him to sell you some supplies.

Fritz is one resident who does not even try to hide it. He lets you into his lair: green shag carpet, bright, like unclipped grass. He is barefoot, enjoying the heat from his illegal wood-burning stove.

"Maddie Muffin!" He kisses both of your cheeks. "I'm making Turkish coffee. You're in time." He stands next to his hot plate, watching the little spouted saucepan, waiting for it to boil. His lop-eared rabbit hops over and sniffs your woolly socks. You reach down to pet its impossibly soft fur. The other rabbit crouches timidly next to a beanbag chair. You sit on a stool and look at Fritz's work on the walls, hanging from metal clips, curly fiber paper. On one wall hangs his real work: small prints, bright, saturated colors, of the inside of arcade machines, filled with stuffed animals. Neon yellow Winnie the Poohs and purple Barneys invite you to dive in. One stuffed rabbit hangs by the metal claw, a squished trophy. On the opposite wall are the money shots: huge, black-and-white, clean, pearly prints, with good, glowing grays: fleshy storm clouds and the bright surprise of jagged lightning into the Chrysler Building, the Empire State—popping white ejaculate from the towers, shooting into the sky.

"Fritz, I've said this before, but you have really got the hang of these big prints. You need to show me your technique."

"So let's do it! I've been waiting! Come up. We'll have a printing party." Fritz has a very equipped darkroom. It's tempting.

"Hmm, I don't have the right negative." It's a big deal, making big prints. It had better be worth it.

"I don't believe you. Bring them up to me! I will pick one." His bushy gray hair is uncombed, beard coming in. Thick horn-rimmed glasses over blue eyes. He smiles big, showing the spaces on the side where he's had extractions. He's wearing nothing but cowboy pajama bottoms and a giant black T-shirt over his skinny frame. You can't see your breath at all. It's a different world up here.

"No, thanks. I'm waiting for the big one. The dream negative."

"Your earthquake. The Big One." The coffee is ready. He brings you a demitasse. It's bitter.

You swallow. "God, Fritz, it's been forever since I shot anything worth printing. I think I did my best work when I was twenty. Who wants to peak at twenty?"

"How old are you now?"

"Twenty-five."

Fritz just laughs, as if this explains everything. You remove your gloves and hat, drop them on the floor for the rabbit to sniff. It's feverish in here, under your layers. The other rabbit, the timid one, grows bolder, tiptoeing away from the beanbag chair, past a yellow mushroom-shaped table, toward Fritz at the counter. Then three tiny rabbits follow, hopping through the green grass carpet.

"Fritz, what the hell?"

"Oh yes. We had an accident. I thought this one was a boy." He picks up the mother rabbit, scratches her ears. "Then, I thought he was getting fat."

"You can stop calling him *he* now."

"I know." He holds the rabbit prone, nuzzles his face in her belly. "Little Victor, you are the problem."

"What are you going to do?" You count six rabbits, the parents and four offspring. All the babies are pale brown, like their daddy.

"I don't know. Get them splayed?" The she-rabbit has gone limp in his hands, adoring the attention.

"*Spayed.*" The baby rabbits hop in line, so perfect, with snow outside, and Turkish coffee, and Coltrane, and plush carpet, a cozy chaos. You are dying to photograph it all. You have your camera over your shoulder, but no film. "Fritz, I'm in a jam. Can I buy some supplies off you?"

"What you need?" He opens his fridge, which is full of food on the top half—milk, eggs, vegetables—and photo supplies on the bottom half. You're tempted to just ask for the eggs, skip the middleman.

"Black and white, thirty-five. And some paper. For a job."

"I'll throw in a baby rabbit." He pulls out two boxes of paper and half a dozen rolls of film. Then a bag of carrots, with bushy tops.

"My place is too cold for rabbits."

"They make a delicious stew. Don't you, little Victor?" Fritz nudges the mother with his toes as he begins chopping the carrots and tossing them into a Crock-Pot. You load a roll into your hungry camera, lie on the soft floor, and try to get one of the babies to approach the lens. "Here, they like these." He hands you a carrot top. You reach out and tease the baby with the greens. It wiggles its tiny nose, then sits up to nibble, floppy ears all over the place. The father rabbit grabs a piece. You focus, click.

"What's this job you're printing?" Fritz asks. He's chopping potatoes now with a giant knife. You roll on your back to frame him, his blade in the air, catching sunlight.

"Actor headshot. Some guy."

"He is cute?"

"They all are. It's their job to be cute."

"I would hate to be an actor. I hate actors."

"Hey, what are you making?"

"Stone soup." He tosses a piece of celery to Victor, his apparent favorite. "Come by tonight if you want some."

When you've got a good negative, you always know the second you expose the film. You may not know why. It's more of a feeling, a spark of grace. Photo students call it the Decisive Moment. You call it dumb luck. Sometimes, your trigger finger is in tune. And you don't have to develop the film to figure this out. You just know.

You think about this as you agitate the two rolls from this morning. Because you are certain of at least six lucky exposures in this very developing tank. The baby bunnies, Fritz and his knife, the inside of the horse. Not earthquake negatives, as Fritz put it, but lucky.

You hang the negatives to dry, take a bite of fruitcake (which you've learned improves greatly in the toaster oven), then cut yesterday's Dudley rolls into strips for the contact sheet. Expose the paper, watch the tiny images materialize in the developer tray, under the red glow of the safelight. One is a definite, even unmagnified in the stop bath; you decide to print it first.

It's the one just before he took your camera away. He's looking not at the lens, but through it, straight into something deeper. When you shot it, you thought it was mysterious. But now, as you watch his features become clearer, your thoughts get clearer too. He is concerned, but he also wants something. *What do you wish for?* He's curious. Puzzled. But also knows more than he lets on. A hint of smile at the corner of his pale eye. That thing that looks good on movie film. The background tossed out of focus, the eyelashes crisp. This is a picture that gets an actor a job.

You phone Dudley at his temp job. "Hey, it's me, Maddie. I think we have a good headshot here."

"Maddie. How are *you*?"

"Seriously, you have to see this." You want to address him by name, look down at your notes. "Paul," you say, a little too late. "I can drop it by tonight, with the contact sheet, if you want."

"No, no, I'll come to you. I want to see how you live without looking like you are living." True, you did talk about this last night, with your mouth full, about hiding underwear and dishes, the fire-inspector drills.

You look at the horse, smiling at the window, where you left him. "OK, I guess. But dress warm."

You arrange for him to come by on his way home from work, hang up the phone, and hear a crash downstairs. Olga, the trapeze artist. It's more of a thud than a crash, something soft—or someone maybe—landing on her wood plank floor. You wait for another sound. You crouch, put your ear to the floor. Nothing. You run to the old steam pipe in the corner. It's defunct, corroded, and holey but makes a great lo-fi intercom. "Olga!" you shout into the pipe.

"I'm OK!" she shouts back up. "Sorry about that."

"What are you *doing*?"

"We took down my heavy bag to *make room*."

If Olga is *making room*, chances are it's worth witnessing. You turn off your space heater, grab your camera, and walk downstairs.

A statuesque, busty blonde opens the door. You recognize her, one of Olga's day-job colleagues. Inside is another one, that exotic green-eyed Brazilian who fascinated you on your sole trip to the Blue Spot.

You can't bring cameras into the Blue Spot. But you remember this girl, the Brazilian, as if you had taken her picture anyway. The way she bent backward, all the way, buck naked, her thin torso forming a sharp peak. Shadows of her ribcage like stripes. Her long hair streaming onto the floor in the garish stage light. You wanted her. Not to sleep with—women aren't really your thing—but to study. What light does to a body in an impossible contortion. What that body does to the light.

Today, her hair is in braids, and she's dressed. A normal sweatshirt and leggings, like the other two women. "I've been promising the girls flying lessons," Olga says. "You remember Tessa," indicating the chesty one, "and Gia," the Brazilian. "This is Maddie."

"You guys mind if I take pictures?" They all shrug. You take this as a no. Tessa is stretching, shaking out her long arms in preparation. Olga is taping Gia's hands.

A single trapeze hangs in the center of the room. A ladder is fixed to one wall, ending in a small platform, about twenty feet up. Thick tumbling mats line the floor and fore and aft walls.

Tessa is the first victim. Her hands are taped and ready. Olga tightens a web belt around Tessa's waist and another around Gia's. Gia climbs the ladder and hooks her belt to the wall. Olga attaches lines to the sides of Tessa's belt. The lines run up to taut wires near the ceiling, then back down on one side, into Olga's hands. "OK, Tess; ready?"

"Nope." Tessa has a certain innocence, one you never would have noticed at the Blue Spot, what with her pasties and red sequins and va-va-voom. You catch a close shot of her face through the rungs of the ladder. Her tight ponytail gives her cheekbones a bare girlishness. She looks terrified. She joins Gia on the platform. Gia holds Tessa's belt while Tessa grabs the trapeze bar.

Olga's all business, with her spiky, cranberry-red hair—a streetwise rooster. Both hands clasp the spotter's rope, ready for Tessa's weight. "Tess, get a good wide grip. No, wider. Good. Now when you're ready, push up and lift your feet like I showed you."

Tessa eventually manages to leap. A high-pitched *aaaaah!* escapes from her mouth, and you click the shutter as she swings by. Olga stays on task. "OK, like I showed you, timing. Knees up NOW! Flex your feet. Good. Hands down NOW!" Tessa's hands drop, and she's hanging from her knees, a full back-and-forth, blood rushing to her face, bosom weighted down toward her chin.

"Hands up NOW!" Olga barks. Tessa struggles to bend her torso back up, and you see why you will never try this. Tessa is a fit woman, obviously does sit-ups in her spare time. "Legs down NOW!"

"I did it!" Tessa hangs by her hands, lets her swinging fade, slows to a vertical, and drops to the mat. She flops on her butt, and you get a good shot of her lying back, arms wide and feet up like a baby, taped hands open, fear erased. "Can I try it again?"

Tessa improves a little with each jump from the platform. Less initial hesitation, more momentum, building her swing by bending her body in the middle. You don't stop shooting. You try longer exposures for the blur of movement. Backlight, from the windows on the far wall, fills her blond hair.

Then it's the Brazilian's turn to fly. She's petite and aerodynamic, like Olga, and fearless too. You breach the safety code, crawl onto the mat to focus on her as she flies overhead, her arms reaching toward the camera, schoolgirl braids flapping and swinging, pure glee and freckles on her flushed face.

You photograph the women for over two hours. Tessa takes another turn, then Gia, then Olga gets up there, no safety lines, shows off a little. She stands on the bar, jumps, catches it on her way down, flips into an inverted split. In your last remaining frame she is airborne, a swift somersault before landing on her feet, chest heaving.

Afterward, you sit around on the mats, like a harem, drinking beer from bottles. The conversation falls into the inevitable: work. They're talking about a certain patron, a wealthy, eccentric Blue Spot regular, who occasionally brings his wife. The man has a bulbous red nose and horrible breath, but he's good tipper and therefore a necessary compromise of the job. "He put three hundred-dollar bills in my G-string last night," Tessa says, and you have trouble hiding your surprise at this figure. You look up at the expensive rigging overhead, the humming gas heater in the far corner, even the beer in your hand, and realize it was all paid for in hard work. "He asked me to go to a bar with him after my shift, but I couldn't bring myself to do it. I know it would have been another three hundred, at least, but my God he smells. Like *dentures* or something. I just couldn't."

Gia and Olga smile privately at each other. Perhaps they have given in to the patron's wishes, on other nights. All this time you've envied Olga for her athletic body and Olympic discipline. Now, you're not so sure.

Dudley rings your bell just as you're hanging the new negatives to dry. You blow into your hands to warm them up and go downstairs to let him in.

He's loaded down with plastic take-out bags. "Chinese. Thought we could eat." He eyes the mailboxes with fascination. "I wasn't in the mood for rice and sugar."

"I have fruitcake too," you remind him, hiking up the stairs. "It's good if you toast it, I swear."

"I'll take your word for it."

Inside your chilly space, he walks straight to the horse. "Hey, you didn't tell me about this thing."

"I just got him last night."

"He just showed up on your doorstep?"

"Yeah, actually. Literally." You can't tell if he thinks this is weird or not. His gloves are off, stowed in the pocket of his huge parka. He's sticking his finger in the horse's plastic mouth, flicking the teeth. You wonder if it was a mistake to let him come here.

"Got any plates?" he says. "*Hidden*, right?" He walks into your kitchen area, without invitation. "Don't tell me. Let me *find them*."

You wonder what else he'll find. No mice, too cold for them. Probably some crud on the plates. You usually just eat out of the saucepan. Less to wash.

He holds a dusty plate up to the fluorescent bulb over the sink. It's really sinking in now. This is a research trip for him. He's an actor, looking for a new *experience*, like *finding plates*. He sets them on the table, a beat-up oak desk you found once in the loading dock. You offer him the sole chair. You sit on the high stool yourself, lean over to unpack the food, trying not to make your hunger too obvious.

He feels sorry for you. The way you feel sorry for homeless people on the subway. You give them something, pocket change, or a bagel, to reinforce the difference, to prove to yourself that you can afford to give. Otherwise the line between you becomes too fuzzy.

You think of Fritz's stone soup. "You know, you didn't have to bring me food. My upstairs neighbor invited me up for supper."

"Oh. Oh, Maddie, hey, I'm sorry." Dudley misunderstands completely. "I didn't mean to mess up your plans. I just thought—" He stops.

"Well, it wasn't really a *plan* plan."

He's blushing. You feel like a jerk.

You get an idea. "Hey! The picture!" You jump up from the table, grab the best print from the drying rack in the darkroom, run back, and place it beside his carton of kung pao chicken. "Whaddya think, hey?"

"Wow. Look at me. I look—" He wipes a hand on his pants, picks up the print to study his own head closer. "I look like, like I don't know. Like Montgomery Clift right before he kisses Elizabeth Taylor. Like I'm about to do something."

"You were about to open your refrigerator."

"Oh, yeah." He laughs, mouth full, still looking at the print. "OK, that makes sense. Hey, can I see the others?"

You're happy to oblige. It's what you're used to, actors talking about themselves. You go into the darkroom for the contact sheet, ready to hear him complain about the mole on his cheek or his huge canine teeth.

"I have a theory," he shouts from the other room.

"What's your theory?" you say as you return with the tiny images. You hand him a magnifier, reposition a gooseneck lamp to bring more light to the table.

"Hold on." He looks hard, scanning in sequence, like a minimovie. "Where's the one you printed? Oh, here. Yeah. Did you notice this? They all get better after that."

"Lemme see." You lean over next to him, put the little scope to your eye. He's right. After the impromptu dinner, you had taken a few frames of him sitting at his kitchen table asking questions. He's far more natural in these, his smile less rehearsed. Looking at you, not at some phantom casting director in the future.

"Quit *acting*, Paul!" he shouts over your shoulder. "You're *acting*! Quit *acting!*"

"Excuse me?" You look up.

"What my teacher always says."

"To be ironic?" You look back through the lens. "I kind of see what she means." In one in particular, he's leaning forward, with a half wink and overtly seductive smile. Nowhere near as sexy as the final frame: slouching back, shrugging his shoulders, on the verge of a goofy laugh. "Hey, I promised you another print. What about this one?"

You expect him to look immediately, but he doesn't. He takes off his parka, lets it flop inside out on the chair behind him. Looks at you instead. "I suppose you do this with all your clients?"

"No."

He smiles, seems glad to be the special one. He takes the magnifier from your hand, bends back over the tiny images. Takes his time. You use the opportunity to inhale some lo mein. You don't want him to watch you eat. You'd rather have him look at himself.

"So, Maddie," he says, not looking up. "You said you were dreaming of horses. Did you conjure this horse of yours? Are you a witch?"

"I'm not a witch."

"Uh-*huh*," he says. "So you didn't wish for the horse."

"No, I just asked for him."

"Who did you ask? God?"

"No, some neighbor dude. His dog was barking at it."

"I see." He's still looking down—smiling, though—into the contact sheet. You get the feeling he isn't really examining it at all. You put down your chopsticks. He keeps talking into the photos. "Do you always get what you wish for?"

"I told you, I don't wish."

He sits up, looks you in the eye. "Bullshit."

You grab the contact sheet. "Did you pick one to print?"

"I trust you. You pick." He grins, pointing at you with a chopstick.

You shrug. "OK. I can get them to you by tomorrow night, if you want."

"No." He takes off his knit cap, apparently growing accustomed to the cold air. "I'd rather watch you print it. *I wish* I could watch you print it. Can I?"

You're not God, but it's a grantable wish.

The darkroom is crowded. You feel the urge to narrate, take extra steps, do a test strip, dodge some darks just for demonstration's sake.

You show him how to agitate the developer tray while the image comes, then let him do it. Because it's magic, the first time you see it, the blank page slowly turning into something familiar. You can tell he's never done it before. The smile is genuine, his teeth pink in the safelight. You coolly pull the print by tongs, slide it into the next tray. It could be garbage and still impress him here, you remind yourself.

"Do you ever take pictures of yourself?" he says.

"No."

"Why not?"

"There are far more interesting subjects."

He turns your head to face him. His hand is cold against your cheek. You expect him to say something, but he just studies your face. You can see his breath, from his nose. The room feels small. It's rude, grabbing a person's face like that, staring like that. You turn back, pull a fresh sheet from the black bag, place it in the easel.

"Here's how you burn in the shadows." You form a circle with your hands around the problem area, fan out fingers like wings to cover the rest.

He watches. "I wish you would take a picture of yourself. I'd like to see what you see when you look in the mirror."

"Yeah, right." You drop the sheet into the developer. He's lost interest in his own face, is looking at the hanging negatives now, the day's booty, fingering them.

"Hey, handle by the edges, please."

"Sorry, boss." He drops the strips, puts his hand in his pocket.

"No problem, just—I just don't want anything to happen to those."

"Why not? What are they?"

"My neighbors."

"Your upstairs neighbor? Of the dinner invitation?" He won't look at you.

"Yeah, him, and some others. And the horse."

His face brightens at the mention of the horse. "Can we print them now?"

You've actually been dying to print them. You were going to do it the minute he left anyway. "Sure," you say, grabbing your scissors.

You've never worked with an assistant before, and you can see how it would get addictive. Dudley mans the trays, while you work the enlarger. Of course he keeps talking, but you let him. You're learning how to tune it out.

"Hey, is this guy chopping up *rabbits*?"

"Hmm. Is this the one who asked you up for dinner?"

"Is this horse really shooting light out of his ass?"

"Hey, I suppose you get used to this chemistry smell. No?"

"Your neighbors have a trapeze? Where?"

"Downstairs," you say, not looking up.

"Hey, I know her."

"Who?" You squeeze in beside him and look in the tray.

"Her." He points in the stop bath at the shot of Tessa lying back on the mat, legs and safety wires all over the place. "I swear I know her from someplace."

"Hmm." You drop the next sheet into the developer, wait for the picture to materialize, a zoom on Gia's freckled face flying overhead.

"Her too! I know her from someplace." He stops agitating the bath, racking his brain. "Damn. I can't put my finger on it."

"The Blue Spot," you say, trying not to laugh.

"Oh . . ." he says. "Uh."

"She looks different with clothes, huh?"

"Now I'm embarrassed."

The Artstars

"Busted." You try to picture him among the desperate hornballs, or the Wall Street guys buying lap dances for each other, waving twenties like trade tickets. It's a very un-Dudley activity. "I've been there too," you say. You drop Gia into the stop bath.

"You have?"

"Olga, she's my friend. She lives downstairs. She invited me."

"Which one is she?" He takes the tongs and pokes the rubber tip through the prints in the wash.

"Here. We'll print her next." You put a new strip in the enlarger. It's Olga, hanging from the trapeze in an upside-down split. Her sweatshirt flops, exposing a tattooed belly with a ring.

Dudley watches her emerge in the bath. "Is she in a circus or something?"

"No. She's trying. She practices every day."

"Don't we all." He's shivering.

You get an idea. "You want to meet her? We could go down. She has *heat*."

Outside Olga's door, you hear loud hip-hop music and repetitive thuds and grunts.

"Dang," Dudley says.

"She's beating the shit out of her heavy bag. She does it every night before she goes to work."

"She must really hate someone."

"Olga!" You rap hard on the door.

"It's open!"

Inside it's warm enough for her to work out in nothing but a tank tee and spandex shorts. She gives the bag a high kick with her sneaker, then follows up with two hard jabs. Then she notices Dudley. "Oh! Hey! Sorry."

"This is my new client," you say. His real name escapes you.

She walks over and offers her puffy, gloved hand. "Hi, I'm Olga."

"So I hear. I'm Paul." *Paul. Don't forget. Paul. Rhymes with tall.* He towers over Olga. Accepts her boxing glove in both of his hands. Looks around at the rigging, the neatly stacked gym mats, the clean kitchenette, the diminutive bed loft, like a hat, over the bathroom. "Nice setup." He looks back at her, still holding her glove. He seems to be trying to recognize her from the Blue Spot, unsuccessfully. She looks sportier without her long wig.

"Yeah. My mom hates it, but it works for me." She removes the gloves, takes a big drag from her water bottle. Dudley, true to himself, walks around, touching things. The heavy bag, the spotter's rope. The big, gold hoop, Olga's latest acrobatic experiment, hanging just at his arm's reach in the center of the room.

"He's a curious fucker, isn't he?" Olga says under her breath.

"Wait until he starts asking questions. He's on a *research trip.*"

"Are you shtupping him?" She's checking out his butt.

"No, of course not."

"What do you mean *of course not*? He's a fine specimen." You wonder if he can hear her through the loud music. "I swear you're like a goddamn nun."

"He's my *client.*"

"Well, he's the first *client* you've brought around here."

Across the room, Dudley flops onto a pile of gym mats. "I love these things. I'd love to fill my whole apartment with them."

"I like him," Olga says to you in a flirty stage whisper. "Are all your clients this excitable?"

"No, just him."

Dudley tries to catch your eye from the mat. You look away. "Hey, Olga, we were just printing up those trapeze pictures Maddie shot," he says. *We.* Olga raises her brow, reading in way too much. "You should be in a circus. I'm serious."

"Well, I'm trying."

"What do you do with that hoop over there?"

"Hard to explain."

"Show us."

She shrugs. "Sure, but Maddie will have to spot me." You've spotted her before. All you have to do is stand underneath and pray she doesn't fall on you.

"Can I spot you?" Dudley says. "I'm good at it, I swear. My baby sister is a gymnast. Back in Vegas."

"I didn't know you had a sister," you say. "I didn't know you were from Vegas."

"You didn't ask," he says. He's already taking off his sweater, loosening his tie, untucking his starched white office shirt. Claps his hands, then rubs them together. "OK, let's go."

"Hold on." Olga is taking off her sneakers.

You're stung over Dudley's comment. *You didn't ask.* Normally you don't have to ask; actors just talk.

"Vegas, I love Vegas. I want to live there," Olga says, tossing her sock.

"Well, I hate it, but there's a lot of jobs for people like you there."

People like you. You wonder if he means strippers or acrobats. "Are you going home to Vegas for Christmas?" you ask.

"Oh, you care all of a sudden?" he says, and you can't tell if he's teasing or not. "No. I can't afford it. I had to *buy new headshots.*" He winks, but you don't know if he means it. "Plus, I can't stand Christmas."

You're rattled. It seems un-Dudley-like to hate Christmas. "What's wrong with Christmas?"

"*Some people* don't do homemade presents. *Some people* spend five minutes with a catalog and a telephone. Then all go to church and sing about what blessed, good people they are. It's dumb. I gave it up."

"You know, I never understood Christmas myself," Olga says.

"That's different," you say. "You're Jewish."

"I'm just saying."

She looks at you for a second, then turns off the stereo. She tosses a couple mats under the ring, takes a running leap, and catches it. You sit on the floor, pull your camera from over your shoulder.

The room is quiet, save the buzzing heater and Olga's deep breathing, the occasional click of the shutter. You love watching her practice in the silence on the stationary swing, after the aggressive, loud boxing workout. It's a meditation for her—just the ring and the body, the limbs and the breath. The ring is like a tire swing, only delicate and sleek.

She is still learning the hoop, so she starts slow. Dudley stands below, facing you, arms out ready to catch. Olga slips a leg through her arms, does an inverted split, one leg through the ring, swinging up to straddle it. Dudley looks up at her flexed ass with naked appreciation, and in the stark, bright light from Olga's halogen lamp, he looks pervy and sinister. Suddenly, you can imagine him as a Blue Spot regular after all, a smelly bill in his outstretched fingers. It feels like a sacrilege next to Olga's focused, yogic stretch, and you look away but can't get the thought out of your mind: Dudley, ordering a lap dance from giggling Tessa or lithe Gia, just another lecherous wallet.

You walk around to the other side, focus on Dudley from behind. Now, without his underlit grin, you're closer to an image worth preserving. Both figures are between you and the light. All the camera will see is silhouette and negative space. You sit on the floor, shoot Dudley's broad back, the light halo from his white shirt. With one hand, Olga grabs the top of the ring, flexes her arm, then lifts her legs and torso straight overhead. A long hold, by one hand. It's enough time to get a crisp image. Long breath. Then she clasps the ring with her other hand and flops her body back down. Exhales.

"That wasn't what you were going to do, was it?" says Dudley.

"No." You wonder how he can tell.

"So, try it. I'm strong, I promise."

"OK." She rests for a second, then inverts her body again. Her arm trembles. Her hand slips. She bangs her elbow on the lower half of the hoop as Dudley shoots in, catches her by the shoulders, lowers her to the mat.

"You OK?"

"Yeah." She shakes out her arm.

"Wanna try again?"

"Yeah." She catches her breath, and Dudley lifts her back up to the ring by her waist. She's more confident now. Far more confident than she ever was with you.

She finishes the stunt this time, flips upside down, then slips her torso through the ring, drops her arms, hangs by the small of her back, spinning slowly, like a spider on a silk thread. She slips down further, hangs by one knee. Dudley clasps her hand in congratulation.

"Hey," she says, "I want to try that again."

It's an opportunity for her, trying something new in the silence of her home, a solid human safety net underneath. You don't speak. They have forgotten you're even there. It's an opportunity for you too. Invisibility is useful.

A loud knock on the door breaks the magic silence. Then Fritz bursts in with a big paper grocery bag and skips right over to you. "Maddie Muffin!" He kisses you wet on the cheek. "Sweetheart, I was worried when you didn't come up for dinner. But I *found you!*"

"Don't worry. I ate. I'm sorry, Fritz. I should have called."

Olga lowers herself to the mat. Dudley looks at Fritz, making the connection with obvious unease.

"But I brought *dessert!*" Fritz cries, reaching into the bag with a mad grin. He pulls out a lop-eared rabbit, and you giggle involuntarily. It's Victor, the cute black-and-white ball of fur. "Whoops!" He hands you the rabbit. She's wiggling, and you fumble for a second before setting her at your feet. "*Dessert!*" he cries again, flourishing an enormous bottle of Maker's Mark. He's had a head start on it.

Olga chuckles quietly, watching the bunny hop around her floor. Dudley seems unsure what to do with his hands.

"Glasses! Maddie, where are the glasses?" He bangs through the cupboards, finds three coffee mugs and a chipped brandy snifter. "Olga, honey, you must get some real glassware. Steal some from that lovely job of yours."

"Fritz, this is my studio, not a bar."

"A bar! You could put it right over here. Wouldn't that look nice, kids? More like a *rec room*. Would make it more *homey*." All eyes on him, the Swiss tornado.

"Fritz, we're not supposed to make it *homey*," you say. "You'll get us all evicted."

"Oh, yes. Little Maddie and her flip-around closet," Fritz replies. Dudley looks at you, seems to be wondering exactly how much Fritz knows about your closet. "Maddie's *fire drills. Please.*"

"I sublet. That wasn't my idea."

"Oh, yes, your law-abiding, conceptualist neighbor. Have you *seen his work*? Who is he kidding? He's here for the *real estate*, that's what I think. Because they're coming. Oh, yes. The yuppies are coming. In their *kayaks and ferries*, they're coming. Right over the East River and up Newtown Creek." He pours himself a generous one in the brandy snifter. "Mark my words, ten years and this'll all be rich fucks in luxury lofts. I'm living in luxury *now*, baby. 'Cause when they get here, we're *all* outta this place. Everybody but your rich, no-talent landlord."

"Please, Fritz," Olga says. "He's right upstairs."

"THEY'RE COMING!" Fritz shouts right at the ceiling. "Get out your checkbooks! THEY'RE ON THEIR WAY! See, LOOK!" he says, pointing right at Dudley. "There's ONE NOW!"

"He's not a yuppie," Olga says, though in his tie and stiff white shirt, he does indeed look like one. "He's an actor."

"I'm a temp, actually," he says. "I'm a secretary."

"Ohhhhh." Fritz looks at Dudley, at you, then back at Dudley, his wheels turning. "Ohhhhh. I get it. This is *your* actor, right, Maddie?"

"He's her *client*, yes," Olga says.

"Hmmph." Fritz takes a swig. "*Acting*, huh?" He is sizing him up now, his tone brittle and pushy. "So are you *cute enough*? That's what Maddie says, it's your *job* to be cute."

"Depends on the job," he replies, looking at you. You pull your camera in front of your face.

"So, Actor—what's your name again?"

"Paul."

"So, *Paul*, how do you deal with the *rejection*? There's what, a million of you in New York, right?"

"Fritz," Olga says. "Settle down."

"No, I'll answer that," the actor says. "I think about that a lot. Until I turned thirty, I was always getting my hopes up. Afraid to talk about stuff like I might jinx it. Know what I mean?"

Olga nods. She's superstitious.

"Of course," Fritz says, flippant, but he may actually be listening. "So now you're thirty, and—"

"Thirty-one," he says. Your guess yesterday was way off. "And all of a sudden, there's no way I'll ever be one of those young rising stars, you know? And I just started being honest about it instead. And suddenly I don't take it all so seriously anymore." He looks Fritz in the eye. "Next thing you know, I'm getting more calls." He looks at you. "Plus, there are way bigger disappointments in life. *Way* bigger."

"Disappointment." Fritz grunts, looks down at the rabbit, then back at Dudley. "Wait'll you get to my age and your friends start dying on you."

He goes over to the stereo and turns on some bossa nova music, begins dancing a silly, melancholic, back-and-forth by himself. Then picks up his beloved Victor from the floor and holds her like a miniature dance partner. He's sad and sloppy, and even Dudley has to laugh. Olga pours Dudley a drink, then helps herself. You try to get a photo of Fritz dancing with Victor, the mother of his rabbit children. He spins his partner in a pirouette, then sets her down gently on the plank floor. You zoom in on her floppy black ears in the stark, directional light.

"Maddie, c'mon, put the camera away," Olga says. "Have a drink with us."

"She's a workaholic, I think," says Dudley.

Fritz snickers. "Nah, Maddie's just *shy*. She hides her pretty face behind the camera."

"Shut up, Fritz." You've had enough.

"No," Olga says. "He's right."

"I'm not shy."

"No," Olga persists. "You're *pretty*. Fritz is right."

Dudley says nothing. You pull your camera up for protection, get a good one of his big sober eyes looking right at you. Click. Your only comment.

"I think we need to take that thing away from her," Fritz, fellow photographer, slurs. "It's for your own good, sweetie. It's fucking up your work."

"It *is* my work."

Fritz is on you already, pulls the strap from your neck while the others laugh, takes your livelihood away, and carries it like a disease over to the other side of the room. "You need bourbon, not this fucking thing."

"OK. So give me some bourbon."

Your hands are empty. You feel naked. Fritz pours you a mug, a big one, but pulls it away when you reach for it. "Maddie Muffin. Please. Don't be angry. C'mon, smile." Teasing you with the drink. You hate being told to smile. He puts his arm around you. "Baby Maddie," Fritz says into your ear, "how are you going to see The Big One with that thing in front of your face?"

"I'll see it in the mirror," you say.

You mean the mirror in your camera, but Dudley misunderstands. "Right, Maddie! Like I was telling you before, you should *take a picture of yourself.*"

"That's not what I meant." You are boiling hot under your layers, under Fritz's heavy arm. "Why is everybody looking at me? Can we please just go back to what we were doing?"

"*I know* what you meant, Maddie," Fritz says quietly, tightening his grip on your shoulder. "But you can't play the odds forever. You'll have a roomful of negatives and go broke."

"I'm already broke."

"Here." Fritz finally hands you the drink. You take a big gulp. "I think we need a toast." He lets go of you. "To our shy, broke friend and her roomful of negatives."

They all laugh, clink their drinks together. You hold yours firm to the chest. "It's not funny," you say. You look up at Olga's humming heater and well-equipped gymnasium. And Dudley's fancy-pants starched office shirt, and Fritz's huge, expensive bottle of bourbon. "I think I'm done drinking," you say. *Broke. Broken.* You set your half-empty mug on the counter and leave.

You trudge up the cold stairway.

"Maddie, wait." Dudley is climbing the stairs behind you. "You left your camera."

"Whatever."

"Why are you running away?" He catches up, places the strap over your neck.

"Christ. Fritz. He drives me crazy, with his damn rabbits and stupid advice. He can afford to say whatever he wants."

"He's just messing with you. You let him get under your skin. What was it? When he said you're pretty? He just wants to sleep with you. You must get that all the time."

Not exactly. You look away. "That's not what pissed me off." You pause. "Fritz is right." You feel like punching the concrete wall. "My *work* is making me broke. I should just go to school to become a fucking accountant. Improve my odds."

"What did he mean, about the odds? I didn't get that."

You look back at him. "It's all stupid luck, you know? Photography, I mean. So you just keep shooting, and it's expensive, and maybe ten percent is decent, if you're lucky. Which I'm not. I'm totally not. Not like him."

"He's good?"

"Yeah." You take a breath. "Or *lucky.*"

"You don't have to just wait around for luck. You don't have to be so passive about it. You know?" He touches your hat. He looks you in the eye. "You keep saying you don't wish. But it's good to wish. Say it out loud, what you want. Right? Just say it, Maddie. What do you really *want*? Huh? What do you *wish for*?"

You've had enough of the actor psychology and name-calling. *Passive. Broke.* "You wanna know what I *wish*, Dudley? I wish you would quit analyzing me. I wish you would cut the questions. You sound like a goddamn three-year-old. I wish you would just *stop talking.*"

He freezes on the stair behind you, squinting in bewilderment, like a puppy with its ears folded back. "Who's *Dudley*?"

Oh. Fuck.

You feel your face go hot. "*Paul.* I'm sorry."

You realize something now, like turning off the safelight and seeing what is really there, in the wash, in plain black and white: He's just a man. He's not researching. He's not nosy. He never was. He's simply lonely. Hungry, same as you, but for something else. No wonder he didn't want you returning to his apartment tonight, with his unopened gift packs—cold, refrigerated obligations from relatives who are checking him off a list. He considers you his friend, and you can't even learn his name. "*Paul.* I don't know where that came from."

His face goes chilly. "I don't even *want to know* where that came from." He steps back and away, down the stairs. He doesn't even have his coat. On gut impulse, like your shutter finger, you grab him by the arm, turn him around, look him in the eye, and kiss him square on the lips.

At first he resists. But then he kisses back. Aggressive. Angry. Hard. Then his mouth softens. And then he's pressing you against the concrete wall of the stairwell, as if it were his idea all along. Maybe it was.

Back in your space, he pulls you by the hand to the ugly sofa. He sits beside you, kisses your wet eyes, removes your hat, your camera, your ponytail holder. Kisses your falling curls. You see the dead horse smiling, out of the corner of your eye, like he knows more than you. You burrow your hands under Paul's undershirt. You feel hair around his navel, a soft arrow to the button of his pants. He giggles, ticklish under your cold hands. He tickles you back under your sweater, and your other sweater, your thermal undershirt, your crew neck tee, your tank tee. You can feel his lips smiling against yours, and you're grateful he doesn't hate you. His hands move up under the layers, finding your armpits, making you laugh too, then slowing over your bare breasts. He inhales sharply. Then his mouth goes serious and hungry over your face, your neck, and he's pulling the layers over your head in the cool air.

By the time you're down to the tank tee, you are covered in goose pimples. "Let's go upstairs," you say.

"To the rabbit guy?" he says, backing away.

"No, no," you laugh. "Up the ladder."

The Artstars

"Ahhhh, the *ladder*," he says, and complies readily. Up in the bed loft, electric mattress pad on high, naked under comforters, you close your eyes and happen to think of snow angels. You're lying in a clean blanket of white, aiming your whole body at making an impression. An impression that will probably drift away by morning.

"Maddie," he says, bringing you back.

You open your eyes, and he's looking right down at you. No anger, no desperation, no hunger, not anymore. He wants to give you something, and not out of pity, either. And maybe it never was—the Chinese food, the cold dinner at his apartment—it wasn't pity; he simply did not like to eat alone, maybe even craved your company. The thought sends a red surge to your abdomen. His bare feet push into the arches of your feet. His gray eyes, his naked belly against yours. You tighten around him, feel a high, hot tingle, and the snow angel melts into clear water. He falls on top of you, liquid, exhausted, warm.

It's hot under the covers, with Paul sound asleep beside you, thick bare arm over your chest. The light is still on downstairs, softly illuminating his head. You slide out from under his arm and the covers, into the cool air. It feels good against your sweaty skin. You go down the ladder to turn off the light.

Something catches your eye across the room. It's your reflection in the glass of the windows, your skin pale, your hair wild and messy. You walk over for a closer look. A smooth shadow curves around your waist and the underside of your small breasts. Highlights wash your forehead and collarbone, the muscles of your thin legs. Round lips, rounder hips, soft, mossy pubic hair. Maybe you are pretty. Maybe this is what Paul sees when he looks at you. The horse is looking into the glass too, appears to be checking you out. You grab your camera from the dirty couch, where Paul left it. You focus on the woman and the horse, side by side, in the glass. Just two subjects, and the rest darkness. You shoot.

But something is missing. Your face. You lower the camera, let the strap go taut between your breasts. Your left hand is free now. You take the lead from the horse's halter, hold it up, and look right at yourself. Not smiling but not frowning either. You are simply a woman leading a horse. You press the button.

It's your last frame, again. You are shivering. It's crazy to be walking around naked in here. You drape the camera over the horse's neck, turn off the light, then crawl up into the warm dark bed, slide back under Paul's arm.

You can't sleep. You have an idea, and your brain is already spinning in high gear. *Relax, breathe, it can wait*, you remind yourself; just go to sleep. Morning will come, and Paul will go home, and you can lock yourself in your darkroom for as long as it takes. But you don't exactly want Paul to go home. And your eyes are wide open in the dark.

You get up, feel around for some clothing, put on your usual five layers, and go down the ladder. In the darkroom, you develop the new roll, hang it to dry, then start paging through contact sheets, looking for the landscape inside of the horse. You find the negative, slip it in the enlarger, then place a sheet of black sketch paper in the easel. You trace the contours on the paper with a pencil: the big valley, the curving hollows. Then throw another negative in: the father and son rabbits, nibbling their carrot tops. You bring down the lens until the rabbits are tiny figures perched at the edge of one of the tunnel holes. Trace their outlines on the paper, jot down the enlarger settings. And another one, two baby rabbits, side by side, hopping into the horse's neck. You trace their outlines too. One by one, you add figures to the drawing: Fritz, blown up large in the bottom right corner, just half of his face next to the glinting knife. Tessa and Gia, swinging by their knees, tiny as the rabbits, suspended from the top of the picture.

The newest roll is dry now, and you cut it up too. Olga, in negative, is a white silhouette, gripping her big ring with one flexed arm. Paul is a small silhouette below her, arms open wide like wings.

And finally, in the foreground: You. Naked, leading your smiling horse, eyes looking straight into the box over your belly.

It's a collage technique you used to play around with in school, where the darkroom wasn't so cold and claustrophobic. It's time-consuming and requires more precision than luck. You're usually too lazy or hate your negatives too much to make the effort. You pull the sketch paper out of the easel and carefully cut out an empty space inside each one of the outlines.

You expose the photo paper in the same order. First the landscape. Then you place the stencil over the sheet and, with strips of old reject prints, cover all the holes but the father and son rabbits. Throw in the negative, check notes, and expose the piece in the hole. Cover it, then shine a new negative in the next hole. You work slowly, use the timer, recheck the notes often so you won't have to start over. Fritz's knife, the trapeze girls, Olga and Paul, you and the horse. Finally, you drop the finished sheet into the developer and wait.

You hold your breath while the image emerges under the liquid. There's a vignetting effect around the picture, from the horse's tail hole, a soft, dark, circular frame like an old-fashioned portrait. The frame obscures some of Fritz's features, making him sinister. The rabbits are a soft gray, with enough shadow to look like they are really standing in the snow, peering down a rabbit hole. Gia looks like she's readying to catch Tessa. Paul's dark silhouette is an evangelist, praying up into the cave of the horse's neck. Olga is a black insect caught in a web. You, you are Lady Godiva, with your horse, your pale skin, your dark eyes, the black leather strap between your breasts. Emerging from a crazy dream, a shadowy halo around you as you peer up through the chemicals into the real, frozen world.

You drop the print into the stop bath and blow into your hands, then look at your watch. It's five thirty already. You've been working on one picture for four hours. You rinse the print thoroughly in the sink. The cold water is unbearable. You put it on the drying rack, run some warm water over your hands, and decide to make some coffee.

You have barely enough left for a pot. While it brews, you dig through a box in the front of your space, trying not to make a racket and wake up Paul. You find it, finally, your ancient large format camera. You set it up on its heavy wooden tripod, facing the bare wall behind the horse. Outside, the sun is coming up. You're pretty sure you have one sheet of four-by-five film left, in your hollow refrigerator, years old, horribly expired.

Paul comes down the ladder just as you emerge from the darkroom with the film, loaded into its old wooden frame. "Hey," you say. "Why you getting up so early?"

"I have to go to work. I should go home and shave."

"Oh. Yeah."

He follows you over to the tripod. "How's my workaholic?"

"I fell off the wagon."

"It was lonely up there without you."

"I'm sorry." You turn around and look at him. He's dressed already, in yesterday's clothes.

He puts his arms around you, and you rest your tired head against his chest. He kisses your head, your ear. "That was nice last night," he whispers. You remember his thin, naked body in the soft tent light under your covers, and your heart flips over.

"Yeah," you say. It was more than nice.

"I'm coming back tonight, OK?"

"OK," you say. It is more than OK.

"But you're not sneaking off again. You're staying in bed with me."

"All night, I promise."

He exhales into your hair. "Good girl." You feel him lift his head to look at the old camera. "So what is this thing? Like an Old West rig?"

"It's a view camera. I'm rephotographing a photograph. Look." You pick up the new print, still damp, from the floor next to the tripod, tack it to the wall.

"Wow." He steps up closer to look. You turn on a floodlight, move its stand closer, and shine it onto the image.

"See? There's you, and Olga here, and of course Fritz—"

"You're beautiful." He could care less about the rest of the picture. "Look at your skin. Maddie. When did you shoot this?"

"Last night."

He smiles, eyeing your body in the photograph with proprietary recognition. "Your face. You look like you know something," he says.

"I don't know shit," you say, ducking under the black cloth to put the film into the camera.

"Maddie, wait."

"What?"

"Look." You come out from under the hood.

A pale spider is lowering in the air by her silver thread, just above the picture. You don't speak. Paul has the same instinct. You both wait, while she lets the silk come from her little body, until she is hovering next to the print, just between you and the horse, sending a clean, tiny shadow onto the snowy background.

You slip the film in. You expose it. The spider cooperates. She holds still, her arms reaching out in her own kind of prayer.

Three Lessons in Firesurfing

THE CRIT STARTS IN THE FOUNDRY COURTYARD, WHERE PATRICK Larsen's steel "thing" keeps growing. I've noticed Patrick tends to work without a plan. But he shows up at nine o'clock sharp every day, pours black coffee from his thermos, puts on his welding mask, and sets to work. Adding more and more rusty steel crap to this giant, heroic, but essentially shapeless amoeba made of I beams and rods and discs. He breaks at eleven thirty for lunch from a metal lunch box, teamster style. After eating, he picks his teeth, smokes a cigarette, walks around the piece. Then puts his mask back on. Sparks fly steadily until four o'clock. Beer time. Turns off the welder, puts leftover rods and mask and gloves in his locker.

I share the thought. "I find Patrick's process interesting. His work habits. He has a punctuality. A routine, I guess. Almost like a portrait of the American work ethic."

Patrick chews his afternoon toothpick, scruffy blond beard framing a half smile. He seems to appreciate the comment. Steve Pak, dressed in head-to-toe big-city black, disagrees. "Come on, Sara. Can you really see that in the *work*? His *habits*? Why not talk about the *piece*? That's what we're here to critique."

Steve intimidates me terribly. Huge vocabulary. Works hard. Knows every sculptor who ever lived. Bachelor's from Northwestern, full-ride fellowship here. The rest of us have "graduate assistantships," cleaning undergrad studios and maintaining equipment, filing shit for Professor O'Malley.

O'Malley, we call him *Boss*. It fits him. He's a big ruddy guy with big arms and a big truck. I think he has a big brain too, but I'm not sure yet. Mostly I just see him collecting money for beer. Today's our first crit of the year. My first year. My first chance to hear him for real.

"I'm with Steve," says Boss with frank authority. "We can talk about process, sure, but would you really see this 'work ethic' if this piece were in a gallery?"

I give in. "No, I suppose not."

"So, look at the *work*, Sara," Boss says. "What is it giving you?"

"It's giving ME the HIVES," says Karla Wells, nearly kicking it with one of her steel-toed boots.

"You'll have your chance, dear," says Boss, pulling her away from it by her tattooed arm. She glares angrily at the blob of steel and its creator.

"I'm not exactly sure what it's *giving* me," I mutter, ready to pass the buck.

"There's kind of an architectonic thing happening over here," offers Mary Sark, our token ceramicist, crouching on the cement floor, pointing with a dirty fingernail.

"See, I think it's more biomorphic," says John Truman in his high, nasally voice. John should know biomorphic. His sculptures are literally alive with fungus. "I like the tension he's created between these two massive verticals." He squints up at it through his nerdy wire-frame glasses. "Reminds me of the crotch of a tree."

"Or the CROTCH of SOMEONE," Karla says with a snort, perpetual, damp cigarette dangling from her lower lip, her muscular arms akimbo in her battered tank tee, battle position.

"*Excuse* me?" Patrick says, actually puffing out his ample chest.

"Dear MOM, I miss your STEELY THICK THIGHS," Karla spews.

"*Mom*?" Patrick only has one syllable in defense.

"Hey, that's what the work is GIVING ME," Karla says, pale chin up.

The crit has gotten off to a lovely start.

Karla's a force field. I met her my first day here, in my studio, as I unpacked my sewing machine and fabric and books. She wandered in, without knocking.

"Hey."

"Hey."

She was wearing what I would soon learn is her uniform: sleeveless undershirt, no bra, crew cut slicked back with pomade, nose ring, worn men's jeans, and boots covered in paint and resin. She's a big person. Six feet tall.

"I'm Karla." She held her hand out like a man for a shake.

"Sara."

"I know. I saw your slides." She's second year, got a say in our selection. "Fiber artist."

"Well . . . " I said, not crazy about the label. "Let's just say *artist*."

"You're not a *painter*," she said, poking through some raw wool I put out on the table earlier.

The Artstars

It's the test, her question, the one I'll take again and again while I'm here. "Strictly 3-D for me."

"Good. I hate painters. Paintings are what you back into when you're looking at sculpture." I passed the test, at least for now. "You know, I voted for you," she confided. "I've had enough of this macho steel shit." She lit a cigarette, without asking. I don't smoke—I hate it—but I dared not object. I was going to need an ally.

"What kind of stuff do you do?" I asked. I handed her an empty soda can for an ashtray. She flicked onto the floor anyway.

"Polyester resin." It's a point of pride among some sculptors, working with horribly toxic materials. Macho in its own way, but I didn't say it. "And tampons, lately. *Used* ones," she said, with a spark in the eye just for me.

The crit moves into Steve Pak's space, just off the woodshop. He's first year too, but you wouldn't know it. He has at least ten objects arranged on the floor in a spiral. They're heavy, fruit-like, rounded, carved from large hunks of wood. I watch him sometimes in the courtyard, going at an oak stump with a chain saw. It's a loud process. I doubt he even notices me watching his wordless contemplation of the wood, as if he doesn't even hear the saw. He works fast, but mindfully, paying attention to knots, leaving many intact. He leaves bark in places. But then, back in his studio, he coats the pieces with metal cladding. Copper and bronze mostly, some aluminum, affixed with hundreds of little nails. He leaves the wood surface selectively, sometimes on the inside of a gourd-like form, meticulously sanded and oiled to bring out the grain. It's hard to resist the urge to touch them.

"OK, who's going to start?" Boss breaks the silence, the respect and jealousy evident on all our faces.

"I love how the cladding here echoes the bark on this other piece," says Mary the Ceramicist.

"There's a real respect for the materials," I say. I notice Karla has given in to the urge and has begun stroking the soft wood on the inside of one of the forms.

"Can you elaborate?" Boss says. Steve stands silent. Critique etiquette, waiting for responses. He doesn't seem nervous at all. Hands in the pockets of his black jeans, listening. He pushes his long black hair from his face, around an ear.

"Well, I don't know." Again I am tongue-tied.

John Truman rescues me. "Well, like Mary said, it's imitative. Like the copper over here, it imitates the rough bark over there. But it's not trying to be anything but copper. The copper is copper, the bark is bark. But they also comment on each other."

"Good," Boss replies. "But let Sara finish her thought."

"That's it. What he said. That's my thought." Boss looks at me patiently, waiting for more. Steve Pak looks at me like I'm absolutely stupid.

"How did you get this patina?" Karla touches a part of the copper that has been blackened, but not really. The black has tinges of blue. The surrounding wood looks a little burnt, the patina feathering naturally from the metal.

"That one, just a propane torch," Steve says. Just a propane torch, like it's nothing. Obviously, there's some technique to his application. We are all taking mental notes. Figuring out what we can steal without looking like we are stealing. He takes a short glance at a plastic jug of some liquid suspended from the ceiling, a slow drip engineered overhead, a bright green patina growing on the pointy copperized tip of the form beneath it, spreading slowly and elegantly from its center.

"What's in that jug?" says Karla without hesitation, voicing the thought we are all having. "Ammonia? It smells like ammonia."

"Ancient Korean secret," says Steve.

"You won't share the recipe?" says Boss, with a conspirator's grin.

Steve just smiles, basking in Boss's approval.

Steve is a hard act to follow, and due to the proximity of my space, I'm the lucky one. I have only one piece to share, and it's not big. It's on a table in the middle of my space. I cleaned up a bit last night, put unused materials in boxes against the wall. The piece looks lonely and tiny in the middle of the room now, miles from the collective awe we felt in Steve's studio.

I've been getting into felt lately. It's such a magic process. Just a little soapy water and manipulation and the wool shrinks and thickens. I've discovered it hardens and dries nicely around objects, which is my main experiment now. I made a good-sized felt bowl, then filled it with felted objects I brought in from home. Important objects, to me, like an old sketch journal, or a kitchen timer my mother gave me, or a framed photograph. I shroud each object in the natural-colored wool, then submerge them in a soapy bath, one by one, and let the materials take over.

Karla has helped herself, picking up the kitchen timer, shaking it to figure out what's the heavy thing inside. "It's OK," I say, breaking the critique code. "You can handle them. I want you to."

Everyone follows orders, inspecting the little things, passing them around. "Well," says John, "there is the obvious comparison to Steve's work. The fiber is almost like the cladding. A coating of a contrasting material."

"True," says Boss.

"And the contrast of the weights of the different objects. I like that," says Mary, hefting the journal.

"My hands are getting greasy," Karla says, setting her object down, wiping her palms on her pants.

"That's the lanolin of the wool," Steve says.

"How do we react to that?" asks Boss. "The fact that she's asked us to touch them, and they are spreading oil on our hands? Is it a dirty trick?"

"I'm not crazy about it," says Patrick. "What if you were allergic?"

"ARE you allergic?" counters Karla.

"No, I'm just saying."

The crit is getting offtrack, I feel. I decide to steer it back where it belongs. "The objects are precious," I say. "They're personal objects from my life. Like this one—it's a rag doll from my childhood. And here is a photo of my sister Becky from fifth grade. She hated that photo."

"But I don't know that. I can't *see* the photo," Steve says, clearly disappointed in me for speaking, for not letting the work do the talking.

"But it's still true," I say, feeling a blush coming.

"This one is personal too?" says John, waving a shrouded toilet plunger in the air with a laugh. I've lost my footing. I'm the target now.

"Yes, it's personal." I resist the urge to grab it from his hand.

"Why does it matter to you so much? The source of the objects?" Boss says.

"Look," I say, feeling anger in my belly. "Like Steve's stuff. It's obvious he loves his wood and copper and whatever the hell is dripping from that patina thing. How is this any different?"

Boss is cool, but he's not letting me off the hook. "But you're focused on *backstory*. You hit it on the head. It's *obvious* Steve's in love with his materials. It's just not coming through here. You actually have to *give* us the information."

"What, you mean like stand next to it and explain? Write it out?"

"No, of course not. That's not what I mean. You think about it. We need to move on. Any last comments?"

"I don't think it's finished yet," Steve says. I can't tell if it's encouragement or an insult.

"It's all one color," says Patrick. "Can't you dye the wool, maybe give the piece more variety? Make it more visual?"

More *visual*? I am communicating nothing here. "I could, if I wanted to," I say.

"But you don't WANT to," says Karla, my lone defender.

"No, I don't." I can't look anyone in the face.

I'm rattled. It's hard to concentrate and contribute now. In Mary's space, we see a collection of coil-built female figures, whimsical, unfired, all brown clay, but no one complains about it being monochromatic. And John's towers of fungus—tall, skinny, phallic, their stench assaulting our nostrils—no one complains of the smell being a dirty trick. No one comments about allergies. I find myself holding my tongue.

Karla's space is big and messy as hell. Pack rats are common in the sculpture world, but this borders on mania. Boxes, milk crates of crap everywhere—under tables, on top of them—a half a dozen dirty electric fans, pieces of salvaged furniture leaned against the wall. She has a lot of light—four big windows—a requirement for ventilation when using resin. But the light fills her work too, her "aquariums," becomes one of the materials.

It's been interesting to watch the aquariums evolve. For me, anyway. First, she lays dozens of bloody tampons out on a table, like wedges of fruit, to dry. She puts a big fan on them and sometimes a hairdryer propped up on a crate, to speed them along. I approached the table slowly the first time she invited me in. I thought it would smell horrible, the old blood, but it didn't. "I know what you're thinking," she said. "Once they're dry, they're practically the same as your hunks of wool. Hardly any smell. And look, they're kind of beautiful." Like beloved collector toys, the way she arranged and rearranged them on the table. "No two exactly alike."

I had to laugh. "Snowflakes, fingerprints, tampons . . ." I edged over to look at them. Almost like dried flowers, each with a little stem, meticulously arranged. "Hey, these are different," I said, pointing to a group with blue strings instead of white.

"You're very observant," she replied, in mock teacher mode. "I figured, why not change brands and see what happens?"

I noticed a bushel basket of tampons, like dried plums, in the corner. "Damn, girl, maybe you should see a doctor. You bleed a lot."

She laughed, seemed relieved I was not calling her a freak. "Nah, people send 'em to me. My sister, some undergrad friends."

"Wow." I wondered if I would ever have the courage to make a donation. If mine would measure up to those of her friends. Probably lesbians too. Lesbians make me uneasy sometimes. I'm never sure how friendly I should get.

The crit ends in Karla's space. She's made a real effort to clean the space around the four blocks of clear resin she's placed under the windows, tampons suspended inside them like swimming fish. They really are beautiful and technically remarkable, the way she keeps the resin from getting too cloudy and injects bubbles over some of the creatures as if they are breathing. Some of them face each other, in little conversations. The sculptors all stand back, not close enough to really see the gesture and uniqueness of each swimming tampon. Karla is tense, chain-smoking on the edge of the group, slouching, waiting for someone to speak.

Mary is not afraid of it. She approaches, peers close. "It's whimsical. Random and not random. They remind me of sperm."

"I don't get it," says Patrick, sneering in disgust.

"Can you be more specific?" says Boss, tired now, maybe a little squeamish himself, operating on rote.

"I don't get *why*. Why we should want to look at these things." Patrick can't even bring himself to name them.

"Why don't *you* want to look at them?" Boss says.

"Isn't it *obvious*?" He looks like he is going to be sick.

"But it's natural," I say, finally unable to keep quiet. "What could be more natural?"

"That?" Patrick points, his hand still an arm's reach from the nearest block. "*That* is not natural. Saving those things? Some things shouldn't be shared."

"But they *are* shared. YOU just don't share it," Karla says. "It's something HALF THE POPULATION recognizes intimately, right, SARA? Right, MARY? Why are YOU so afraid of it? IT'S NOTHING. LOOK." She digs into the bushel basket in the corner, brings up a handful of them by the strings, dangles them in Patrick's face like snakes. Taunting him as he backs right into Steve Pak.

He kicks at her in self-defense. She throws the bouquet of tampons at his head. Some scrambling, yelling, and Boss grabs Karla by the waist as she tries to slap Patrick. Steve and John hold him back—he's big—until he cools down and brushes himself off, then faces her, hatred in his Nordic blue eyes. "I'm outta here," he says, then turns, adjusts his army jacket, and leaves.

"OK," says Boss, trying to resurrect the discussion. Karla, fuming, stomps her boot on the concrete floor. Mary and I wordlessly do what women do: clean. We pick the tampons up from the floor, carefully, and return them to the bushel basket.

The crit is unquestionably over.

I go to my studio, close the door, put Joni on the tape deck, volume high. Sit on the lone chair, looking at my stupid basket of stupid precious objects. *California, I'm coming home*, Joni sings with a clarity I wish I had. I miss home. This is no place like it. Whoever said Midwesterners were polite never had to deal with this lot.

Unfinished, Steve Pak called it. This experiment, full of so many hours, careful selection of mementos, sacrificing them for the piece, that sacrifice appreciated by no one but me. A lump of useless felt. A blob, no more meaningful than Patrick's steel monstrosity, which at least has scale going for it.

Unfinished. I'm pissed, because I know in my gut Steve is right. I'm looking at it now, and it doesn't move me. I hate it.

I grab a pair of scissors and begin stabbing at one of the objects on top. The kitchen timer. It slides around. I can't even stab it effectively. I pull it out of the bowl and begin cutting at the felt with the sharp shears, a surgical slice right over its heart, then around the top, releasing the object inside.

I'm surprised by what falls out of the skin onto my lap. The timer is now unrecognizable, nonfunctional, its old tin caked with rust. I never really considered this possibility. Far from protecting the thing inside, the skin of felt has changed it. And the skin itself is beautiful too—a perfect, rusty negative, a clue, a *story. Focused on backstory,* Boss complained, but this is different. Not backstory but present tense. A new story. Here, now, free of nostalgia. Free.

Eagerly I use the scissors to free the other objects. The ink from the journal has run onto the inside of the felt, pages buckled now in a natural ripple. The wood of the picture frame is rotten. The photo, surreal colors now, has reacted with the detergent bath, making my sister Becky's corkscrew curls look clownish and sublime. The colors on the rag doll's face are runny, like she is crying, the fibers of her hair and dress sticking now to the inside of her mold in a crosshatched pattern. I liberate all the objects, then lay the skins on one side of the table, opened like dissected frogs, and the transformed objects on the other side. I toss the felt bowl under the table. I don't need it now.

Joni stops singing. The tape is over. I hear music outside, something more hardcore, driving drums, tribal, people yelling and laughing. I take a last look at my table of specimens, turn off the light, and go outside to investigate.

Someone has lit a bonfire in the middle of the gravel parking lot. A cooler of beer sits on the tailgate of Boss's truck. Karla is feeding wood to the fire, broken furniture I recognize from her studio. Everyone is smoking and laughing, beer going down like water.

"Sara! Where you been?" Boss says, opening me a bottle.

"Working."

"Good girl." He tousles my hair with his big rough hand. Then laughs from his belly, watching John and Patrick lay a plank of wood on the top of the fire. John, his nerdy glasses yellow in the firelight, stands rocking at the edge of the fire, then leaps, his boots gripping the rough plank, into the middle of the flame. He stands there for a moment, whooping and beating his chest like a gorilla before jumping to safety.

"You ever seen firesurfing before?" Boss asks.

"No. I can't say I have." I take a nip of the icy beer.

Patrick leaps onto the plank right after John. Sideways, legs apart, crouching for balance, like a true surfer. He lets out a lion's roar, leaps off, making a surge of sparks behind him. Boss, beside me, cheers.

Karla lays another board and jumps onto it without hesitation, waving a stick overhead like a sword. Not to be outdone, Patrick jumps on after her, bottle of bourbon in his hand, then releases a mouthful into the air, sparkly in the firelight. "Oh yeah?" Karla says, full warrior now. "Watch THIS." She sets a wooden chair onto the board, sits on it like it's nothing, legs crossed demurely, stays a second too long for my comfort.

"Atta girl!" Boss shouts. "Show 'em how it's done."

There's an art to firesurfing, it seems. Caught up in the spirit, Mary and Steve, my fellow first-years, join the fray, jump onto the board together, hand in hand, half dare, half pas de deux. Some coaxing, and even Boss steps into the fire. This is crazy. He is seventy years old. He could fall. I remind myself there is a fire extinguisher in the foundry courtyard.

"Sara, come on! It's fun!" says Mary, goading, pulling me by the hand. I'm terrified. My hair is long and flammable. I'm wearing sandals. She pulls me through the flames onto a piece of plywood. Sparks shoot up and all around us, and heavy smoke and heat and orange make everything else invisible. I almost want to stay there, in the hot orange world.

"Go, Sara!" I hear Boss shouting as Mary pulls me to safety. A laugh wells up from deep in my abdomen, pure giddiness and lightness and freedom.

"Want some of my mushroom tea?" says John, appearing beside me with a pitcher and a stack of plastic cups. There's something different about him, a wildness in his eyes behind his sparkling glasses, an internal fire, something animal.

"Sure." Hallucinogen, presumably. It tastes bitter. I sip slowly. He downs a full cup, glug glug, wipes his mouth with his sleeve, skips off. I abandon the tea, return to my beer.

The feeling around the bonfire is changing. Karla throws on another board and jumps up and down on it, crushing live coals under her weight, howling like a coyote. Patrick practically pushes her off, then balances on one foot. It's a contest now. Between Patrick and Karla, the latest battle in a long war. Karla jumps back on with a pitchfork, strikes an American Gothic pose until her jeans catch fire and she jumps off, slapping the flame down with her bare hand. Patrick, again, with a cigarette in his mouth, does a goofy pirouette. Karla, fierce, hops on and lets fly a karate kick. It's getting joyless and angry. Boss should take charge. Someone's going to get hurt.

Suddenly, John Truman comes dashing from the building, screaming wildly, waving his arms, wearing nothing but cowboy boots and white briefs, hair a sticky fright. We all stand agape as he sets a metal stool on the board and stands on top of it, arms overhead, his skinny body a gleaming white tower in the fiery fountain.

I wake up with something wet and rough touching my ear. And a horrible smell. Dog breath. Karla's pit bull, Louise Nevelson, is licking my face, burrowing and sniffing in my hair.

I crashed in my studio after the bonfire last night, too late to walk home alone, and everyone else way too fucked up to trust for a ride. I'm on the floor under my table, on top of a bunch of fabric and wool, my retired felt bowl a surprisingly comfortable pillow. Karla strides in, freshly showered and wide awake. "Hey! Hey! Are you ready?"

"Ready? Huh?"

"Today's our trip to government surplus."

"Oh, yeah. I forgot." Louise the Dog is curling up beside me, as lazy as I feel.

"Hey, you cut open your felt things." Her feet stop beside the table, as she doubtlessly handles my objects without asking. "This is cool. Look at this rust."

"Yeah." I get up. Stretch. Sore back.

She surveys the skins on the table and their liberated guts. Nods her head, smiles. "You may be onto something."

I hear voices and laughter in the courtyard. "Is there time for coffee?" I croak.

"C'mon. I got a thermos in my truck."

It's John riding with Patrick, Steve riding with Boss, and the girls bringing up the rear of the three-pickup caravan. Louise Nevelson rides in the back of Karla's truck. Mary wedges between Karla and me in the cab. Karla's coffee is too sweet, but I drink it anyway, grateful. I'm the only one with any apparent hangover.

"What happened with John Truman last night?" Mary asks. We've reached the edge of town. Strip malls give way to cornfields and flatness all the way to the horizon, miles away. "Seriously. Jumping into the fire in his *underwear*?"

"He does that. He's an exhibitionist."

"I never would've guessed," muses Mary, shaking her close-cropped head.

"Last year, someone started calling him John Truman Capote."

"Ah." Mary laughs. "As in dweeby intellectual by day, world-class hedonist by night?"

"I guess," Karla says with a shrug. "I never read him."

"Capote? Didn't you ever see *Breakfast at Tiffany's*?"

"Me?" Karla cackles. I say nothing. I can see Boss laughing ahead of us, probably at Steve Pak's wit. Damn teacher's pet.

Karla downshifts around a turn. "Mary, you gotta see what Sara did to her piece last night. She *dissected* it."

"Really?" Mary turns to me.

"Yeah," I say, not quite ready to talk about it yet. "How far is this place?"

"About a hundred miles," Karla says in an exhale of smoke. "But don't worry. It goes fast. It's *coming back* that takes time."

I don't ask why. The smoke assaults my sinuses. The flat Midwestern fall speeds by outside the window. Louise's pink snout, in the passenger side mirror, joyfully sniffs the clean country air.

The government surplus warehouse is a candy store for sculptors. Room after room of junk, dirt cheap to institutions. Circuit boards. Spools of wire. Plumbing supplies. Antiquated medical devices. All of us are wide-eyed, not sure where to begin.

John gravitates to the chemistry gear: boxes of dusty 1950s-era beakers and test tubes in racks. Patrick, Boss, and Steve are thumping on a large, rusty, decommissioned propane tank. They can fight over who gets to cut it up; I don't care. Mary is fascinated by an old iron lung. Karla is checking out a pile of pink rubber tubing.

I find myself in a room full of uniforms, haphazardly folded on a table. Not just camouflage and military, but also lab coats, wet suits, surgical scrubs. Scrubs—*yes*. Maybe this is what I need: a proper uniform in which to *perform surgery* on my felt objects. I pick out a blue scrub suit, about my size, set it aside.

I find an old felt park ranger's hat, khaki tan, like Smokey the Bear's, turn it over to examine its construction. The felt is much tighter and harder than the felt I have been making. The brim springs back after I bend it. I pop it on my head. There are no mirrors. I step up to the window separating my little room from the next one, fall in love with the hat on my head in the dusty reflection.

"Hey! You look like Joseph Beuys!"

I nearly jump out of my skin. It is Steve, peering through from the other side.

"Sorry. I didn't mean to startle you." He disappears, reappears in the room beside me. Begins trying on a lab coat. Then a flight suit. With a nurse's cap. Gleefully, like a kid playing dress-up, only on speed, he's shifting personalities rapidly and seamlessly. Dispensing with modesty, he takes off his pants to try on a cop uniform. "Well, little lady, how fast do you think you were going?" He seems to want me in his game. I'm flummoxed. He's a different person. Swim fins and a gas mask. With a chef's apron. And a life preserver. Trying to get me to laugh. Some goofy safety glasses. He tosses me a pair. "Look!"—in a paper hazmat suit and goggles—"I'm DEVO!"

I don't know what to say. Mr. Serious Teacher's Pet and Critique Etiquette, prancing and squealing, with a four-year-old's energy and imagination? "Sara, check this! *Watches*. We can *synchronize* them for *beer time*." A box of a dozen of them, white faces, green web bands, army issue. He puts the whole box on his pile. "Enough for *all of us!*"

I'm speechless, but his joy is contagious.

"Oh. Oh. Sara. This one's yours. Definitely." He tosses me a man's red sleep shirt. I put it on over my clothes. "Yes!" he cries, handing me a khaki utility vest to put over it. It feels right. I look at my reflection in the window.

"What the hell?" Karla steps in to see what the commotion is. We must look ridiculous, Steve in the Devo ensemble, me dressed like a goofy hippie in nightshirt and vest and big-brimmed hat. She shakes her head like a proud but befuddled parent and leaves us alone to our impromptu performance.

"There's one rule of sculpture. If you can't make it *good*, make it *big*. If you can't make it *big*, make a *lot of 'em*." Boss is drunk, dispensing his wisdom, holding court at the bar of a dirty dive called Smokey's, in a little town I think is called Springville. It's the third bar we've been to on our trip back. Now I know what Karla meant: *it's coming back that takes time.*

I'm tired. I look at my new army-issue watch. It's past midnight. I go to the other end of the bar, order another Stag beer. Across the room, Patrick absorbs Boss's advice like gospel. Karla joins me. "Same old shit," she mutters, putting money on the bar.

"Yeah."

Steve squeezes between us. "Joseph Beuys!" he says, tweaking my new felt hat. "I've been thinking about that. I don't know why I never thought of it before. The felt—you know how Beuys used felt because it *saved his life* during the war? Some peasants wrapped him in felt and fat, so it *became his material*."

Karla, awakening now, grins. "You're right! Why didn't that come up in the crit?"

"But I've been thinking," Steve continues, his black eyes bright with epiphany. "That's what's missing in your piece. *You*. Like Beuys. You need to *be in it*. Forget wrapping stuff—what if you wrapped *yourself*? To see what it feels like? As an experiment? Then there would be no question about the personal aspect! You wouldn't have to explain anything!"

"Yeah!" Karla affirms, slamming her bottle on the bar.

I try to imagine it, logistically, creating the felt around my body. A bathtub full of detergent. I'll need help. Modesty will be out of the question. But the idea intrigues me. Like trying on a cop uniform, to see what it feels like. Trying on my work, to see what the objects feel. To transform myself, like the objects were transformed. To see the skin after it is removed. I smile. "Thanks, professor," I say.

"And *you*," Steve says, pointing rudely, but not rudely, in Karla's face. "Talk about *involving the body*. You scared everybody! *Tampons!* The look on Patrick's face! You scared *me*! I never seen those things before, bloody like that. *Damn.* But I like that! I like being scared. It's *power*."

Karla looks down at him gratefully, a welcome warmth at this end of the bar, constructive and invigorating. "Really?"

"It makes me think." Steve's a little drunk, on a roll now. "You know? I admit I adore formalist stuff, but I'm in a rut. I wish I could be more like you guys. Really laying something on the line. Putting the *self* out there, you know? Like a true experiment." And the jealousy in his face is genuine, like everyone else in his studio yesterday, all of us wanting just a little of his technical accomplishment. I'm humbled.

"Hey, O'Malley!" The bartender shouts to Boss. They are friends, from years and years of these sculptors' bar crawls. "I gotta joke for you. *A hippie, a Chink, and a dyke walk into a bar*."

Silence. I realize he is looking at the three of us. I must be the hippie, still wearing the red nightshirt and khaki vest over yesterday's smelly clothes, my long hair stringing out under the Joseph Beuys hat. And Steve, the only Asian in the room—or indeed the whole town, probably—we know which one he is. All faces are frozen on the other end of the bar. Mary looks like she wants to die. Meanwhile, Karla—the dyke—is red and might kill someone.

And then Steve does the impossible. He laughs. Giving permission to everyone in the joint. Boss and Patrick and Mary and John laugh with nervous relief. Others—strangers, farmers, barflies—laugh along, their motives harder to read. Even I laugh, maybe to make the comment go away. To bring back the warm camaraderie from a moment ago.

But it is gone. Karla throws her beer at the bartender and storms out the door. I wait a moment, then, concerned, go after her.

I find her in the back of her truck, drinking a tallboy from her cooler, arms around Louise Nevelson, her rock. "Karla." I climb into the truck bed, then touch her shoulder. "Are you OK?"

She is crying. "I'm sick of this shit. I'm not a dyke. I'm not gay. Why does everyone think I'm gay?"

You're not? I don't voice the thought. I sit on the wheel well, next to a large mound of new rubber tubing.

"Mary's gay, but no one calls her a dyke," Karla says.

"Really?"

"Yeah, she's been hitting on me since she got here."

Louise licks Karla's cheek, the salty tears. It's quiet out here in Springville, or Springfield, or wherever the hell we are. Karla's upending her beer, spilling it on her face, and something is making sense to me. Karla's focus on Patrick. His blue eyes and manly work ethic and blond Viking beard. She doesn't hate him at all. Not at all. A heartbreaking impossibility. He is oblivious, will never see what I can see now, clear as resin, in her raw, inebriated face. She lights a cigarette. "I hate it here."

"Me too." The voice startles me. It's Steve, climbing into the back of the truck. "Sorry. I was lost without my hippie and dyke sidekicks."

Karla laughs. I laugh too. Steve sits next to me, on the pile of tubing. Pulls a bottle from a pocket inside his jacket. "Want some Jägermeister?"

"What the hell," I say. It is sweet and pungent, its hot assault welcome in the back of my throat. I pass the bottle to Karla, then lean against the cool steel of the truck, look up at the sky. A nearly full moon. Stars bright, like they can only be in the country. Louise settles next to Karla's feet. I breathe the cool fall air, quiet, steady.

"Hey, Pak," says Karla, passing the bottle back to Steve. "I'm dying to know what your formula is. For that patina."

"The ancient Korean secret?" I venture. I'm curious too.

"Ach. It's nothing," Steve says, stretching out his legs. "Promise you won't tell anyone."

"I promise." My hand over my heart.

"Me too."

"Skim milk, kosher salt, blue food coloring, and piss."

"Whose piss?" Karla pushes.

"Who do you think?"

"And you were worried about putting yourself in the work," Karla says, accepting another drag from the bottle. The dog sighs and repositions herself. Faint music drifts from the jukebox inside the bar.

"True," Steve admits. He leans against the wall of the truck bed, his long black hair beautiful in the moonlight. A truck passes on the bumpy little highway, washing light over us, three foreign freaks and a lazy dog in the back of a rusty green pickup, banded together for safety, armed with nothing but rubber tubing. The neon Pabst sign buzzes in the roadhouse window. Next to it is a feed store, closed for hours, kudzu vines creeping up the silent building, arrogant and thick, choking it to death.

The bar door opens, and noise gushes out. John Truman, dressed only in white briefs and cowboy boots, runs yelling into the empty road. Boss chases him down, grabs him roughly by the arm, drags him to his truck, throws him in. Then Patrick dashes out, arms full of John's discarded clothes, and Mary runs up to us, giggling nervously. "I think we've worn out our welcome," she says.

"Yup, time to go," Karla says. She hops into the driver's seat, puts the truck in gear.

Patrick is speeding away already, Boss too, crazy John in tow, not wasting any time. "Hang on," Karla shouts through the window, as Mary slams the passenger door, and Steve and the dog and I are thrown onto the truck bed floor, a pile of limbs and teeth and rubber tubing. Something jabs into my shoulder.

"Damn. What the hell was that?" Steve rubs a sore elbow. We're back on the open road. Good. Good riddance, Springwhatever. Back into cornfields, straight highway, aiming for home.

I sit up a little, lean against the cab. "Here." I help Steve to an empty spot beside me. "Louise!" The dog is hopping back and forth over the rubber tubing, making me nervous. "Sit! Sit down!" She obeys, settles between us, rests her bony chin on my knee.

"Well, I guess we're here for the long haul." Steve digs through the cooler, opens himself a beer, passes one to me. I'm already drunk, I realize, taking a pull of it. All of us are. None of us is in any condition to drive, Karla especially. This might very well be the last beer I ever drink. The last ride I ever take. Steve doesn't seem nervous at all. Hangs his arm over the side of the truck. Looks straight up at the sky. "I'm glad it's not raining," he says.

A positive comment. He has a point. Rain would make this journey uncomfortable, but there is no rain, and I'm relaxing now, in spite of common sense, into my drunkenness. Karla's doing sixty, probably. My hat flies off, onto the road, and we watch it recede into darkness. "Bye," I call after it, my little felt friend. My hair is flying wild into my mouth and eyes. I lie down completely now to get out of the wind. Steve, above me, relishes the chaos, lets his long hair do what it wants, looks up at the stars.

"I think Karla is in love with Patrick," I say. It's loud out here. She can't hear me.

"Really?" He looks down at me, just a moonlit silhouette now, his expression impossible to read. "I never thought of that. Whatever it is, she's got it bad."

"Yeah." I scratch Louise's chest as she stretches. "You know what, Steve? I'm sick of being afraid of you," I blurt.

I'm not sure why I said it. Maybe losing the felt hat has left my brain exposed and rusty, like the kitchen timer. I expect him to laugh, but he doesn't; he just looks at me peripherally, back in his inscrutable mode, which I realize now is just another costume, its own kind of hazmat suit.

God, *inscrutable*? Did I really just think that? Can he hear my rusted brain thinking it, over the wheels and wind?

He doesn't say anything. He looks straight back at the road.

"Hey, Devo. Snap out of it," I say, and reach to poke his armpit. He winces, faces me, and finally cracks a smile.

Aquaria

Sculpture by Karla Wells: Exhibition Catalogue (excerpts)

Artist's Note

Though they may be beloved family members, it is important not to anthropomorphize our pets. Dogs are dogs. Koi are koi. More useful information can be gleaned from a study of natural behavior in a natural habitat. Toward that end, I present an extraordinary set of species from the Tamponicus *genus, and while we can all agree they are cute as hell, I prefer to keep this discussion in the realm of scientific inquiry.*

1. *Tamponicus fuckofficus*
The bright, saturated crimson of the female *Tamponicus fuckofficus* serves to ward off advances from the males, whose aggression and stupidity they find distasteful. The males, meanwhile, are terrified of the deep red hue, leaving the females free to hang out and shoot the shit.

2. *Tamponicus elegia*
Unlike other members of the *Tamponicus* genus, the *Tamponicus elegia* form monogamous pair bonds and can be observed migrating in tandem during spawning season. Procreation often proves challenging for the *Tamponicus elegia*, and after the eggs are fertilized, both male and female wait, carefully guarding the spawn until they hatch. Failure to produce offspring results in unusual behavior, which appears to the human observer like arguing and blaming, followed by a month of apparent mourning. Females will typically lower their heads and curl

up their tails, following the offspring of other females with their eyes. The males remain close by but clearly have no clue what the females are experiencing.

3. *Tamponicus festivus*
The behavior of the rare *Tamponicus festivus* is often compared to that of the *Pan paniscus*, or bonobo chimp, in which sexual congress is the primary form of socialization, establishing both status and bonding in a complex family hierarchy. Females exhibit brief, casual sexual behaviors with both males and other females, and procreation is a secondary concern. In sharp contrast to the *Tamponicus elegia*, the *Tamponicus festivus* appear relieved at the failure to produce offspring, exhibiting the characteristic "festive" red bloom. Much has been written about the "dance" of the *Tamponicus festivus* over their inert eggs, prompting members of the scientific community to speculate that this species is one of the few on the planet to have mastered voluntary birth control.

4. *Tamponicus cursio*
Noted for their dark purple color, the *Tamponicus cursio* have been the subject of depressing poetry and song for generations. Stricken on the full moon with apparent severe pain and immobility, females of this species are known to refrain from strenuous activity for as much as a week at a time, bobbing with the tide, in small groups, apart from the rest of their colony. Males are, reasonably, prone to avoiding the females during this time, engaging in athletic activities and commiserating among themselves. A word of caution: if females in a colony are displaying the deep purple hue, it is advisable not to put one's hands in the aquarium, as they will interpret this as a provocation to aggression, and their teeth are no joke.

War

THE PLAIN TABLE. THE PLAIN BOOKSHELF, WITH PLAIN OLD DICTIONARY. The lamp, gooseneck. Concrete floor slanted severely. Daybed propped up with stones on one end. Windows facing a stand of fall-turning trees. Walls, white and bare, and an easy chair. I sit in the dusk in the quiet, hollow room, waiting for poems. The room is far too big. It is the inside of a guitar I have forgotten how to play.

Supper is at 6:00 p.m. in the residence hall. Some bring wine to share. Some pray silently before picking up forks. This is the South, Virginia, where pitchers of iced tea cool brows and jump-start brains. I pour myself a glass and try to find my appetite. The woman beside me introduces herself—Sara, a sculptor from California.

"I'm Ben. I'm a poet, or I used to be."

"You're from England?" She smiles at my accent.

"Originally, yes. I'm more of a New Yorker now," I say, and she gives me a look like an apology.

"My sister Becky is there. She's been freaking out. I'm pretty sure she was drunk for two straight weeks."

"There's a lot of that going around."

"It must be strange, being here, especially now, in this quiet place."

"Yes," I reply. "The sirens are gone."

My phone has no reception in my bedroom or studio. I take a walk in the morning, hold out the plastic thing, my divining rod, wait for the tiny antenna display to grow bars. I discover clarity in the middle of a field. Lean against a big yellow wheel of hay to call home.

"Baby, where are you? I've been worried."

"I'm sorry, V. There's no reception here. I'm in the middle of a pasture."

"With cows?"

"No. I'm leaning on hay." It's prickly.

"*Cowboy.*" Virgil laughs, and I can see his mouth next to his phone, mate of my phone, its twin.

Nights, just after dinner, I stand in the center of the field, hold my phone up to the purple sky, wait for it to vibrate with text. Honest couplets and haiku, from Virgil's new work computer:

> *our cafeteria*
> *is full of firemen*
> *(can I have one?)*
>
> *bandwidth low*
> *spirits lower*
> *secretaries crying*
>
> *big plume of black smoke*
> *this thing is still burning*
>
> *dog misses u*
> *(me too)*

The only poems come to me from the Virginia sky, from Virgil, from his eyes. His black almond eyes, the ones I long to kiss. I see him covered in dust, like when it happened, arriving home, finally, his suit and lungs and mouth filled with charred computers, asphalt, bones. Papers still float in the smoky air over Brooklyn Heights. Crying with relief, I take him into my arms. *V, I was so sure you were gone.*

We pick up lunch boxes, each painted with bright acrylic strokes. Mine, *Studio W1*, has Adam and Eve and an apple. I think of Brigitte, a German artist here. She showed me a drawing: twin towers, Adam and Eve, filled with text from Genesis. *The Big Apple*, she calls it. The moment innocence quits, the garden's faults become obvious and palpable.

Inside the lunch box, another apple, a real one, which I save on my windowsill for later. A ham-and-cheese sandwich on perfect whole-wheat bread. A tiny cup of pasta salad. A homemade sugar cookie in a waxed paper bag.

I think of him; I can't stop. Now he's in his cafeteria, overlooking the hole, with the dusty, haunted firemen, with the girls from his temporary office, talking

The Artstars

about the fragile database they nearly lost in the fire. He tells me about it, every night in the field; I wish I understood. *Restoring from backup, onto tiny computers,* and I look at my tiny, waiting computer on the tilted table, wish I had backup or some means of restoring the thing I came here to do, which feels ridiculous now, and I can only eat my sandwich and fall asleep on the daybed, propped up by rocks, the window light warm, the faint, lush piano chords from the composer's studio nearby.

Night, in my bedroom—bags still opened, waiting to be unpacked. I lie naked in bed and hold my cock, lonely for its other: Virgil's honey skin, his dimpled ass, his hairless slim belly against my aging bloat. The dog, warm on my feet, tail beating against my leg.

I hear the composer showering in the bathroom we share, between our rooms. I spoke to him at dinner. He loves poetry, is setting Rimbaud to music. *Rimbaud*, and I get his meaning: we are of the same tribe, and I listen to the water on his body and realize I did not hear the click of him locking the door between us.

My hand moves and blood moves and Virgil disappears, and I am thinking of the man in the shower, whose piano chords haunt my afternoon dreams, his broad pale back under the water, and no poems come, but I do, into my hand and the borrowed sheet. And shame, and I lie awake in my sticky mess, and I should never have come here.

Ladybird beetles are infiltrating my studio, escaping the fall chill. They creep through the cracks around the door, collect like baby basketballs in the corners of the windows. I name one: Sylvia. Another: Emily. Emily crawls, delicate orange creature on my finger. I ask her for a poem; she must have one to spare. She lifts her antennae, questions me, then flies up to the window to join her sleepy sisters.

Next to the door is a plaque, where previous fellows, writers, have signed their names. I pull a pen from my pocket, and under the others, some famous, I write *Bennett Campbell*. The only two words I write all day.

I take a walk to the nearby college to use the library. I'm thinking *Inferno*—been years since I read it—sure to be in the stacks.

A timid doe peeks at me between orange and yellow leaves. The road is hard and empty beneath my sneakers. And I come upon a construction site, the opened earth impossibly red, Southern dirt, the excavated hole a bright vermilion, like fire. Waiting concrete culverts are collected, like gray corpses, for the men to bury them.

It is a women's college. The library is full of women. I look at their young female bodies with relief. No shame, no hunger, only curiosity and a weird longing for Emily, the ladybird I entertained on my finger, stingy with her verse, but I'll forgive her when I return.

At dinner, a fork clinks a glass, and everyone listens. It's Sara, the sculptor; she will have an open studio tonight. I have an urge to impress them, these stranger artists, wish I had a good reason to clink my glass with a fork. I'm not nobody, am I? I'm somebody; Virgil knows. Emily, the ladybird, knows, though she won't share.

I will go. I have nothing better to do. I have no poems to write. I will call Virgil, then go to the open studio, drink wine, forget how little I have to say.

Sara works in felt, makes inverse portraits of people by wrapping them in the fiber. "It's not pure felt," she explains, while we drink wine and look at her work. Her portraits are spread out on the table and pinned to the wall. She's mixing plaster with wool and rag in a large bucket, chalky dust all over her shoes and jeans. On the table: a cup, the clear contour of an ample breast inside. On the wall: an inverse belly, its navel sticking out like a nipple. Fragments of bodies, inside out, skins: a shoulder, an ear, a foot. I pour myself another glass of chardonnay, feel it fill my skin with cool relief. "I have a volunteer tonight, so you can see the process." The composer. He smiles, sits, lays his hands on the table like it's a piano. The hands are large, big enough for the lush chords that cross the courtyard in the afternoons. Sara applies the fiber mixture over his greased fingernails and wrists. It is dusty gray, like Virgil's suit that day, full of particles of unknown origin. Her hands are covered in it too, sticky and sensuous, like mud, and I wish hers were my hands, spreading it between the fingers of the composer. He laughs at the odd sensation, his eyes looking right into mine.

That night I wait in bed, naked, listening. Crickets rub legs to wings; laughter floats up from the TV room downstairs. I hear the sound of water in the bathroom next to mine, the sound I have been waiting for. I sigh into the pillow, my skin empty, my head spinning with wine. The water continues for a long time, like a dare, and finally I can't hold my curiosity anymore. I stand up, try the door to the bathroom.

It is unlocked. Inside, through the smoky wet air, he is waiting for me, soapy cock in his hand, bits of felt and plaster on the floor of the shower. I don't speak; I hurtle forward, as if pushed, to his waiting mouth.

"I need to be fucked," he says, his vowels long and Southern. "I am so lonely here."

I love the coarse honesty of his admission, pure American, *to be fucked*, to push away loneliness. I pull my fingers through his watery red hair, kiss his piano hands, the vermilion fur of his chest, like Southern earth. It's what I have wanted, but my throat fills with bile, and my body won't cooperate—a wave of self-loathing spreads through my chest. I close my eyes and see Virgil, insistent, dusty, exhausted. Virgil's eyes. I pull away.

"This is wrong. I'm so sorry. I'm married. I can't."

His countenance fills with naked anger. He turns, takes a towel into his room, and clicks the lock behind him. I close my door too, crawl sopping wet and cold under the covers.

Emily and Sylvia have friends. Thousands of them, and not cute anymore. I wake from a nap, and they are all over my sun-warmed studio—on my blanket, in my hair, dotting all four walls like ladybird-patterned paper. I stand up and shake out the blanket. I am still wobbly and hungover. I can feel them crawling under my pants. I see them all over the plaque of famous and not-famous names, on the lone dictionary, on my powerless computer, creeping between the lettered keys, dotting the dark screen in mockery.

At dinner, I ask Sara if she will make my portrait. The felt reminds me of something, I tell her—the ash all over Virgil's suit and skin. She listens intently.

"That must have been frightening, waiting for him to come home."

"I have never been more frightened."

"You miss him."

I nod. "It's strange—no one is talking about it here. In New York, everyone's talking about it all the time. It's all we talk about."

"The towers, you mean?"

"Yeah. And where we were that day, and who we knew inside. Everyone knows someone inside."

The composer sits at another table, eating and laughing, not looking this way. "I have ladybirds all over my studio," I say. "I can't work."

"Ladybirds?"

"Ladybugs. They're everywhere. Millions. I want to kill them."

"*No way.*" She thinks I am joking. "Not ladybugs. You can't kill them. It's bad luck."

Virgil asks me how my work is going. I don't lie. I tell the truth: there is no work, and nothing is going, and I wish I never came here. I want to confess the real truth, how I kissed a Southern composer with beautiful hands and we were both naked and what a horrible husband I am. I am sitting in the middle of the field, midnight, the sky dotted with lights, the crescent moon, beautiful, but I am only sick for home. "I miss you" is all I can say. "I don't think I can last another two weeks."

"It'll go so fast, B."

"I know. How is the database? How are the firemen?"

"The firemen aren't coming much anymore. I think they hate seeing us with all our laptops and Hugo Boss suits and shit. And there are tourists all over the streets. Can you believe? It's a damn *tourist attraction* already, and they haven't even put the fire out."

"I wish I were there." I imagine him in the bed, dog curled next to him for warmth.

"Oh, no, you don't. You earned this."

"There are ladybugs all over my studio. A swarm of them. Like the plagues of Egypt."

He laughs.

"Seriously, I want to kill them."

"So kill them. Get a can of Raid. It's your studio, not theirs."

I'm not so sure that's true, but at least he knows I'm not joking.

Sara applies Vaseline to my cheeks and eyelids. She will make a mold of my face, like a death mask. Then she glops the gray mixture on my skin, muddy and warm. She warns me that the plaster will heat up, then places drinking straws in my nostrils, and I focus on my breath. She covers my wordless mouth, my cheeks, then my eyes, and I am blind. I feel her long hair, falling soft against my bare arms. I can hear everything now, in full volume, in the dark—Sara's breath, the squishing material, the composer's piano wafting in through the open window.

"Mind if I put on some music?"

"Mm-mmm."

I hear her putting a CD in the player, clicking it shut. Joni Mitchell, her mountain dulcimer, straightforward and simple open tuning, her high, honest soprano. "Mmmm," I say, unable to move my mouth.

"You like Joni?"

"Mm-hmm." I do like Joni; I like anyone who can drown out the drifting piano. She's another expat, like me, choosing American life and American instruments, trying to adopt the simplicity of this place, its frankness of expression, its innocence. I feel the mask going hot and stiff on my face, making permanent this American moment. I feel tears pushing against the hardness over my eyes.

Night, in my studio, it is much cooler. The ladybirds have collected in high clumps, huddled for warmth—easy targets. I spray them liberally with the pungent chemicals, watch them panic and drop to the floor; dead poets, short lives.

After sweeping the corpses out the door, I sit and turn on the computer in the dark. My hands click on the keys, falling over themselves in their impatience:

Fuck ladybirds. Or ladybugs, or whatever the hell they call them here. Fuck Emily, that stingy rhyming bitch, fuck Sylvia, American whiner. Fuck this place with its stupid slanted floor, fuck the bed, fuck the bookshelf, fuck the table, fuck the window. Fuck the famous writers on that plaque over there. Fuck the piano chords I can't get away from and fuck iced tea and the South and smart people clinking their glass at dinner and fuck art. Fuck mobile phones that only work in the middle of a fucking field, fuck the field, fuck the hay, fuck the red dirt under me, fuck the stars over me, fuck the clean air.

Fuck those fuckers in those fucking planes, fuck them for trying to kill my Virgil, and those fucking arrogant towers, good riddance, fuck them too. And fuck Virgil for writing cleaner poetry than me in a fucking mobile phone, and fuck him for seeing what I can't. Fuck my American husband, fuck him for surviving, fuck him for making me wait, fuck him for being so rational, fuck him for letting me come here, no, fuck him for making me come here, fuck our fucking home I miss so much, fuck time.

And fuck me. Fuck me especially. For this bad American rant and its lazy American vocabulary, and for killing fucking ladybugs and nearly fucking a composer, and for not fucking the composer when he needed to be fucked, and for not writing a fucking word, and for leaving the fucking dog, and for leaving the man I love alone to clean up the fucking mess.

Pink

HELEN MARKS USED TO HAVE A THING FOR THE HAPPY MEAL. IT WAS worth the wait in the amorphous queue, at the Wall-Street-themed McDonald's, under the streaming ticker board. Oh, the sad little patty! Oh, the mushy white bun! The lone salty pickle, the blob of sugary ketchup! And the hamburger wasn't even the point. The point was the tiny prize. She always asked for the girly prize: a Beanie Baby, or Hello Kitty, or spokescritter of the latest Disney offering. All in shades of pink. Shocking, or rosy, or tender, or loud: *pink*.

She had them arranged, her mute, smiling audience, along the top of her monitor and around the sides of her cubicle. Virgil Feliz, her friend from the Help Desk, was creeped out by it. "How can you work with everyone staring at you?" he said often, popping his head over their shared beige wall.

"How can I work in general?" she said, though she was managing, sort of. Productivity was important. It was patriotic. They would stick it to the terrorists through productivity.

"I hear you," Virgil said, then returned to his gargantuan task—answering a perpetual phone ring, reassuring the weary and traumatized, telling them where to point and click, encouraging the reboot.

Helen didn't go to McDonald's much anymore. It wasn't worth it. She would have to hike around the giant gaping hole in the sky. Back through police checkpoints, through workers laying new power and telephonic cable under the streets of Tribeca, streets dug into channels like the canals of old Amsterdam, then down to Broadway and into the sickening pack of lookers. Grungy memorial gifts were everywhere down there, tacked to fences and walls—teddy bears growing crusty with ash, strings of faded origami birds. Tourists were having their photos taken in front of it: Miss, please, do you mind? The fire wasn't even quite gone yet. Look, Ma, I was here! That, plus the fife player tweeting God Bless America over and over—it made her brain go spongy. It made her fists do something ugly. It made her lose her urge for a Happy Meal. The corporate cafeteria would do just fine. At least in there, they were among their own. Everyone had the same emptied stare. Everyone had their work cut out. No one wanted pictures.

The world knew the layoffs were coming. *Wall Street Journal*: "Singer Martin to Cut 5,000 Jobs." People discussed résumés in the elevator. Virgil had a running joke: *Nice to see you! Nice to be seen!* Whole departments were likely to get the chop.

When Helen got the call from Human Resources, she popped her head over the wall, but Virgil was on the phone. His look told her he knew already. The tech guys were "prenotified," just in time to cut off network permissions.

The HR guy, Nick Bartoni, looked exhausted. He was clean-shaven, but his face looked scraped raw, like he was fighting serious grown-up acne. He wore a suit, which was no longer required, probably intended to give the goodbye meetings a professional air, though the air had worn off by 3:00 p.m. He gave her a short, tightly canned speech: cost cutting, market woes, the need to reconfigure the organization as a whole. "The Quant department is just too big," he said. Meaning they were keeping some of her colleagues, but not her. Her boss had gone through the roster and picked her.

"How many of these have you done today?" Helen asked.

He sighed, ran a hand through his sandy hair. This was the same guy who drank mojitos and danced a silly Electric Slide with her at the holiday party last year. He looked hollowed out. "You don't wanna know."

"Really. I do."

He sank back into his generic chair. There was a stack of folders on his desk, at least twenty deep. "You're the sixteenth."

"Damn. How many you got left?"

He looked at the stack of folders. "You mean today or altogether?"

He obviously didn't want her to reply, so she didn't. He looked her in the eye, a man on the edge of an abyss. Behind him was a sealed picture window. Outside, a big gap where the North Tower used to be. Light streamed in over the still-smoldering pit. Clouds, wispy cotton, dotted a stark blue sky. Helen took a deep inhale, looked up at the blue. He slid a thick white packet across the desk.

"No pink slip?" she said.

He didn't laugh. Her question was as old as the Catskills. "The package is as generous as we could make it," he said.

"Thank you," Helen replied, automatic. It's what you say when someone gives you a package.

Helen had met Virgil on the day of the main event. She had been hearing him for over a year, on the other side of the wall, cooing to his lover on the phone or patiently talking down hysterical users. Once, she had even wandered by to connect a face with the voice, but she didn't say hello. She had pictured a Chelsea butch guy in a tight white T-shirt and wallet chain, but Virgil was small in stature and wore the nerd uniform of his techie brethren—a decent gray suit with the labels cut out, jacket draped over the back of his chair, white shirtsleeves rolled up over skinny forearms, lunch-stained tie. Next to his monitor was a framed photo of a fierce little mutt in a rainbow sweater.

But she didn't talk to him, not until she got an e-mail from a London colleague: "Is it true a plane flew INTO the World Trade Center?" It wasn't possible. That was right next door. She hadn't heard a crash. Then people started running in the halls around her. Helen froze. And Virgil, bless him, strode right into her cubicle, laptop under his arm, stuffing phone and keys into his suit pockets.

"Grab your gym shoes," he said. "Don't leave your bag behind. You'll need your phone." He held out his hand. She took it and didn't let go, all the way down twenty flights of fire stairs and into the panicked streets. They stood outside their building, trying to get phones to work, looking up at the tiny blaze. The fire was so far away, so high overhead, unreachable.

Virgil had started to cry. No one was in charge. "Don't look at it," she said, turning his head away, just as she saw something she knew she could not unsee. She gripped his hand, marched him to the mouth of the Brooklyn Bridge, and hugged him goodbye. Then, she took off her suit jacket and began the long hike to her apartment uptown. She did not look back. She was in Chinatown when the towers fell. She kept walking as the people around her stopped and stared at the spectacle, as if they were not going to see it over and over, forever, on their televisions. Virgil was still at the bridge when it all collapsed, Helen learned later. He was helping a stranger, an asthmatic. They both got a mouthful of ash, but they made it over the river.

They didn't see each other again for a month. The office building was powerless and unsafe. Helen telecommuted. She called the Help Desk once, and Virgil answered. His voice was cool again and tired. "This problem is expensive," he kept saying. "There's no way they can pay us all."

"They won't have layoffs. Not after this. That would be just cruel."

But Singer Martin was not their mother. And he was camping out on a cot in a server room, some nights. He had smelled the rotten entrails of the dying beast.

After a month of cleanup, the headquarters was reopened. Helen's Happy Meal characters welcomed her back to the warm cubicle. The apples she had left on her desk had been removed. She had been expecting a pool of decayed fruit flesh on her desk and the smell of hard cider, made the hard way.

She had lunch with Virgil, her first day back, in the third-floor cafeteria. They didn't talk much. People stared out the window, forks frozen in hand, all with that same far look. Feeling lucky and unlucky at the same time. The plaza outside, normally full of lunching suits, had been turned into a staging area—a flatbed truck and a shipping container plopped amid the stone picnic tables. On the plaza railing, facing the Hudson, was inscribed, in letters a foot tall, a quote from Walt Whitman: *City of tall facades, of marble and iron—proud and passionate city—mettlesome, mad, extravagant city!*

"Wanna hear something sick?" Virgil said, stabbing the yolk of his hard-boiled egg. "The attacks are spawning new industries. The guys on the Desk are all talking about this biometrics outfit—you know, those retinal scanners? Booming. The stock is about to take off. Is that blood money or what?"

"All money is blood money," Helen said, quoting an old Econ professor. "The veins of New York are pumping with blood money."

"More like bleeding out," he said.

At the table next to them, a group of firemen hunched over their free lunches. They ate silently and slowly. They were keeping to themselves, avoiding the clean people with clean clothes and clean jobs.

"I think I'm done with New York," Virgil said.

"How can you say that?" she replied. "There's no place in the world like this."

"New York is full of itself," he said.

Helen disagreed. It seemed, to her, to be emptying itself out.

For two days, she didn't tell anyone about getting sacked. Virgil didn't call. Maybe it was one of those kinds of friendships—the trauma-spawned friendship, the kind that doesn't last past the trauma. She toyed with the idea of calling the Help Desk to ask for some Help. But he was busy enough, processing all the firings, killing off permissions.

She sat around in her apartment, flipping through channels, unable to get up and turn on the computer and mess with her résumé. She didn't even bother looking at her mail. Not until it was unavoidable, a messenger with six file boxes labeled MARKS PERSONAL EFFECTS, packed with care by one of the temps, each Happy Meal toy shrouded in bubble wrap. She cried as she unwrapped them and arranged them on her cramped desk. The phone rang.

"Helen? What's going on?" It was Mom. "I called you at the office, and there was some girl on a recording saying you were no longer at the firm. Did you quit?"

"No. I'm a statistic."

"You're what?" Pause. "Oh. Oh, Helen. Oh, I'm so sorry."

"I'm fine. They gave me a package." She tried her best to sound fine, wiping her nose on the sleeve of her sweatshirt. "I still get paid for six months."

"Dick? Dick?" Mom shouted into the house. "Pick up the phone. It's Helen."

"Helen?"

"Helen's been laid off," Mom said.

"Oh." His disappointment struck Helen in the gut. She didn't try to hide her tears anymore. She couldn't, not from him.

One of her salient Singer Martin memories: Waiting for a client lunch on the forty-second floor. The client was over a half hour late, and Helen had brought nothing to read. So she looked out the window. At the Hudson, filled with big chunks of ice floating slowly to the Atlantic. The park along the shore, way, way below, dogs and children running like dots on the snow-covered grass. And inside, on one wall of the executive dining room, portraits of the CEOs of the last fifty years, all authoritative, portly gentlemen in blue and gray suits. She inspected the portraits closely, noticed a slight evolution of style in the application of paint, a mini-art-history lesson for those who paid attention. In the earliest ones, the look was flat and no-nonsense, poses stiff but flattering, faces confident, the peaches and whites of skin blended seamlessly. But then there came a gradual softening of the brush marks, as time passed and artists were replaced. She put her face up close to the latest one, interesting for the dewiness of the man's pink cheek and for the glazed highlight in the corner of each blue eye, almost like a tear.

It was time to network, to put feelers out there, but Helen had no energy and no feelers. She finally gave in to Mom's suggestion and went home for a little suburban R and R.

There, she found her twin bed packed with stuffed animals, each with its own story and name and personality. The *Dogs Playing Poker* print still hung on the wall, a gift from Dad for her tenth birthday. She had forgotten the softness of her pink blanket, which she kept folded under her pillow and stroked as she went to sleep.

In New York, she hadn't been sleeping well, but here, the dark, country quiet enveloped her, and the dreams came, the ones she had been expecting. Some were almost goofy, like one with her and Virgil getting on the elevator to go for drinks at Windows on the World. Halfway up, the elevator stops, and everyone gets out. "I'm sorry," says a guard on the fiftieth floor. "The rest of the building is gone. This is as far as it goes."

"They couldn't tell us that in the lobby?" Virgil says.

"We are all on a need-to-know basis," the guard says.

The worst dreams were nothing but memories, brought back into real time by sleep. Replaying that day, the endless trek down the crowded fire stairs, walking away from her office and wondering if she will ever go back. The smoke and papers flying, and her hand turning Virgil's head away, so he won't see that thing, the thing Helen can't unsee: a figure in a navy-blue business suit, back first, then turning, flapping pink tie becoming closer and clearer.

Finally, she closes her eyes, shutting out the man, the suit, the thing. Shutting it out.

"So, what are you going to do while you're here?" Mom asked over the breakfast table. Her cheeriness was grating sometimes, but not now. Now it was refreshing and restorative, like orange juice. "You know your painting stuff is still in the basement."

"She should work on her résumé." Dad put down his newspaper. "I can look it over for you, maybe show it to some of the guys at the club."

"Dick, shush. The résumé can wait." Even if Mom was wrong, Helen was relieved to have a spokesperson.

Dad gave one of his self-assured shrugs. "Maybe not, Marian. Gotta stay in the game while you still have some decent cards in your hand."

"Cards!" Mom lit up. "What a great idea! Why don't you come with me to my bridge club tomorrow? There's bound to be room for you, Helly. Do you still play?"

"Not really." Helen had learned when she was nine, much to her mother's pride. Dad's pride too, though he didn't play. Bridge was a smart game, for smart girls, in his view.

Helen jabbed a toothpick between her two front teeth. They were crooked, crowded just enough to trap food at every meal. "I hate my teeth," she muttered.

"What's wrong with your teeth?" Dad said. "They're perfect."

"Look." She bared them under the pendant kitchen light. Dad leaned in, the gray hairs of his nostrils huge. She could hear his wheezy breath as he studied her mouth. "They're getting more crooked every year," Helen said through frozen lips. "I can't smile for photos anymore."

"Let me see," Mom said, leaning in too now, her floral perfume enveloping the trio. Something to focus on. A family barn raising, right here in Helen's mouth. "Hmm," she said, and stood up. "I never noticed that before."

"They look great," Dad said, reraising his shield of newspaper.

"You know, a lot of adults get braces now. Cindy, the church secretary, has them."

"Mom, I'm thirty-four."

"Why not?" Mom's object was clear. Her mind was made up. This would be Helen's big project while she was home. "Isn't your friend Jerry Steloff an orthodontist, Hon?" Dad snapped his newspaper and humphed the affirmative. "Well, great. Good. Helen, we'll get you an appointment." Maybe it wasn't such a bad idea. Come home, straighten her head, straighten her teeth. Go back to New York a new person.

Dr. Steloff's assistant, Cheryl, was mixing putty in a little plastic dish. She was cute, pixie red hair and a Hello Kitty smock, probably for the younger patients, but Helen welcomed it. "OK, Helen, this stuff tastes nasty, but I can flavor it if you want. Do you want strawberry, mint, or piña colada?"

"Do you put rum in the piña colada?"

"That's the best one. It covers up the plastic taste."

"Make it a double."

"Just taking an impression," Cheryl murmured as she placed the curved cup over Helen's upper teeth. "Bite down." She put a suction tube in Helen's mouth, which grew loud with her saliva, her gums dry and uncomfortable. "Sorry. It's disgusting, I know."

"Mmmmph." Helen replied, trying not to gag. She let her mind drift while Cheryl pulled out the putty, then put another round on the lower teeth. There was a poster on the ceiling, an orange kitten hanging by his claws from a tree branch, the old saw caption below: *Hang in there, baby, Friday's coming.* The kitten looked scared. Helen had never noticed that before. Mortally terrified, like the fall from the tree was many stories, would be his last. It wasn't funny at all. *Friday's coming.* The kitten knew better than to count on that. Cheryl rinsed, asked her to spit. Helen obeyed.

"Well, Helen," said Dr. Steloff, sweeping into the room with a big perfect smile. He rode a rolling stool over next to her, focused a light on her face, and leaned in, his red beard showing hints of gray beneath his plastic face shield. "Let's take a look. Open." Helen obeyed again. His tie was dotted with tiny Elmer Fudds, mimicking the ruddy, round face inches from hers. "OK, now bite down on this paper. Open again. Hmm. Bite again. OK, I think we can help you."

"Gooth."

"I'm sorry?" He let go of her jaw.

"Good."

He went in again with a tiny mirror, his blue eyes terrifyingly close. "Your dad says you work on Wall Street. What do you do?"

"Quanthithathid analytht."

"Quantitative analyst? Interesting. I hope you're enjoying your vacation." *Vacation?* "I imagine you need it. The market has not been easy, has it?" Helen shook her head. "How soon do you have to go back to the city?"

How to answer that? Had Dad been lying about her status? Dr. Steloff smiled, inches from her face, just another workday, hanging on cheerfully for a Friday that was surely coming. His fat wedding ring was studded with diamonds under the latex glove.

"I go bhack nextht week," she said, before she could stop herself.

"But you'll be able to come back here regularly to continue the orthodontia?" He pulled his fingers from her mouth, then ripped the gloves off and tossed them in a foot-controlled bin by his feet.

Helen stretched her jaw. "Sure," she said. Why had Dad lied?

Steloff had rolled over to the counter, was looking in her chart, probably at the full-head X-ray from that mysterious booth Helen had sat in half an hour before.

"I'll just hop on Metro-North," she said. "A good excuse to see my folks."

"Good girl." He rolled back over and handed her a Dixie cup of water. He pulled off his face mask, rubbed his beard thoughtfully, looked at her straight on, like one would a peer. "Say, you would not believe what has happened to my stock portfolio."

"I probably would."

"I'm getting creamed. Bought a bunch of Internet stocks, like an idiot. And now this terrorist thing."

Helen didn't answer. She knew better than to invest in tech companies with no foreseeable revenue. And she really didn't feel like thinking about this terrorist "thing." But she had lost money too.

Dr. Steloff wasn't done talking. "But I keep thinking, there has to be something. If you don't mind my asking. Your dad says you're a real crackerjack. Isn't there some way to invest, given the terror attacks? *Awful*, I know. Awful."

"It's a normal question." Maybe it was a normal question, or maybe it was a horrific question, or maybe she just wanted him to think she was smart. "Aerospace defense maybe," she said, thinking aloud. "Or, this other new industry—"

"What? Tell me." He rolled his chair closer, looked down at her with an intensity and desperation that she had seen plenty in her macho colleagues, day-trading addicts, glorified gamblers, everyone ready to pounce. The cartoon tie kept her talking.

"Well, security. Biometrics. There's this company I like, RetImaging Systems. They are developing those retinal scanners."

"Oh yeah, I've heard of that, for identification."

"Yeah, only these guys have patented a lot of the technology. And they also are developing the database aspect of it too, like a plug-in package you can use for, say, a corporate office or whatever. Building security. You know, or for secure computer log-ons."

Dr. Steloff was sold. "What did you say they were called again?" His pen at the ready.

"RetImaging Systems. R-E-T-I-M-A-G-I-N-G." Helen rinsed her mouth, spit into the bowl. Steloff wrote the name carefully. "They're on the NASDAQ."

"Wow. Superb. You're my new favorite patient."

Helen dug her old painting stuff out of the cabinet in the basement. She found a small canvas she had stretched and gessoed over a decade ago, dusty but decent, and a box of paints, still alive with the addition of a little linseed oil. She set up a studio on a tarp on top of the pool table, laid the canvas under the hanging tavern light, and got to work. First, an undercoat of deep blue, then she scratched in the outline of five figures around a table: portly, authoritative men in business suits. Some had cards laid out on their felt tabletop; others held them to the breast. At the end of each jacket's sleeve, she sketched in the paw of a bulldog or mastiff or collie or Saint Bernard. She giggled to herself as she mixed lead white, burnt umber, alizarin crimson, and vermilion with shiny oil on her glass palette, seeking the perfect shade of whiteboy pink for each of the faces of her five CEOs.

Dad stepped out of his office on the side of the house and through the sliding glass doors into the basement. "Whatcha doin'?" he said, peering over her shoulder.

"Don't you recognize it?" Helen giggled again, feeling the ache of the new spacers between her back teeth. "It's the *Dogs Playing Poker*!"

"They don't look quite like dogs."

"No, but that's what they really are." Helen had forgotten the heady smell of the pigments and the linseed oil, the feel of the paint's squish under the palette knife. Something in her welled up with each squish.

"Hmm," Dad said with a bemused shrug. "Interesting." He headed for the stairs, for his punctual lunch in the kitchen, then turned. "Have you made any progress on that résumé?"

"Not really." She did not look up.

He squared back. "How long are you going to do this?"

Until you stop lying to my orthodontist? She didn't have the balls to say it. "I don't know."

"Your mom needs help with the Christmas party."

"Don't worry. I'll help her."

"You can't do this forever. You've got to stay on your game."

Helen didn't answer. She had found it, in the squish under her knife—the exact hue she had been looking for to shape the nose of her favorite CEO.

Dad turned, finally, and walked up the stairs.

"Well, how's my favorite patient?" Dr. Steloff beamed and wheeled his stool over to the reclining chair. Bugs Bunny tie today. "Ready, Brace Face?"

"Ready." She opened her mouth wide for him, and he swabbed her gums dry with cotton, then wedged several pieces in to catch the spit. He was trying bands on her molars for the right fit, then setting the winners on the tray beside him. The lamp was hot, and she couldn't look at the kitten poster. She closed her eyes.

"I'll be putting some cement on your teeth here, so try not to swallow."

"OK," she said through the cotton.

"You know, Helen, I owe you a debt of gratitude. I bought RetImaging Systems at sixteen, the day you told me about it. Today it's at twenty and a half! I can't believe it. You found me the one stock that is going up." He stuck the suction tube in her mouth. "Close your lips for a second. OK, open."

She felt a surge of pride in her good suggestion. Then a surge of something else. She thought of Virgil and the haunted cafeteria, the silent firemen eating their gift lunch. *Mettlesome, mad, extravagant city!* Paint squishing her glass palette. Blood money. Lunch. Lunch, squish, lunch.

"So what should I do now, boss, huh?" Steloff said. "Bite down on this stick." She could feel the steel band closing around her tooth. "I love this stock! Should I double down?"

She hadn't been following the story, but it didn't sound right. There was no way the price could hold up. "I don't know," she struggled to say. "I habhen't reawwy researthed it." He held the stick again for her to bite down. Her jaw ached. "I think you thould thell."

"Sell? It's just getting good."

"Trutht me." She was annoyed at herself, at the phony confidence of her cotton-addled voice. She didn't know. She was only following her gut. Lying to this innocent person in Looney Tunes attire. It violated every professional standard.

He backed away, set down his hands on his lap, still holding a pair of skinny pliers and that painful biting stick. "You sure? Sell? Hmm. OK. OK, I trusted you before. OK. OK, I'll do it."

"You won't be thorry," Helen said. She tried to smile as he inserted the suction tube again.

Steloff smiled, spun around on his chair, then returned from the counter with a handful of little plastic brackets in bright candy colors: red, green, black, baby blue. "These go on your front and side teeth. You can pick your color while you wait for the cement to dry."

She reached into the cup of his latexed hand, sorting through the tiny dots until she found the one she wanted. "Thith one," she said, holding up the pink.

Helen dreamed she was sitting in the X-ray booth in Dr. Steloff's office, her body covered with a lead apron. The machine moved slowly around her head, clicking and buzzing, making her heart race with panic. *It is taking a picture. It is taking a picture of my brain. They will know everything.*

The panic didn't fade after she woke up. She had to do something. She grabbed the primordial princess phone from her nightstand and dialed the old Singer Martin Help Desk, hoping for a familiar voice. Maybe Virgil had heard more about RetImaging, or maybe she just wanted to know he was OK, or maybe she needed a deeper kind of Help now, as she wound the tired pink coil of cord around her finger again and again, the way she used to back in junior high, talking to her girlfriends.

"Help Desk." The voice was high and nasal and fussy. It wasn't him.

"Is Virgil Feliz on the Desk today?"

"Virgil left the firm."

"Oh. Was he . . . downsized?" The tech guys probably process themselves last.

"Maybe. Who is this calling?"

"Helen Marks."

"Weren't you . . . ?"

"I was one of them. Yes. Do you have any way to reach him?"

"We can't give that information out."

"Of course. I'm sorry."

Helen's forefinger had swelled purple with blood. She unwound the cord and watched the color fade.

Mom's party had a big turnout: the ladies from the bridge club, Dad's clients and golf cronies, a few friends from church. Mom kept talking about somebody's

The Artstars

kid, who was Helen's age, a good-looking fellow named Brent. "He's definitely coming. Single! You never know!" She kept winking, as they put Ritz crackers and cheese cubes on a tray with a little cup of toothpicks. Helen ate a piece of cheddar, then had to poke a toothpick at the wires in her mouth to get the residue out. If her teeth were catching food before, they were starting a real collection now. The insides of her cheeks were full of canker sores. A swish of whiskey was good to dull the pain.

For a while she helped Mom, as she had promised, refilling chip bowls and relish trays, refreshing people's drinks. Helen came to this shindig every year, but this year was different, people commenting, or not commenting, on her pink braces. Awkward remarks about her job status from Mom's friends, who all knew she had been laid off, and disturbingly cheery questions from Dad's friends, who knew nothing at all. "So how is Singer Martin treating you? Your dad is so proud of you." Proud, indeed. So proud he couldn't bear to share the truth: she was not good enough to be indispensable.

Helen answered with noncommittal smiles, hoping the pink teeth would prove distracting. She found herself refilling her glass more than she ever did at home. She had never been drunk in front of her parents. As her equilibrium started to give, she retired to the basement with a gaggle of men, among them Dr. Steloff, who challenged her to a game of pool. Her art studio had been removed, tarp folded up, paints stowed away, the *Dog-CEOs Playing Poker* nearly done, propped against the wall behind the bar. She accepted Steloff's challenge, racked the balls, rolled them around and into place, then picked her favorite cue from the rack on the wall.

"Care to make it interesting?" he said, chalking his own stick.

"Nah. I don't gamble."

"No, you don't, do you?" he replied, looking at her intensely now, reading her. "You're no dummy. I never thanked you for suggesting I sell that RetImaging Systems. Have you been following it?"

She had. After failing to reach Virgil, she had taken matters into her own hands, on her father's computer. "Yeah, it closed at eighteen today," she said. "Rumors of litigation."

"You got me out just in time, Helen. I'm telling you guys, this woman's a real crackerjack. Your dad is right." *Woman*. No more *good girl*. Some appreciative smiles from men twice her age, Dad watching quietly from the corner, pretending to listen to some guy blabber.

"Your break, Dr. Steloff," she said, standing back, leaning on the cue for balance.

"Please. We're not at work. Call me Jerry."

"OK, Jerry. Your break."

Jerry Steloff had a couple drinks in him. It was a weak break, pocketed nothing, left several striped balls open for the taking. Helen zeroed in, the whiskey bolstering her confidence, and sunk the ten ball into a side pocket, leaving a clear shot at the fourteen ball. There were advantages to growing up with a pool table in the basement.

She pocketed four balls before she got stuck but was able to leave Steloff without a clear shot. The big rule—in pool, and life—as Dad had taught her: if you can't make a shot, don't leave one open. Steloff chalked his cue excessively, surveyed the table, seemed to be realizing he might actually lose to a woman, here, in front of his friends. He wore a boring gray sweater without any cartoon faces on it at all. "Helen, you're good," he said, his admiration adult, baldly sexual.

"I had a good teacher," she said, looking up at Dad for approval, but he didn't hear. Steloff aimed for the corner but missed, leaving her a clear shot. She chalked, moved some people aside, and aimed.

"So what's your next tip for me, huh, Helen?" interrupted Steloff. "There's got to be something hot you've been hearing about at work."

He rattled her. She made the shot but left nothing for the next one. She looked up at Dad. He was deep in his own conversation. Steloff smiled with his crafted teeth—an overture, or desperation, or greed; she couldn't tell. She paused, aiming for the cue ball, looked straight at her opponent, and said firmly, "I am not working now." Then shot the nine ball between his cue and the rest of the balls, leaving him empty.

"I know, I know," Steloff said. "I'm sorry. You're not at the office. I'm sorry." He made a clumsy attempt to shoot, but his face was flushed. "I'm sorry, Helen. It's a party. You don't ask me about braces, I don't ask you about stocks." He backed away from the table, smiled into his bland sweater. The room had gone quiet. The men were all looking at the table.

"Actually, *Jerry*, what I meant was, I *have no job*." Whiskey and bile rose in her throat, her voice a little louder than she meant it to be. "I was LET GO. I am UNEMPLOYED." She paused. "And I cannot discuss your portfolio anymore. I REALLY DON'T WANT TO HEAR ABOUT IT."

And only the sound of balls hitting balls, as she sunk the rest of the stripes and focused the yellowed cue on the final black one. Steloff was blushing fully now.

She looked over at the corner of the room, at Dad. He was looking right at her, pity and shame and disappointment shading his normally steadfast face. She held his eyes for a second until she couldn't anymore, then overshot. The cue ball followed hers into the pocket. A scratch. Game over.

The Artstars

She walked over to Steloff, shook his clammy hand. "Congratulations," she said. The room was too quiet. Dad, in the corner, looked right at her, shook his head, then turned and walked upstairs.

Helen needed another drink. She walked, as steadily as she could, to the bar, then behind it, dug through bottles to find the bourbon. A young man was leaning on the bar—handsome, dark hair, dark blue suit, brave pink tie. "Can I make you a drink?" she said.

"No, no. I was just looking at this painting." He had a lilt to his voice. Helen suspected he preferred boys. His eyes were honest and harmless. She trusted him immediately.

The painting was still wet but was turning out just as she had imagined it. Hours and hours of work had produced five CEOs, like the ones in the old executive waiting room, their faces dewy and pink, their canine claws clutching cards in the highest-stake game of all.

"You did this?" said the man. She nodded. "It's funny. But not really funny. It's beautiful." He was sincere, thoughtful, his gray eyes meeting hers without greed or fear. "This one especially." He pointed to the CEO in the center, her favorite. Face soft brushstrokes of pink and white and a hint of yellow, a highlight in each blue eye that looked almost like a tear. The stranger looked straight into her for a second, understanding something, then back at the man in the painting. "It's his skin tone, I think. It gives him an air of innocence. You almost feel sorry for him. He doesn't know what's about to hit him."

"Yeah."

Helen looked at the man looking at the man in the painting. His calm smile, working at nothing. He looked familiar. She had seen him somewhere before, she was sure.

"Helen!" her mother shouted down the stairs. "Can you help me in the kitchen a moment?"

"Thank you," she said pointedly to the stranger, and made her exit.

Mom was freaking out a little in the privacy of the kitchen. "Your dad told me what happened downstairs. I wish you'd be nicer to Jerry Steloff. He's one of our biggest clients."

"You mean one of *Dad's* biggest clients."

"I mean, we can't *afford* to make him uncomfortable."

Afford. It was possible Helen had never before heard the word cross her mother's lips.

"I'm sorry." Helen gulped. "I might be a little drunk."

"It's OK. We just have to be careful now is all."

Silently, Helen helped her mother rinse glasses and put them in the dishwasher. Mom looked tired. Her Christmas sweater had a blob of tomato sauce staining the snowflake over her heart. Her hands were old, a hint of arthritis in the knuckles, liver spots haloing her diamond wedding ring.

"Who's that guy, Mom? The one in the navy-blue suit? The young one?"

"I didn't see him." Mom wiped the counter now with a sponge, her mouth firm, deliberate, too exhausted to smile.

"He was downstairs. By the bar." Mom showed no recognition. "Was that this Brent dude you were talking about? Because if it was, I don't think he likes girls."

"Helen, honestly. Your *negativity* . . ." Mom let her pursed lips finish the sentence.

Helen closed the dishwasher. Its click punctuated the silence. And in a flash of clarity, she remembered where she had seen that blue suit before. On another stranger, burned into memory: his back first, then spinning slowly in the air. Falling, pink tie flapping, limbs helpless against gravity and time, his whole body resigned to the fact that everything had already changed.

Down the Slope

Dear Rebecca,

Thank you for considering Williamson and
Associates to represent *The Thinnest Line*.
Unfortunately, we have to pass. In this tight
fiction market, you will need a strong advocate,
and sadly, we are not sufficiently enthusiastic.
Please feel free to send us any future projects.
Best of luck.

Warm Regards,
Judith Lightfoot
Williamson and Associates

At least it was a personalized letter this time, with the title of her novel in it, even. Warm regards too, not just regards. She had to take the warmth where she could. Others had sent photocopied quarter sheets with unique logos and generic apologies. Maybe warm regards meant progress. She swallowed, then stuck the letter in the file with the others and slammed the cabinet drawer shut. *War of attrition*, she reminded herself, looking at the sign she had taped to the drawer: *DON'T ATTRISH*. An old teacher's standby advice, along with its correlate—favorite advice of her hippie sister, which she did not commit to signage: *BREATHE*.

Topper was twitching and dreaming on the couch, breathing deep, oblivious to the file cabinet and its contents. But a few favorite words—*are you READY?*—would get his curly tail wagging, and he would relish the ritual sit-down at the door while she clicked the lead to his collar. His whole body reacted to that click—the joy of the routine, legs springy and ready to go where he knew they were going. She stuck the leash in his eager mouth. Topper was reliable. No rejections here. There was still time to make it to Prospect Park before the morning off-leash cutoff.

Outside, the fragrant Slope summer. Brownstones had miniature front yards grown wild with tall hollyhocks and sunflowers. Stoops were crammed with container gardens—fresh herbs and strawberries and coleus, barely room to climb steps. Leggy bachelor's buttons bloomed around trees at the curb. Topper sniffed some purple morning glories twirled up a low iron fence. He left his mark on the flowers, then pulled Rebecca up the slope, toward the park. Up ahead, a group of kids rode scooters, racing down the gentle grade of the sidewalk.

One of the kids, a girl, about ten and a little overweight, dropped her scooter and walked right up to Topper. The others held back. Topper was big and loud enough to be frightening. But the girl wasn't scared of a little bark.

"You want to give him a cookie?" Rebecca offered a biscuit to the girl, who held it properly for the dog, not snatching her hand away. "You like dogs?" The girl nodded. She wouldn't look Rebecca in the eye, only Topper. Her kid belly stretched out a daisy-printed T-shirt. Thick black lashes framed downcast eyes. "You can pet him if you want," Rebecca said. The girl touched Topper's head gently, then grew bolder and knelt to hug the dog's thick, furry neck. He licked her face. She giggled.

"What kind of dog is he?" she asked quietly.

"Angelica!" A curler-headed woman leaned out a third-floor window. "Get *away* from that dog!"

"It's OK, Mami," the kid shouted back.

"*Angelica*, what did I say?"

The girl held on, buried her face in Topper's neck, then finally stood, looking up at Rebecca with a blush.

"Angelica! Come! *Now.*"

She hopped on her scooter and headed back to the voice. Topper barked. Rebecca jerked the lead. She hadn't meant to get the kid in trouble.

Idea: LETTUCE

Angelica is a shy but smart kid. Not that her teacher notices. She's quit raising her hand. Her arm was getting tired, and what is the point? Does she really feel like talking in front of these fourth-grade fools? She prefers animals. She wants to be a veterinarian. Begs for a dog but only gets a guinea pig. She names him Fatty. She brushes his orange, chunky fur with her own hairbrush. She tries to get him to kiss her or follow her around the apartment, but all he cares about is lettuce. He doesn't care whose hand is offering. He doesn't even notice the hand or the love behind it. Only lettuce.

Sometimes, at night, she brings Fatty into her brother's room. The three of them lie in his bed, make a tent of the covers, while their parents forget they are there and argue about money in the kitchen.

Oh, great. The shy-but-smart trope? Teacher, teacher, look at me? Hiding from fighting parents? Latino parents to boot? So many levels of wrong. Abandon this, unless Angelica can get a better problem.

In the grassy middle of the Nethermead, Topper found a new friend, a female Jack Russell puppy named Pinky. Topper liked to be chased, in wide circles, and Pinky seemed to enjoy chasing. Topper could kill this little thing with a shake of his mouth, like he did with his stuffed animals at home. But Pinky didn't seem scared. "How old is she?" Rebecca asked Pinky's mom, a white, wealthy-looking woman with a tennis-perfect ponytail and tanned face.

"Five months," said the woman, beaming at her dog.

"She's adorable. That's such a great age. Before the adolescent rebellion sets in."

Pinky's mom laughed. "We'll see. We've just gotten through house-training."

"Oh, yeah. That's a joy. I tried crate-training him, but I couldn't bear to hear him crying in the cage. So next thing you know, I let him out, and he's peeing on my bed." Topper had a stick now and was play-growling at Pinky while she tried to steal it.

"We had a similar experience. Not the bed, but an antique rug from my mother-in-law. You can bet that was good for my marriage. Oh, and the chewed shoes. Once, I got to the office before I noticed teeth marks on my kitten heels."

Topper's growl sounded less playful. Both women zoomed in. Rebecca gripped Topper by the collar, made him sit. "No. Topper. No." She pried the stick from his jaw. "I'm so sorry. He has a possessive streak." She lobbed the stick out and away. Topper tugged at his collar, ready to run after it, his part of the stick game. She didn't dare let him.

The woman held the terrier in her arms, belly up, and cooed to her. "Little Pinky, are you OK?"

Rebecca dreaded the *look*, the chilled glare she had gotten plenty from dog owners: *How could you let him get like this? Don't you train him?* But the look didn't come. The woman focused on the creature in her arms, desperately maternal. Rebecca didn't want to interrupt this moment, the yuppie Madonna accepting kisses from her substitute child. "I think I better take Topper home."

The woman looked up and smiled. "No worries. Next time we'll just make sure there are no sticks." Rebecca sighed. Maybe yuppie lady was not so bad.

Around the corner from her house, Topper pulled her toward a scruffy drunk sitting on a sheet of cardboard on the threshold of the bar that rarely closed. She saw him there often, mornings, eating rice and beans from a take-out container. He looked to be in his fifties, with a graying beard and long greasy hair, beaten brown tweed suit jacket, bent eyeglasses. She found him a little frightening, the haunted blue stare he often gave her as she walked past, her eyes avoiding his change cup. She realized Topper might smell his food—and be looking to steal it. "Topper, no. We have food at home."

"That's OK, miss," said the guy. "I'm done eating." He surprised her with an English accent. He set his near-empty container on the ground, and Topper pulled toward it. "Come on, puppy. It's just rice. Can I let him have it?" She decided it would be impolite to refuse. Topper had a strong stomach, besides, the way he scarfed chicken bones and bits of bread from the gutter, the memory of his own home-less past too ingrained to break. She relaxed the leash. Topper licked the container clean while the man laughed, showing darkened teeth. He scratched the base of the dog's spine. "What do we have here, a little collie blend? Some Siberian husky?"

"I think of him as a breed of one."

"He is peerless, isn't he? A beauty."

"Where are you from?" she asked, realizing she was being too forward, might give the man ideas. She was simply curious. The fiction writer in her took over sometimes, pushed shy out of the way.

"Manchester."

"That's a long swim from Manchester to the Slope." She wasn't quite sure of the etiquette, talking to a homeless man. Was he, in fact, homeless or just a person who sits on cardboard, waiting for the morning barman to arrive? Was it OK to ask?

"A long swim indeed," he said, slurring a little too much for this time of morning. He stroked Topper, who licked his dirty face like it was any face. She impulsively reached in her pocket, pulled out a wrinkled five-dollar bill.

"Here," she said. "For later. Topper's and my way of saying thank you."

He accepted the bill with a smile. "Topper!" he said, scratching that furry butt. Topper flattened his ears and wagged. "Thank you, friend of Topper," the man said. Her gut told her he wasn't talking about the money.

Back in her apartment, she sat at her desk, looked out the window, her mind blank, her fingers silent on the keyboard. The mulberry tree outside gave her nothing. The blank screen flickered its ridicule. The rejection letters nagged from the file drawer. She decided to look at some student work instead.

Rebecca was teaching a fiction workshop at a writer's center in Gowanus. It was a great gig, and she knew she was lucky to have it, considering her sketchy publishing record. A buddy from grad school had found her the job as a favor, knowing how deep she had gone into her credit cards.

She pulled out the two stories the class would be discussing this week. One was by a quiet, older woman named Bea. It was a gentle, subtle piece about a housewife taking her youngest kid to college and then having trouble filling her days, finding herself working alone in her plot at a community garden. The detail of the story was rich, its protagonist not quite aware of her own grief, the plants themselves providing the emotional gut work: some dying, others self-sowing and blooming shamelessly, taking over the dirt. Rebecca penciled notes in the margin: *Good image. Fill it out more. Good verbs here. Aggressive plants! Nice!*

The second story was less fun to read. Peter, the student, was fresh out of college and had obviously digested bookfuls of screenwriting how-to. He spoke out a lot about *third acts* and *raising stakes*. Sometimes the advice made sense, but mostly it just kept others from voicing their views. And his work was clichéd, O. Henry wannabe stuff, neat ironic endings with pat moral messages. This one starred a liberal arts major who blew too many smoke rings and bedded too many gorgeous women. A poor looker looking for the right funky-sexy girl to make his life complete. So reliably unreliable, this smoke-blowing narrator, as he climaxed into his comeuppance. Was this supposed to be *feminist*? Peter probably had the actresses picked for the Hollywood version. Rebecca imagined the grimaces on the female students' faces, slogging through this stuff, trying to be positive. Her pencil slashed through ugly paragraphs, ham-handed diction, rhetorical darlings. She managed to find a couple keeper images, wrote a half-hearted *nice!* in the margin.

It dawned on her that she could simply ask Peter to leave the class. Tell him that his critiques were disruptive and that she would arrange a refund. It was a disservice, really, to encourage a writer like this. Someone should tell him he was delusional.

Idea: PINKY'S MOM

Iris and Charles have been trying to get pregnant for two years. After failures with a fertility monitor and scheduled sex, disrupting both of their careers, calling him home from sales trips to fuck, hormone injections stealing her equilibrium in meetings, they fork out the money for artificial insemination. The process is degrading for both of them. He provides a cup of semen in a sterile, clinical bathroom. He has trouble producing it, the idea of sex too fraught with expectations and results. She finds the syringe painful, and Charles's sympathy is inadequate. Home, they fight. Charles misses the life they used to have and is ready to give up trying. Iris can't. Not yet. She is heartbroken when her period comes. Blames him for it, as if the egg could hear his talk of quitting. Charles consoles her with a new puppy, a Jack Russell they name Pinky. Iris holds the dog constantly, can't let go of her, cries into her little soft body, overcome with sorrow and failure.

Think more on this.

The evening of class arrived. Rebecca started with a group chat on a favorite Chekhov warhorse, then moved on to Bea's story. Most of the students appeared affected by the detail, by the freshness of Bea's voice, but their opinions were interrupted by Peter.

"I don't exactly *get it*. It really needs a *plot*." He leaned back in his chair, smug in his wire-frame glasses, the beginning of a beard darkening his symmetrical face. He would be attractive if he weren't so full of his attractiveness. He was exactly the type of dude her sister Sara used to chase, or be chased by. Rebecca had never understood the draw. They only enraged her.

"There is a plot, though, if you think about it. A *garden plot*," Rebecca said, noticing Bea's red-faced silence. Bea had a habit of touching her face with her chapped hands. Gardening hands. She kept covering her mouth, as if to keep her words contained. Rebecca wanted to hug her.

"It needs a real *conflict*," Peter went on. "There's no *conflict*. There's only *one character*."

"But don't you think there is an *internal* conflict?" Rebecca suggested. As usual, the class had gone from a group discussion to a two-way contest, everyone clammed up—everyone but Rebecca and her sparring partner.

"I think she needs to raise the stakes. Sending the kid to college isn't enough. The kid has to have a real problem, I think. Something *serious* for her to worry about, like an eating disorder or a drug habit. Or bad grades."

"I disagree," Rebecca countered. "It's not about the kid. I think the narrator is learning about herself. The plants are teaching her something about her own need to nurture. About her own latent anger and fear of failure. Those kind of issues you suggest would only turn it into melodrama."

"What's wrong with melodrama? That sells. How about this: the plants *make her sick*." Peter was excited with his own helpfulness. "Maybe she catches a *serious disease* in the garden. That would *raise the stakes*."

Rebecca tried to catch Bea's eye, to share a private moment, encourage her. But Bea looked down at her notebook, blushing, overwhelmed with how little her story had communicated. The evening was getting long. Rebecca dreaded moving on to Peter's piece.

Another letter came, addressed to Rebecca in her own handwriting, her own saliva under the stamp on the corner. No names on this one, just page one of her short story—a little dog-eared—and a tiny printed slip, barely bigger than a business card:

```
We regret that we are unable to use the
enclosed material. Thank you for giving us the
opportunity to consider it.
The Editors
```

Rebecca plopped it into the fat file folder. She turned on her computer. It greeted her with a mocking *ta-da!* Welcome to the widemouthed world of nothing to say. Topper settled his furry body on her bare right foot, his favorite spot. It was the push she needed. The dog was in position; so was she. She closed her eyes and began typing.

Idea: THE SLOPE

Simon is a music promoter from Manchester's '80s heyday. Comes to NYC on tour with his band and meets the woman who is his undoing. A manipulative, gorgeous cocaine addict who cheats on him just enough to drive him crazy. He becomes Othello-obsessed with her whereabouts, follows her, forgets his basic survival needs. She bankrupts him. He takes to drinking and sleeping on the sidewalk outside her new boyfriend's Brooklyn apartment; then any sidewalk will do. Loses his passport, but it doesn't matter to him anymore. He's fallen through a one-way hole. Green card or flying home both absurd impossibilities. Talks to himself and dogs on the street. Manchester wouldn't recognize him now. Music wouldn't recognize him now.

How fucking depressing. Down. Nothing but down. What's the point? Or, suppose I make him the foil to some impoverished, self-pitying, unsuccessful, over-reaching artist like me? The artist sees poor Simon drooling on the sidewalk and learns her lot is not so bad? Meet the man who has no feet? Oh, the simple epiphany. Cue the music. With the right actress, there might even be a sequel.

I am so sick of this shit.

At the park the next morning, Topper and Pinky found each other immediately, their past skirmish forgotten. Rebecca watched cautiously and silently, ready for the diving-in moment. Pinky's mom, "Iris," seemed less concerned. Pinky, who looked bigger now, lay prone and submissive and let Topper sniff her privates. An intimate moment between pals. They were on the Long Meadow, no sticks around. "She loves big dogs," Iris observed. Topper broke away and ran in a wide circle, changing directions, faking out his buddy. Then rolled on his back, scratching it against a grassy slope, letting gravity pull him down the gentle hill, his belly white in the sunlight, while Pinky barked encouragement. "He's really cute," Iris said.

"Thanks."

Rebecca found herself staring at Pinky's mom without meaning to, her story notes fresh in her mind. The woman had a runner's body. More lean than muscular in biker shorts and a crimson Harvard T-shirt. Fanny pack. Her face was tired, too tan, dehydrated. She was probably much older than she looked at first. A hint of gray peeked out at the temples of her chestnut hair.

"The house-training holding in OK?" Rebecca ventured, hoping the woman would provide a bigger clue.

"She's doing great. We were thinking of rolling the rug out again, but my husband is going on a business trip next week, so we decided to hold off. Expect some regression. She's gonna miss him."

"Yeah," Rebecca said.

"I hope your dog wears her out. What's his name again?"

"Topper."

"Look at them." The dogs continued to run in a wide circle around them. "They're gonna sleep today. I hope. I brought a lot of work home this weekend."

"What do you do?" Rebecca was thrilled. The information was coming with barely an effort.

"I'm an attorney. Intellectual property. I've got three contracts that need a bunch of revision. I'm so tired." A lock of hair had escaped from her ponytail. She sighed and pulled it around an ear.

"I should get your card. I'm a writer. Trying to get my first novel represented."

The woman laughed, more sympathy than derision. "Good luck. The market's tight now."

"So I've been told."

"I don't have cards on me." She reached in her pouch. "But I have liver treats! Can Topper have one?"

Rebecca tried not to cringe. The dogs were getting along so well. Food was Topper's biggest bugaboo, bigger than toys and sticks, sure to start trouble. Pinky was already running to her mom at the sound of the emerging plastic bag. Topper followed, ears perked, head cocked. Both dogs sat in front of Iris, begging the right way. Iris, thankfully, waited for Rebecca's permission.

"Probably not a good idea," Rebecca said, clicking on Topper's leash. "But thanks. He has food issues."

"Ahh," said Iris, with a knowing nod, and she held the treats tight until Rebecca and Topper were a good distance away, up the hill from the Long Meadow. Rebecca looked back. Topper barked. Pinky jumped high, Jack Russell style, for the liver treat. Iris laughed at her beloved.

"Sh, Topper. That's enough. Here." Rebecca handed him a cookie from her own pocket. It wasn't liver. She didn't bother trying to make him jump.

Iris fields a phone call while Charles is away on business. His mother. She is concerned, asks after Iris's health. Iris confesses that her work deadlines are wearing her out. The mother-in-law suggests that her job is the reason the artificial insemination didn't work. That they can afford to have Iris stay home. Iris has never argued with her mother-in-law before. Usually, she just puts Charles on the phone. But she defends herself, her choices, knowing it will only result in Charles's anger when he returns.

She manages to produce three eggs for an in vitro procedure. It is cold and clinical, and in the cab on the way home, she confesses to Charles that she never wants to do it again. He is surprised and relieved. He starts talking about how liberating it would be to give up. To retire wherever they want. No college tuitions. Freedom. They make a pact, in the cab. If this doesn't work, then they are done trying. He kisses her, romantically. She finds herself hoping the expensive procedure has failed.

Back in their brownstone, Pinky greets them at the door, barking and jumping. Both of them laugh, forgetting the fertilized eggs inside Iris, focusing their energy on the object of their love. Already feeling the freedom of a childless future as, quietly, triplets quicken in Iris's belly.

```
Dear Rebecca:

Thank you for considering us, but we have
decided to pass on your novel. We found the
voice far too discursive for contemporary
audiences. The manuscript would require too much
editorial work for us to take it on. Further, the
narrator's romantic naivete is a bit simple for
our taste.

Good luck,
James Tarragon
Tarragon Curtis, LLC
```

Maybe a generic "no" would have been better. She had been saving the letter for three days, reading and rereading it, torturing herself. Now, Saturday morning, she still didn't want to put it in the file. She wanted to burn it. She gave it to Topper to have his way with. He obliged, joyfully, leaving scraps of the horrid onionskin all over the apartment. She ripped her old affirmation sign off the cabinet, wadded it up, and attrished it across the room.

On their way to the park, she thought of Iris and Charles, of the lightness and freedom of her characters upon their decision to give up. She tried to remember the last time she had felt any kind of lightness. Rebecca let Topper tug up the slope, the familiar route to his favorite place.

Topper found Pinky instantly in the Nethermead. Rebecca looked around. Iris was nowhere. Instead, a little boy, maybe five, came running after Pinky, then picked her up clumsily under her forelegs. "Jack! Jack!" shouted a man behind him. "Gentle, please." Pinky's belly was shaved, a fine bit of hair growing back over a new spay scar.

"Where's Iris?" Rebecca asked the man, then immediately realized her stupidity.

"Iris?" he said, catching up to his son and dog.

"Uh, Pinky's mom." She felt herself blush.

"Oh, my *wife*. Jennifer. She's home with our daughter. They're both sick."

"Ah." Rebecca's gut tightened. She hadn't anticipated this, that her imagination was so far from the truth. Or that she would have such a strong reaction.

"These guys are friends?" the man said, pointing to the dogs.

"Yeah." She felt cloudy, suddenly, unable to make simple conversation. Topper started running his laps, followed by not only Pinky but the little boy, Jack. *Jack*, the number one Park Slope child name. *Jack*, who was not supposed to even exist; there were probably three of him in his kindergarten class. She tried to conceal her disappointment. Jack's dad sported a bland haircut and bland golf shirt and bland khaki pants.

Jack, apparently, had little instinct for big dogs. He picked up a stick, and upon discovering Topper's desire for it, he began waving it teasingly, then ran away, making Topper chase him for it. "Uh," Rebecca said, her tongue numb. "Maybe that's not such a—"

"Jack. Stop," said the father. The boy kept running. "Jack." The boy giggled and taunted Topper. "Jack, I mean it. Cut it out." The kid stopped finally, tired, and Topper grabbed one end of the stick, bared his teeth, began a growling tug-of-war.

"Jack. Drop it," the father said sternly. Pinky hovered near the duo, barking a play-by-play. "Jack. I mean it."

"He's just playing, Dad," Jack shouted, not letting go, then squealed, pushing Topper over the line into a big-dog growl. Topper outweighed the boy and was not playing now. Still, Jack did not let go.

Pinky's barks crescendoed in defense of her little master, and on instinct, Rebecca scooped the little dog up under her arm, where she couldn't instigate or get hurt. "Topper, no!" she said firmly. "Drop!" But he was beyond listening. He jerked the stick—and the boy's arm nearly out of its socket—guttural, wolflike anger rumbling from his throat.

Jack's self-preservation kicked in. He dropped his end of the stick and ran to his daddy, hiding behind khaki legs. Topper dropped to the ground to chew his winnings.

Rebecca had almost forgotten she was still holding this man's dog. He held out his arms to accept the bundle, and unmistakable in his eyes was the *look*, the one Rebecca had been expecting—pure judgment and disapproval of her unruly mongrel. She tried to ease the mood: "I see you've had Pinky spayed."

He refused to smile. "You should put a muzzle on that dog." He held the terrier protectively with one arm, his child with the other.

"You should put a leash on that *kid*," she replied. She hadn't meant to. She couldn't help it; mouth and brain had disconnected, and the tight turn of his lips told her she had crossed a far bigger line than Topper had.

"You need help," he said, then turned and steered his son away, lapdog under his arm. Topper continued to chew his victory stick. Rebecca clicked his leash onto his collar and pulled him in the opposite direction. She let him keep the stick. He would need a souvenir, because they would not be coming back to the park for a while.

Topper pulled her down the slope toward home, and Rebecca felt tears coming. *You need help.* Maybe the cruelest thing to say, because maybe he was right. *Fool*, she had been falling in love with Iris and Charles, fake people in a fake story. A story that wasn't even written yet and probably would never be. Their liberation could be hers too. *Giving up!* What grace! There were plenty of ridiculous and impossible goals to let go of.

Topper sniffed garbage bags as they approached her corner. He had no idea how disruptive and rough he was, how everyone else saw him. Just like Peter, her student. There was a time when she, like Peter, had had pure confidence in her chosen vocation, in her own potential. A time of innocence and productivity and lightness. She decided there was no point in kicking him out of the class. The world would tell him the truth.

Topper pulled her toward the entrance to a liquor store. The homeless man was emerging, opening a bottle in a paper bag. The dog walked right up to him, oblivious to his stench and inebriation.

"Topper!" the man said, prompting full-body wags and folded-back ears. He knelt to give the dog a proper scratch. "How are you doing, big fella?" Topper dropped his stick and licked the man's dirty face. The man grinned fully and looked up at Rebecca; then his expression changed. "Hey, are you all right?"

"I've been better." She wiped a stray tear from her cheek. She wanted so badly to go into that store, to buy a bottle in brown paper, even at this hour of the morning. Her big sister would kill her if she knew.

The man did not pry. He took a swig from his paper bag. "Me too," he said. He scratched the dog's ears, then stood with effort, holding a sore back. "You're lucky. You have a beautiful dog."

"He'll do," she said.

She gave Topper a tug, and they moved on. Turned her corner, and the dog led the way home. She paused at the wrought iron gate in front of her stoop. The sidewalk was covered with black stains, trampled fruit from the mulberry tree. The same mulberry tree she always stared at, hour upon hour, from her chair upstairs. Funny, she had never noticed the stains. Maybe because she never looked down. Maybe down was where she should have been looking. Maybe down was where the truth was.

Inside, she would not write. She would not even sit in the chair. She would give Topper a scratch and a marrowbone from the freezer, then lie still in her bed, close her eyes, and wait for the day to dissolve.

Volunteer

BEA BLOOM DROPPED HER KID OFF AT JFK, THEN CAME HOME AND sank into child's pose for nearly an hour. It usually reassured her. Forehead against cool mat, shoulders releasing over knees, palms open next to bare toes. She could feel her fleshy belly over its old cesarean scar, expanding and contracting against her thighs. Long inhale—stretch of vertebrae—long exhale—surrender of the spine. Private, like hiding in her father's old closet: power in smallness, in stillness, among the polished dress shoes, smell of woolly pants and starchy shirts. Here, in Brooklyn, there were no shirts, no father. Tears fell quiet on her yoga mat. The reassurance did not come.

That morning had been the opposite: the frantic last gathering of treasure for Sadie's duffel bag, like her old stuffed elephant with the crank over its navel and music box inside. "Sadie, we can ship anything you need," Irv kept saying. "Just call and ask." But Bea had understood and helped Sadie ransack her rooms for tokens of home: a small framed photo of the family—Irving, Bea, Nina, Sadie—in front of the old granite fireplace. A sachet of rosemary from Sadie's plot at the community garden. Sadie's first night at Berkeley might be lonely. The tokens would keep her company.

Sadie had wanted to ride to the airport by herself. She had always been a me-do-it kid. But, last minute, the black Town Car pulled up to the brownstone and Sadie took a panicked look around the kitchen. Bea said, "You want us to come with you?" Sadie had nodded.

Irv could not go. He had a patient that afternoon. So Bea went, held Sadie's hand along Eastern Parkway. Sadie watched Brooklyn go by, seemed to take mental photographs of the library, the museum. Bea took mental photographs of Sadie. Round baby cheeks, with a hint of their childhood freckles. Innocent but righteous. Berkeley was the right place, Bea hoped.

Bea generally did her best to disappear while Irv was in session. Patients entered through the main front door and worked with Irv in a porch-like room up front, behind a pocket door. It was private. Nonetheless, the nearest bathroom was off the dining room, and patients didn't need to bump into family members along the way. It had been harder when the kids were little, trying to keep them quiet in the kitchen. They used to make a game of it, tiptoeing through the living room to the stairs or the front door. Later, keeping quiet was habit, broken only by sudden arguments between the girls, which hadn't happened for at least three years, since Nina had gone off to college.

That evening, Bea went into Irv's office to wait for Sadie's call. It was quiet, if you wanted it to be—shuttered windows and filled bookshelves insulating the walls. The air conditioner was a pleasant white noise. Bea came here often after supper, especially in summer; it was the only air-conditioned room in the house. Bea objected to air-conditioning—a luxury, a waste of power. But on hot nights, her principles faded, and she would find herself lying on the patients' couch to read or to close her eyes and try to imagine what patients said from this spot. Irv never spoke of them in detail. Bea did not ask. She knew that one of his patients, a young man named Trevor, had been hospitalized last year. What did Trevor talk about, this mere boy Sadie's age, who lay on this couch, wishing his own death? Bea tried to slow her heart, watched the quiet cordless phone rise and fall on her chest.

"Bea, let's order. I'm starved." Irv walked into his office in nothing but his blue Speedo-style briefs. This would be Irv's summer uniform, if propriety allowed. His round belly sagged over the waistband. Snowy beard, fluffy eyebrows, tan skin, and ubiquitous white body hair, which used to make the girls laugh and call him Mr. Yeti.

"What if Sadie tries to call? And gets a busy signal?"

"Then she'll call again. Aren't you hungry?"

"I wish we gave her a cell phone. Why didn't we just buy her a cell phone?"

Irv grabbed the phone from her chest and dialed the number she wished he hadn't memorized. She could hear Mr. Manfredi through the cheap earpiece. "Dr. Bloom! How ya doin'?" Manfredi's had been in Park Slope since before the yuppies and hippies and tofu-eaters took over. "The usual?"

The usual was a meat extravaganza: pepperoni *and* sausage *and* meatball, all on one pie. And a house salad, the perfunctory nod to vegetables, though Bea would end up eating all of that. When the doorbell rang, Bea knew her job—she opened the door and paid. Better than Irv answering in his underpants.

It was her own fault. Irv didn't need any more fat in his veins, but she could have prepared something for him. Irv, left to his own devices, would always call Manfredi's. Her vice was air-conditioning. His was pepperoni.

Sadie finally called after 1:00 a.m. Bea was still on Irv's couch, phone on her belly, listening to the air conditioner. Irv was upstairs, unconscious, unworried.

"Mom, I can't wait for you to meet my roommate. She's a cross-country runner. She's training for a marathon. We're going running tomorrow morning before academic orientation."

"That's wonderful, Sadie. How are *you* doing?"

"I'm totally fine." Generic. Confident. All trace of this morning's panic gone.

"Why did you wait so long to call?"

"We had dorm orientation after dinner. Then I had to wait for the pay phone. I'm sorry. I forgot about the time zones."

Bea had forgotten too. It was still early in California. Yes, she was stupid for worrying. *Don't volunteer for jobs that don't need doing*, Bea's father used to say. Sadie didn't need Bea to keep vigil. "You going to bed now, kiddo?"

"Yeah, we're getting up early to run, like I said."

We, already. Bea had hoped she would find friends quickly but felt a pang of something irrational and unnameable. "Please let us know the minute you get your new phone number."

"I *will*, Mother."

Bea hated the sound of her own voice. Worrywart, *Mother*, such a formal title when Sadie was exasperated. "I'm sorry. I love you, sweetie," Bea said.

"I love you too."

I miss you terribly, Bea wanted to say, but feared it would be too much.

Bea hung up and went into the bedroom. It was hot. Irv snored, on top of the sheets, naked. She stripped and fell in next to him, put her arm around his furry chest, and whispered in his ear: "She called. Everything's OK."

"Good. See? She's fine." He opened his eyes, looked into her face in the dim light from the window. "How about *you*? How are *you* doing?"

"I don't know." She let herself cry into Irv's armpit. He didn't tell her to stop. He wiped her face, kissed the wet spot on her cheek, his beard soft.

"You're a beauty, Beatrice Bloom. You know that." She didn't know, but it was the reassurance she needed. She pushed her naked body against his and kissed his mouth, pulled her hand through his thick white hair. He responded, rolling on top of her, his sweaty mass bringing her back here, to this safe room, his rapid breath and heartbeat anchoring her; they were alone now, no kids to hear, and she let out a loud cry as her body accepted his.

The next morning she awoke alone. She could hear Irv laughing down in the kitchen, probably talking to Nina. They talked nearly every morning, since Nina had taken an office job that allowed her to phone the US for free. She was in Tel Aviv now, indefinitely. It had started as a junior year abroad from Brown, where Nina majored in religious studies. Bea had been supportive. She had always wanted the girls to explore their Jewish side, and Lord knows Irv needed someone to remind him which holiday came next. But Tel Aviv was a scary place, in Bea's imagination. Nina rode buses daily. Ate in cafés. Bea didn't try to dissuade her but ended up obsessing about the dangers, until Sadie convinced her to quit watching the news. "They're trying to scare us, Mom. They need us to be scared."

Then Nina had called, last spring, and announced she was in love. She had found a job at a media company. She was staying. Her rabbinical aspirations were on hold. Irv, such a hot-climate soul, was ready to go visit. Bea was stricken. She found herself avoiding conversations with Nina. She didn't mean to, but she knew she exposed her fear in her voice, and she hadn't raised her girls to be cowards. It got harder, every year, to set a decent example. She envied Irv his casual silliness with the girls, his complete lack of impulse to cover their heads or ask what they ate for lunch.

She got up, put on her yoga clothes, rolled out her mat, and tried some breath exercises while Irv continued laughing downstairs. She punched lungfuls rapidly, from belly to nose—*huh huh huh huh huh*—almost like a laugh, but not really. She couldn't laugh for real. It made the *huh huh huh* feel more like rage. Downstairs, between father and daughter, laughter exploded without effort.

Everything took effort for Bea today. Every pose on this faded sticky mat. She heard Irv at the front door, greeting the day's first patient. She waited to hear his office door slide closed, then went down to the kitchen. Her bran cereal tasted like mulch. She tapped her spoon restlessly against the kitchen table. She washed her bowl, then Irv's. Lord forbid he could wash a bowl. She turned off the faucet. The silent room sickened her. She decided to go check on the garden plots.

Sadie's morning glories tangled up and over the chain-link fence next to her plot, hundreds of green hearts crazy for the hot air. Bea had not visited the garden in three whole weeks, preoccupied with Sadie's readiness. Plenty happens in three warm weeks when one is not looking. Now, among the healthy, aggressive leaves were pods, dried berries, each bearing a star of seeds, like wedges of orange inside a dry skin. Bea had never wanted morning glories here at all but had caved to Sadie's enthusiasm years ago. It went against the ethos of the community garden: natives only, no invasives, managed growth. For eight years, there had been no need to plant morning glory. It sowed babies, generations of flowers mutating to darker purple each summer.

Bea trimmed back the vines and clipped the pods she could find into a bucket, so they wouldn't end up in the compost. That would put her on the garden's shit list. Randie, Bea's longtime friend, a middle-aged tomboy and one of the garden's founders, kept tabs on everybody's habits, logged garden gossip, especially about Mr. Patel, who kept to himself, though his plants crept through borders and up fences, self-sowed in neighboring plots. Bea stole looks over her shoulder as she clipped the pods. Randie wasn't around today. Mr. Patel was harvesting his bright zucchini over in the far corner. They were beautiful zucchini. Bea had noticed them with jealousy on her way in, wondered if he fed them chemical fertilizer, another of Randie's pet peeves.

Beside the morning-gloried fence was Sadie's old pizza garden: a round, raised bed with herbs and tomatoes grown in wedges, like slices of pie. Her father's daughter. Sadie herself had seen the idea in a magazine and taken the initiative to order seeds from the catalog, back when she was eleven. Bea had been proud. That summer, Sadie had cried when the tomatoes were munched by horrible, ugly hornworms, practically overnight. *Honey, I'm so sorry. Let's save some seeds. We'll try again next year, with lots of marigolds to chase the bugs away.*

It had been a disappointment for Sadie, but Bea relished the memory and her daughter's flop into her side for comfort. By the next summer, Sadie had grown inches and toughened, turned to friends her own age for support, would never be seen in her mother's arms in public. She came less often to the plot. Bea had picked off the occasional hornworms herself that season.

This year's tomatoes were rebelliously striking. Heirlooms open-pollinated for several years, some of them giant new breeds, bursting skins of yellow and orange and red. Bea picked a dozen pretty ones and set them on the bricks edging Sadie's circle, then went to her own plot to work on flowers.

"What kind of tomatoes are those?"

The voice startled her. It was Mr. Patel, bending over to inspect the ready fruit she had picked.

"Well, they have no name. My daughter's own variety."

"Beautiful. Ripened on the bush. The best way." His voice had the musical lilt of his home country, high and warm.

"Take some, if you want. We won't be able to eat all of them," Bea said, not looking up from the stems of echinacea she was clipping to take home and arrange. She was afraid to get too friendly with Mr. Patel, could hear Randie already, whispering in her ear: *He plants mint, for God's sake. Mint! The nerve! And he just lets his winter squash climb up the poor cedar tree!* By the time Bea stood up to face him, Patel was gone. On the brick edging, several young zucchini sat in place of the tomatoes he had quietly accepted.

Home, Bea walked up the brownstone steps, loaded down with a mesh bag of vegetables and a thick purple bouquet. The door opened and a young man exited. His brown eyes were puffy and rimmed in red, his face pale and gaunt. His long hair was ashen and greasy, in need of a wash. Still, it had a gentle, wild curl that caught the sun, giving the young man a delicate-dangerous air, like a little gypsy girl on a postcard.

"I'm sorry," Bea said, stepping to the side. The house rule was to avoid the stoop at the turn of the hour, when patients were coming and going.

"You're carrying a sea monster," he said.

"A what?"

"*That*." He pointed to the spiky cone at the center of an echinacea bloom. "Or maybe it's just a flower that flipped itself inside out. A flip-out flower." He laughed at his own observation. Bea laughed along nervously. The young man hopped down the steps, both feet together, then strode up the block, swinging his arms. He was tall, skinny, clothes draped from his frame as if confused, used to a snug fit. And a heavy, unbuttoned coat, too, far too heavy for the season. Bea wore only a light tank dress.

"I'm sorry," Bea repeated to Irv as she closed the door behind her. "I ran into your patient outside."

"He was rude?"

"Rude? Heavens no. He said these were sea monsters. *Flip-out flowers*." Irv shook his head, followed her into the kitchen, and watched her unroll the bouquet from its newspaper wrap. "Hey, is that boy the one who—"

"That's Trevor. Yes." The firmness of his jaw told Bea she was pushing it.

Bea changed the subject: "Zucchini. Beauties," she said, holding up the mesh bag. "From one of the other gardeners."

"Nice," Irv said, though his mind had left the room or maybe never entered it. Bea shrugged and filled a vase with cold water, let the gushing sound fill where conversation couldn't.

Sadie's absence was felt most at supper. Bea served in the dining room, like any old night. The table was half naked with only two plates, and the giant vase of flip-out flowers screamed overcompensation. Bea dished herself some green salad while Irv sat quiet, hands resting flat beside his knife and fork. He stared past her shoulder and out the window a room away, seemed lost in a thought he could not share, the one topic they could not touch.

"Honey, have some ratatouille," she said. "It's Sadie's tomatoes and the squash that man at the garden gave me." Chattering, the way wives do, filling empty air. She exhaled, took a bite of her salad, and shut up to let Irv think it out, the crunch of romaine echoing through her head.

Other wives didn't have to chatter on about vegetables. *Dear, how was your day at work?* This question would never get a straight answer in the Bloom house. Bea sometimes thought, on nights like tonight, that Irv grew so tired of talking all day—talking, and more to the point, *listening*—that he craved nothing more than quiet. He rarely watched TV or listened to the radio after supper. Often, he sat right here, in his dining room chair, in his Speedo briefs, no music, drinking beer and reading the sports section.

Quiet. Bea found herself recalling the first time she took Irv home, to Pennsylvania, to meet her Quaker family. He was a student, then, an atheist, but curious about Quakers, their politics and their meetings, so they took him to one. Their meetinghouse had a reputation for "popcorn"—too much talking, people standing up simultaneously to express. But on the Sunday they went, no one stood up until near the hour's end, when old Mrs. Paxton struggled to her feet and said, "Today is my husband's birthday. I am grateful for the time I had with him." This, as a finale to the human sounds, the rearranging of legs and feet, the clearing of throats, the child sniffles, and Bea could picture Mr. Paxton sitting in the empty spot next to his wife's usual place, clearing his own throat and arranging his own feet. Bea had been overcome with a longing for a husband of her own. Irv, maybe even.

Irv must have had a similar thought, because he had looked a little teary when Bea turned to shake his hand and close the hour. He seemed confused, she recalled, at the formality of the handshake—weren't they lovers, after all?—but he rolled with it, clasped both of his enormous hands around hers.

What kind of wife had old Mrs. Paxton been? Was she a chattering wife, filling up the supper table with empty talk, the daily recap of job and school? No, it didn't seem like her. Did she grow her own tomatoes and discuss them? And Mr. Paxton, did he lose himself out the window like Irv did now, after a hard workday?

"Hon, you remember that time I took you to the Friends meeting in Philly, and an old woman stood up to talk about her late husband?"

Irv's brain seemed to return to the room, his eyes to his plate. "I don't quite remember a woman. I remember the meeting, though."

"Oh." Here she thought they had experienced the same thing.

"I remember how loud all the coughing and sneezing became. And when you shook my hand." He shook his head. "A handshake! Oh, I was so in love with your hand."

"Mmmm." *Was?* Bea chewed.

Irv sighed, looked around, noted the empty chairs with a nod. "Did Sadie call?"

"No, not yet today." She sipped her wine. "How is Nina?"

"If you like, I'll wake you up tomorrow when she calls. She'd love to talk to you."

Bea didn't answer. Her mouth was full.

"Bea, she thinks you're angry with her."

Bea swallowed. "That's just silly. I'm not angry with her."

"Are you sure?" He had that maddening therapist mind-reader look on his face.

"OK. OK. Don't shrink me. Just wake me up tomorrow."

Bea couldn't sleep. *She thinks you're angry with her.* Irv snored steady beside her. The window was open, but there was no breeze. Bea shut her eyes.

It's what everyone thought, she was sure. That she was angry at Nina or just plain didn't like her, not like her sweet Sadie. Could that be true? Could she be that kind of parent, the kind who favored one kid over the other? Could the world see what she heartily denied?

She did worry about Nina. Right? Proof of love?

Oh, there had been unforgettable, awful moments with Nina. Not like Sadie—during Sadie's middle school conformist stage, Bea's greatest crimes had been sack dresses and singing in public. But when Nina was that age, the list of maternal infractions had been so much deeper. *Why do you have to go home and make supper? Dad should learn how! You went to college; don't you want a job? All my friends' moms have jobs.* Which had been true. One an attorney, another an accountant. A copy editor, a college professor, a successful artist. None of them displayed the compulsion to make sack lunches and button up other people's sweaters. *They order Chinese takeout, like NORMAL PEOPLE,* Nina had said. *Why can't we just be REGULAR?*

Bea knew she should let it go. Nina had been twelve. Her friends had been pushy overachievers, not to mention also twelve. Nina had new friends now, an apartment of her own, and a secretarial job unfitting her preteen goals. And she *wanted* to talk to Bea. *She'd love to talk to you.* OK, Irv, so if you're right, what, exactly, does our daughter need to say so badly?

Bea couldn't help but rehearse one conversation after another behind her tightly shut eyes:

Mom, why are you avoiding me?
Oh, Nina, I'm not. Just with getting Sadie ready and everything, you remember how it was.

That's classic, Mom. Sadie told me you're wearing her out with all your "help."
Oh, she's just playing it tough. You know how Sadie is. She's a homebody. And
  she's going much farther away than you did, just taking the train to Brown.
I'm in Israel now, Mom. I think I win the "far" contest.
Well, that was your choice, Nina.
You're on to something. Berkeley was your idea. Tel Aviv was my idea. You
  don't like my ideas!

No, no, no, this was not going well. Bea tried again:

Nina! I miss you! How are you?
I'm great, Mom. Come see for yourself!
Well, I don't want to leave Sadie.
What are you talking about? Sadie's in Berkeley.
And my passport's not current . . .
Mom, seriously? Don't be silly. Don't be paranoid. This isn't Gaza.

It was no use. No matter what, Nina fell into critical mode, and Bea became defensive. Was Nina really like this, so accusatory and pushy? Where did this stinging New York tongue come from?

Mom, get a job. Do something creative.
This isn't creative? Working in the garden? Painting the kitchen table?

Dammit. Bea opened her eyes, got up, put on a robe, went downstairs, and opened the freezer compartment. Irv had some butter brickle ice cream in there, she hoped. The cold air felt good. She rested her head on a bag of frozen okra, like a pillow, watched the white vapor swirl around her head in the freezer light, then out into her dark kitchen.

"Randie, do I need a job?"
  "Why, are you broke?"
  They were amending the soil in Randie's new vegetable bed. Nina hadn't even called that morning, after Bea had been up all night, freezing her head and prepping for a showdown. Irv had suggested the obvious—*are your fingers broken?*—pointing to the phone number on the fridge, but Bea had chickened out. *She's busy. She's at work. I don't want to interrupt.*
  So, Bea had not talked to Nina yet, and her muscles twitched with guilt, and pacing around the kitchen did diddley-squat, so she ended up back at the

garden, offering Randie a hand with the weak soil in the newly claimed corner. The shovel felt solid against Bea's foot. She pushed deep into the ground, then flipped the dirt and stones into a wheelbarrow; she felt her heartbeat quicken, her blood go warmer.

"I thought Irv's practice did pretty good," Randie said. "Does he, like, gamble or something?"

"No, no, no," Bea said. "I'm not talking about money."

"Then I don't follow." Randie shoved her spade into the difficult dirt and left it poking out of the ground, then straightened her spine, wiped her brow with the back of her wrist, the only unmuddy surface left.

"Maybe I should do something more *creative* with my life."

Randie let out a husky laugh. "Ah. So you and Nina are speaking again?"

"Not exactly."

Randie looked at her in that unshrink way, like, *Out with it; I don't have all day for this feelings crap.*

"She didn't call today like usual. But I promised Irv I would talk to her."

"I thought you didn't give a shit what she thinks. *Remember?*" Randie swigged from her water jug, set it down, then took up the spade again.

Bea kept digging without pause, looked down at their progress to avoid looking at Randie. "Don't be silly. Of course I care what Nina thinks. Besides, Sadie's at school now. I have time on my hands."

"So come here! Work the garden! Don't you know how lucky you have it? I wish I could complain about time on my hands. When I don't have my face over a bowl of chicken parts, I'm dog-tired. If I didn't have to report to that piece of hell every day, I'd be here. Damn straight I would." Randie was a sous-chef at one of the new Smith Street bistros, worked six nights a week, often seven.

"But you are here every day, Randie."

"Sure, but I'm not *here* here. I'm only half of myself. I'm half here. The other half is home, sacked out on the couch, sawing wood."

Bea privately wondered if she were *here* here herself. And if she was only half here, like Randie, where was the other half? In her kitchen? In Irv's office, stealing air-conditioning? Dormant?

"Oh, Jesus, will you look at that?" Randie said under her breath. Mr. Patel was over in his plot, bearing three large Pepsi bottles. He poured the contents of one into his already thriving patch of mint.

"I wonder what he's got in those bottles," Bea said, stopping her work. "Do you suppose it could actually *be* Pepsi?"

"I hope to God it's herbicide," Randie replied, then laughed at herself. "I can't believe I just said that." She watched Mr. Patel empty the last drips of

Pepsi. "This place is getting out of hand." One of the cats ran over to his plot. "Holy shit," Randie said, ducking behind a tall hollyhock for a closer look. The cat walked right up to Patel for a scratch on the head. Bea was as surprised as Randie. The cat was feral—they all were. There were half a dozen of them, garden regulars. No one could get close to them. This one rolled onto its back on Patel's feet, as if hypnotized.

"Good morning, ladies," Mr. Patel called out. His shout didn't startle the cat at all. "Mrs. Bloom, your daughter's tomato was lovely. Thank you."

Randie shot Bea a look, like, *Excuse me?* Bea decided to ignore her. "Thank you, Mr. Patel. Your zucchini was divine. I made ratatouille. My husband even took a second helping. And getting vegetables into him is usually a chore."

Patel nodded. The cat wound through his legs. Randie stood frozen, hand on spade. Patel put a hand over his brow and squinted in his stark sunlight. No wonder his vegetables were so perfect. "My granddaughter is the same way. Four years old, and already a princess. Nothing but french fries. French fries with ketchup, like a real American girl."

Randie broke her silence with a *hmmph.* She hated talk of offspring, Bea knew, especially from people she disliked. A confirmed nonmom. Never married, never wanted it. It was part of her appeal. No kids, a perpetual kid herself. Like the tough ringleader in the playground, the one everyone wanted among their friends.

Randie clammed up for the rest of the morning, mixed compost with the native dirt, stringy brown hair hiding her face. Bea worked, flustered, alongside her old pal, spade to dirt the only sound. She didn't dare continue the conversation with Patel.

"Maybe you *should* get a job," Randie finally said later, after Patel had left with a cheerful wave and large harvest. "So you'll get something new to talk about."

The comment, from nowhere, stung. Had Randie really thought her boring, these years? Was talking to a new gardener such a crime? Bea was relieved when Randie locked up her tools in the shed to go home for a prework nap. She wondered if Randie even liked her. Or, was Randie using her for her boundless free time and willingness to pitch in?

Was Bea just a helper? Was that all? A helper with nothing worthy to say?

"What do you plan to do with Sadie's plot?" Randie said as she put on her backpack and pulled her bicycle from behind the shed.

"Well, I'll keep it for her, I guess."

"Then don't let those morning glories get out of hand," Randie said, playfully, but not really, turning away and out the front gate.

Alone in the garden, Bea set to work on some volunteers that had sprouted in a common area, next to the gazebo she and Randie had built two years ago. Wind had lifted hollyhock seeds clear from Randie's territory, several plots over. A long flight. The blooms were likely to be boring colors—wild ones always are—and she found herself yanking hard, chopping them into tiny bits before flicking them into her compost bucket. Who was Randie to bitch about invasives? How come Randie was exempt from the shit list?

Bea heard a cough. She looked up. It was young Trevor, Irv's patient, standing at the edge of Sadie's pizza plot, squeezing rosemary leaves between his fingers. She hadn't noticed him coming through the gate. He didn't seem to notice her. He sniffed the rosemary oil on his hand. Bea held her breath and stood still. Here was the boy, the odd boy, the one who made Irv's eyes go distant at dinner.

Trevor wore that unseasonable trench coat and a white silk aviator scarf flipped over his shoulder. Hunched over the rosemary, his chest was nearly concave. His long hair clumped in an unkempt ponytail today, giving Bea a good look at his gaunt face: eyes downcast, cheekbones large in the waning afternoon light. He had a tiny, blondish beard, which Bea had not noticed before. No mustache, like a Quaker.

Trevor crossed to Bea's plot, recognizing the echinacea, the plant he had christened, touching one of the blooms like it was a woman's face, stroking softly its flipped-out petals. He smiled at the flower, the kind of smile expecting a return smile, then receded in disappointment, like recognizing someone on the street who doesn't recognize you back.

Bea thought about smiles. When the girls were infants, their smiles always struck her as a trained response. In their bouncy chairs or in the stroller, peering up at funny-faced adults, their baby smiles were designed to elicit reaction: applause or laughter or sweets or a tickle on the belly. They knew. Cute Nina with her big sole tooth front and center; little Sadie with her right-cheeked dimple. Even preverbal, they knew. A smile was a contract with the world.

Trevor's smile seemed a broken contract. It was stained with shame—the quiet kind—and a conviction—Bea could see it clearly in Trevor's face, knew it intimately in her gut—that if he weren't here, he would not be missed.

She announced herself by turning on the hose. It was cleaner than speech. He turned and smiled again. Unlike that amnesiac flower, Bea smiled back. "Hello! Are you enjoying our garden?"

His cheeks blanched. "Oh, hey. I'm sorry. I'm, like, trespassing, aren't I?"

"No! Of course not! It's a public garden." Bea wanted to rush over and hug him but knew better. "It's not our garden. I just meant, you know, us, the

The Artstars

gardeners." Her hose sprayed the hosta at her feet, in the gazebo shade, but she did not look down. "Want me to cut one of those echinacea for you? The flip-out flower? You could take some home if you want."

"Nah. I'm not going home yet." Maybe Bea imagined it, but there was a finality, a resignation in his voice. Her face must have shown a reaction. He looked back at her with incredulity, like, *how much has he told you about me?* She wanted to answer, *Nothing! I swear! Just your name!* But even that was a lie.

"Listen, you can come in the garden any time. And next time feel free to cut some for yourself." She paused, then added, "From that patch, of course. That plot, that one's mine." He didn't reply. "And that one behind you, with the rosemary, that's my daughter Sadie's plot. She's away now. At college." But Trevor wasn't listening. Not to this chatter. Bea stopped talking, set her eyes on the big green and white leaves at her feet. By the time the hosta was watered, Trevor was gone.

Back home, the phone had messages from each of the girls.

Nina's: "Dad, sorry. I didn't get to call you this morning. But there's a good reason for it! I have good news! Call me! I love you! Hi, Mom."

Sadie's: "OK, Mom, I promised you my new number. Got a pen?" The number was garbled, but Bea wrote what she heard. "My hamstrings are killing me from all this running. But other than that, all is good." Slight pause. "I guess." Bea heard a girlish giggle and squeal in the background, like someone getting tickled. "Love you guys. Poli-sci. I'm late."

All is good—I guess. Bea heard too much in Sadie's pause and uncertainty. What was that noise? And so early in the morning over there? Did the roommate have a boyfriend? Was Sadie already subject to late night grunting in the next bed? Bea did not even know the roommate's name, she realized, her fingers gravitating to the keypad to dial the new number, foreign now to her muscles, but not for long.

Later, lasagna in the oven, Bea went into Sadie's room, still a mess from their last-minute ransack two days ago. Was it only two days? She had tried Sadie's number repeatedly, but nothing.

Her plan for entering Sadie's room had been to clean, but the plan derailed when she saw the inviting bed, covered in stuffed animals. She fell onto it, crashing from last night's insomnia, and looked up at Sadie's John Lennon poster on the ceiling. *Imagine.* Damn, that kid was born in the wrong epoch. On the closet, Sadie had taped a Greenpeace poster, a picture of the earth: LOVE YOUR MOTHER. This other mother, the big green one, did not love Sadie back as fiercely as Bea did. The earth had too many children. Some, like Trevor, were lost and cold, cold enough for a winter coat in Indian summer.

At dinner, Bea told Irv both girls had called. "But I couldn't reach Sadie back. Her message was disconcerting. I think I heard a boy in her room."

"Bea, Sadie is hardy. Both our kids are hardy."

"I know. I know."

"Wouldn't you be more disconcerted if she called all the time, homesick, like Nina did her first week at Brown?"

"Jeez, I forgot about that. The roommate she had until they got switched? What was her name again? Marilyn? Marylou?"

"Mary Something. Mary Alcoholic."

"Mmmm. Remember the night the girl vomited in her bed? Nina was so hysterical." Bea paused to swallow, overcome with unexpected nostalgia. "I miss her."

"I miss Sadie too." Irv looked at the big vase on Sadie's place mat. "It's too quiet."

"Actually, I was thinking of Nina. So hysterical on the phone."

"Huh. OK. So you miss hysterical American Nina, but happy Israeli Nina not so much?" Irv had stopped chewing, was reading her across his plate.

Bea decided to lay it on the table. "Yes. I miss hysterical Nina. And baby Nina in her stroller. That smile. Do you remember the way she used to show off that tooth? Now, she doesn't need us so much anymore. Or *me*. She doesn't need *me* so much anymore."

Irv looked ready to contradict her but didn't. "And that's why you're angry with her?"

"Yes. Maybe. Maybe I'm a little angry with her."

"You have a right to tell her you're angry."

"Irv, don't be silly. It's not rational."

"Anger never is." He gloated over her confession and chomped a bite of bread. Bea wondered if he gloated like this with patients too, after they purged— hardly the ideal bedside manner. She couldn't look at him. She looked at the echinacea. She thought of Trevor, smiling at the flowers' forgetful siblings in the garden. She turned back to Irv. "I saw your patient again today. Trevor."

"Oh, yeah?" The gloat dropped. He put down his fork. "Where?"

"Wandered into the garden. He didn't even see me at first. He was looking at Sadie's rosemary. He seems lost in something. He was wearing a winter coat and scarf."

"Hmm." Irv seemed to want to say more.

"Something's missing there, I think. He was so—apologetic. So—I don't know. But something was missing."

"What would you say was missing?" Irv could certainly ask questions, even if he couldn't answer them.

"Like Sadie and Nina—you call them *hardy*, you know? Even hysterical, Nina was hardy. And when she was his age, I never feared for her—" Bea couldn't utter the thought.

"For her life?"

Bea pulled her wineglass in front of her mouth and nodded.

"But you fear for her life now?"

"Yes, God yes, now I do. But it's not the same. This would . . . I don't know. This would be worse. What Trevor's mother must feel."

"I know."

"You do know, don't you?" Bea looked at her old man across the table, his hair gone white a decade ago, those hound eyes, downturned at the corners, brow crossed with worry. Perhaps he had fatherly feelings for his patient, he who had wished for a son before Sadie came along. "Do you pray for him?" she asked.

"For Trevor?"

"Bea, you know I don't pray."

"But if you did pray, would you pray for him?"

"Yes." Irv nodded, dark eyes welling up with what he would not say.

Irv's office line rang before dawn. Bea didn't even hear it until Irv was already downstairs, picking up, and a sick feeling overtook her. He never answered that line after hours. He usually snored right through it.

He returned to the bedroom and clicked on the dresser lamp. He looked pale. "Is it Trevor?" she said.

He only nodded.

"Is he OK?"

Irv sat on the twisted sheet, stooped as if carrying a load on his back. "He's in the hospital. That was his mother. They admitted him about an hour ago." He began pulling on yesterday's pants and socks, abandoned by the bed like a collapsed fireman's uniform, waiting for his feet.

"Did he . . . ?"

Irv didn't answer. He sat upright. Color had returned to his face. All business now. He pulled wallet and keys from the dresser into his pockets, called a car service. "I should be back in plenty of time for my noon patient." He kissed her on the forehead.

"Should I stay home and wait, just in case patients show up?"

"No. I'll be back." He turned off the light.

"Will he be OK?" Bea said, like a child into the dark room.

"Today, yes."

He went downstairs to wait for the car. Bea stayed frozen on her side. She heard a honk outside, then Irv's keys in the front lock. Bea lay still, watched the new sun slowly fill the sheer white curtain, listened to sparrows in the tree outside, greeting the day like any other.

Bea waited, not moving, until the light filled the room. The coleus on the sill needed water. It cast a shadow onto the empty space next to her, Irv's wrinkled pillow. A siren cried several blocks away, racing to something tragic.

She closed her eyes, tried to picture something reassuring. She only saw Trevor, standing close enough in the garden yesterday, close enough for her to run to him, pin him in her arms. What if she had done that, instead of keeping her eyes to the hosta? Her stupid eyes, her stupid hosta? Why hadn't she run to this boy? This baby? Held him? Let him rest his unwashed head on her shoulder, rocked him?

She clenched her eyes tighter. She thought of her mother's shoulder, her mother's lap, the old walnut rocker; a sudden, visceral memory, the pillow of her mother's arms around her. Mother smelled like milled applesauce, she remembered, and was teaching Bea to spell her name: B-E-A-T-R-I-C-E, with a little tune to help her memorize it. The chair rocked, and the two of them had sung her name; a powerful chant for a little person, the message so plain: *Your name is important. You are important.* If only repeating the song now could conjure this feeling. She wished she could call her mother, sing the letters through the phone to her, hear her scratchy soprano join through the telephone. She would sing the letters of her mother's name too. *You are important. You were important. I miss you.*

She opened her eyes and thought of Irv's face last night. Not the gloat, after confessing her anger at Nina, but the other look, before that. *She doesn't need me so much anymore.* Irv would have been right to contradict her. Nina called nearly every day. She needed something. If the phone rang during breakfast today, Bea decided, she would muster the courage to answer. Here was a garden she could cross, a kid she could put her arms around. A name to say aloud.

Bea was twisted into a yoga knot when the phone rang, much later than normal. She fell over herself onto the hardwood floor, banged her elbow, and was heaving, grabbing her funny bone as she pressed the answer button.

"Mom? Is that you? Are you OK?"

"Nina. Sorry." She tried to catch her breath. "I was tied up. Yoga."

Nina laughed—raspy, edgy, maybe a little nervous. "Oh. Good. Good for you." Pause. "I expected Dad." Bea could hear a man shouting in the background, then a big belly laugh and a woman laughing too.

"What's going on there?"

"We got a rowdy bunch here. Everyone's sticking around on deadline." Nina shushed the others in Hebrew, that familiar, husky Nina voice, but the words all different. Bea felt a surge of pride at her bilingual daughter. "Nina, you're so smart. I miss you," Bea blurted.

"Mom! Where did that come from?" Nina still seemed nervous. "I miss you too."

Bea tried to picture Nina at her desk, with a console phone and huge computer screen, in the Middle Eastern heat. Or, maybe it was air-conditioned. It must be. "Do you have air-conditioning?"

"Uh, yes. We do." Nina laughed. "That's an odd question. Why do you ask?"

"I don't know." Bea felt frozen and without topic. "Your dad is out. His patient is very sick. At the hospital. But I'll let him know you called?"

"That's it? What are you, chopped liver?"

"No, no!" *You have a right to tell her you're angry with her,* Bea kept thinking; then: *Am I angry with her?* "What about your news? Is this about your deadline?"

Nina took a deep breath. The room behind her had quieted. "Ari and I are getting married."

Bea flopped onto the messy bed. "Honey, that's great." It didn't feel exactly great. Nina was only a kid. Only twenty-one. Bea had not talked to Ari once, not ever. "Are you—"

"Pregnant? I knew it!" She said something in raspy Hebrew to her office mates, then chuckled, the way one chuckles at the stupid.

"Are you guys drinking? You shouldn't drink if you're pregnant."

"Mom, I'm not pregnant. Yes, we're drinking. It's afternoon here, remember?"

"I'm sorry. I just . . . I don't know. I'm just being a mom. It's what we do."

"Here, I'll put him on the phone."

Bea panicked. A shuffle on the other end, then: "Mrs. Bloom!" Ari's voice was deep, like Irv's. He sounded tall. "How are you this morning? How do you like our surprise today?" His accent was heavy, but he was trying, spoke with exclamation points, seemed to bubble over with the English words he had trouble forming in his exuberance. "I love your daughter! I hear you are a garden person!"

"Well, yes, I am—"

"Me too! I am a garden person. I will be happy for you to see my garden. It is small, but we are growing some nice stuff. You will like it when you see it!"

"What are you growing?"

"Oh! Tomatoes, eggplant, dill. Mint. Nina says your thumb is green. My green hand will shake your green hand!"

"Green *thumb*," chimed Nina's throaty voice behind him. Bea heard him kiss her. Nina sounded content, giggling into the body of her beloved in their air-conditioned office.

"You must have lots of light," Bea imagined aloud, picturing a courtyard, tiled maybe, with Ari's plants in terra-cotta containers. "Not *now*, I mean, but, you know. In general."

"I will cook for you! You will come to Israel, and I will cook. My Mexican dishes are famous!" So he knew how to pick up a spatula. Good for Nina. Bea wondered what it would be like to lie on the couch while Irv prepared dinner, without resorting to Manfredi's. How lovely. To have a job, to come home, to have dinner prepared by somebody else.

"Your *dirty dishes* are famous!" Nina squealed. All of this fame, and all of it new to Bea. "Give me that." Nina was back on the line. "You'll love him, Mom. Dad already does."

"Oh." Irv had mentioned speaking to Ari, but not love, not specifically. "Good."

"How's Sadie?"

"Well, I don't exactly know."

"What, she doesn't call?"

"Not when I'm here, she doesn't."

"Huh. She must be having fun, then, right?" Nina said. "Jeez, it's been what, three days? Promise me you won't turn into a worrywart." Nina may have been trying to reassure, but her tone was more ridicule than tenderness.

"I'm aware that Sadie can take care of herself," Bea said with a surprising chill.

"I'm sorry. I know." Nina paused. "Hey, it must be real different in the house now, huh? How are you?" The question was sincere and hit Bea right in her solar plexus. She started to cry. She could not help it. "Mom. Mom, hey. Are you all right?"

The tears came steadily now, and Bea didn't even try to stop them. "I'm sorry, Nina. I thought I could hold it together." Her whole body shuddered, and she heard her daughter shooing people from the room.

"Mom. Breathe. What's wrong?"

"I don't know. Your father's patient, this kid, he's only Sadie's age, and he's such a mess, and I wanted to help, I *want* to help, but there's nothing, and your dad is so preoccupied, and Sadie doesn't pick up, and I'm always scared to talk to you. Do you think I need a job?"

"Do I *what*? Slow down. Do you want one?"

"I don't know. I don't know what I want." Bea stopped and took a long breath. "You know how you used to say all your friends' moms had jobs, and why couldn't I be more like them, you know? Maybe you were right."

"I said that?" Nina's surprise sounded real. No memory of it at all. "That wasn't very kind."

"No, I guess it wasn't." Bea fumbled through the bedside drawer for a handkerchief. "You were kind of a bitch." She found a sock in the dust bunnies under the bed frame and wiped her nose on its scratchy acrylic. "You hurt my feelings."

"Wow. Wow, Mom. Hey, I'm sorry. When did I say that?"

"Oh, I don't know." Bea caught her reflection in the dresser mirror: her short, salt-and-pepper hair sticking out in all directions; her red, runny nose. "Ten years ago? I think?"

That husky laugh. "OK, Mom, and you're just now saying something about it?"

"I'm . . . slow," Bea said.

"Am I really that scary to talk to?" Nina said. Pure Nina. No games.

"Yes," Bea blurted, making it not true, suddenly, not true at all. "I mean no. I'm sorry I waited so long to . . . say something."

"You ever see any of them now? My friends' moms?"

"No." One would think she'd run into them at the Korean grocer. Or glimpse them walking by the garden.

"Who you hanging out with now, then? With Sadie gone? Randie?"

"Yeah." Bea wiped her eye with her palm, leaned into the mirror to flatten her hair with her fingertips. "But I'm beginning to think Randie's a control freak. Maybe she's using me."

"HelLO," Nina replied. "I never trusted her."

"Nina! Why didn't you tell me?"

"I didn't think you'd listen."

It was a hard way to think of herself, as a nonlistener. Bea had prided herself on her big project: a safe home, two strong kids, being approachable. But maybe it was just fantasy. Maybe she was a really bad listener, even—avoiding Nina's calls—and even Trevor had fled her yesterday. She looked at herself hard in the mirror, tried to see what others might. Freckles from the summer's work, of course, but few wrinkles yet around the eyes. Firm jaw, thin lips. Not like Irv, whose crow's-feet and Santa beard gave his face perpetual warmth. And Bea's arms—they were lean, certainly, for her age. Torso straight and unyielding in her black unitard. Not like her own mother's squishy, aproned self, inviting one to dive in for a hug. Maybe she wasn't as approachable as she thought.

She thought of Mr. Patel, the other day, tiptoeing out of the garden with her tomatoes, leaving her alone to her work. Even the exuberant Mr. Patel had a line he would not cross with her. "I think I might have a new friend," Bea said to Nina.

"Good. You need new friends. Who?"

"This Indian gentleman in the garden. He's good with the cats, and he grows the most exquisite zucchini. But I don't really know him."

"Get out there, Mom. Be intrepid. You have loads to offer besides free labor."

Bea felt the rigid freeze waft from her body, evaporate out the window. She sighed. "Oh Nina. *NinaNinaNinaNinaNina.*" It was a new arpeggio, sung from gut to phone, a spontaneous incantation.

Bea went to the garden with something new in her bag: a big slice of last night's lasagna, wrapped in a recycled salad container from Manfredi's. It was an experiment. After talking to Nina, she had replayed the conversation repeatedly—*Be intrepid, Mom. Get out there, Mom*—and her decidedly unapproachable frame in the mirror didn't help. *Good, you need new friends.* But did new friends need her?

The lasagna had turned out well. It did contain Mr. Patel's zucchini. It would be a simple overture of friendship between fellow vegetable-obsessed people.

When she got there, Patel was the sole human in the garden, sitting on a cinder block next to his plot, petting yesterday's cat, a fat brown tabby. He had helped the cat to get this fat and now reaped its affection. The cat swished against his leg. Patel beamed, eyes closed against the bright sunlight. His skin was dark from months of gardening, his hair nearly white, but his body was slim, young, and his hands too, touching the purring animal with a sensuality she found unnerving. She hadn't really thought of him as a man before. Only as a grandfather: old, safe, a foreigner. And here she was with a wrapped dish, like charity or a potluck offering, too much old lady herself.

The way to a man's heart is through his stomach, girls used to say back in college, teasing each other about MRS degrees. She had first seduced Irv with food, in fact. Her senior year, this attractive, older grad student had looked hungry, so she fed him. A wrapped dish, just like this one, brought to his office hours. Such pleasure she'd taken watching Irving Bloom relish her cheese strata as he pretended to discuss her term paper.

And here, she sought Patel in his kind of office. She wondered if he would take it the wrong way.

Irv hadn't made it home by 11:45 a.m., and the noon appointment loomed. She was worried—about Irv, about Trevor, about the noon patient—but felt something else too, something less rational. *Anger never is.* Irv, with all his talk of feelings—her feelings—never seemed to see fit to share his own. Gloated over her confession but confessed nothing himself. She had no idea what to say to the noon patient, since she wasn't allowed to *know* these people, and suddenly decided that door monitor to precarious persons was not her job. She hadn't volunteered for it, and it might not even be a job worth doing. *Nina, NinaNinaNinaNinaNina,* she incanted, slamming through the kitchen, packing Patel's meal. Irv would have to face the fallout of his absence, his crazy clients and their crazy secret needs.

And now, at the threshold of her garden, she took a breath, then strode over to Patel, arm outstretched with the savory offering. "Mr. Patel, have you had lunch? I brought you some lasagna."

The cat jumped for cover under the gazebo floor. "Mrs. Bloom!" Patel said.

She was about to cross a line. She was being intrepid. She stepped forward and handed him the dish. "It's vegetarian. Made with your zucchini and my daughter's tomatoes."

"Wonderful! I am vegetarian."

"Me too, when I can help it."

He gestured to the cinder block next to his, and she sat. He seemed like a lonely kid, sitting so low to the ground, his best friend a stray cat. Ready prey for anyone with ulterior motives. Like Randie, using her for her idleness, for her willingness to be used, her need to be useful. He opened the package, took a bite with the plastic fork she had included, smiled approval while he chewed.

"Mr. Patel, what's your secret with that cat?"

"Please, call me Ganesh."

"Like the elephant guy?"

He let out a silly, high elephant cry and waved an arm like a trunk, spilling sauce onto his chin. She was drawn to the blob of sauce, wanted to wipe it with a tissue and a little of her saliva, like she used to do with the girls. She blushed at the thought of her saliva on this stranger's chin. She looked away at the cat, who crouched a good distance away, watching Patel's pachydermic outburst.

"Please watch, Mrs. Bloom," he said. He set down his lasagna and pulled a can of sardines from his shopping bag.

"Bea," she said.

"*Bee,*" he said, then buzzed his tongue against his teeth and flittered his hands at his shoulders, like wings. "We are an elephant and a bee."

"An elephant can crush a bee," she said.

"No! A bee is the star of the garden. Important! Without the bee, the elephant has no fruit."

He returned his attention to the sardines. The cat heard the key in the can, like the key in a lock, and ran over, forgetting her fear. He set the open can on the ground, next to Bea's foot, and the cat put its face right into it. Bea tentatively reached out and stroked the ravenous animal, while Patel resumed his robust lasagna eating. Bea felt a bulge at the cat's round side, distinct and alien, like a tumor.

"She's pregnant," said Patel, through his food. "That's why the sardines are irresistible. That's my secret. Some kind of secret, eh?"

"Mmmm." Bea's hand grew bolder. The cat was getting used to her. She was getting used to the cat. "I wonder what kind of mother she will be."

"She is not young. She must know what she is doing," he said.

"I've been pregnant. I'm a mother. You never know what you are doing."

The cat finished the fish and licked the oil from the bottom of the can but didn't leave. Gently, Patel lifted her onto Bea's lap. Claws dug through Bea's clothing into her thigh, and the lumpy, furry belly spread into a purr.

It was the same size as a baby, the cat; the same weight. The weight she had been longing for, light and manageable, tugged at the part of her memory she had been pushing back. She wanted to embrace the cat but didn't dare. The cat was relaxed but spring-loaded, ready to leap away.

The Artstars

The Stone Floor

THE STEPS OF THE QUAY DROP RIGHT INTO THE GRAY-GREEN WATER. She says she wants to descend those steps, into the cold rush like her favorite writer, pockets full of rocks. Since we were kids, she talks like this, strolls along edges and fake laughs. I don't slap her. Not anymore. Nowadays, I push the counteridea: I want to descend the staircase nude, cubist, flattened and orange, with my nose over there and my hip up here.

Rebecca swats my head. "Sara, really. Make it yours."

"You're filling your pockets with rocks," I tell her. "That's not yours."

"They're my souvenirs," she says.

I don't say. I'm done saying. Hers, or not hers—who gives a hoot. They are weighing her down. Everything she touches weighs her down.

Down is where she looks nowadays. She scans the gravel for souvenirs, misses the monuments. She misses the meringues too: jumbo, pillowy meringues, a windowful in Easter-colored drifts. "Becky, look. Cloud cookies. Look up."

She does not look up. She snatches a rock from the ground and rubs the dust off with her thumb. The rock is crusty white, like the hilltop cathedral behind her. She holds the rock up and squints, like a drawing student, to compare the rock to the domes. "Look, a scale model," she says.

I am done saying. It is not a scale model. It is a rock. I like rocks. I have nothing against rocks. This is something beyond rocks. She spit shines the rock, then drops the find in her overcoat pocket, and it clanks against her collection. I can see the bulge of her pocket. She scans the gravel for another.

I step to the shop to buy a cookie. "What color you want, Beck?"

"Color, not flavor?"

"That's not an answer." I don't wait for an answer. I buy her a yellow, to eat with her dirty fingers.

The sky darkens, then opens up. Umbrellas dot the air over our sidewalk: black, black, red, black. Up the hill, the cathedral weeps salt. "I'm going inside," I say. There are saints I want to see. I want the high shelter, the placid faces overhead, the gilt halos.

"I'm staying out here," my sister says. "I don't want to get converted."

"You won't be converted. They can't make you believe anything you don't want to."

A puddle forms around her feet, where the street won't drain. "You believe everything," she says.

I hike up the stairs to the church without her. It is a wrought wedding cake thick with frosting, pearly and crowded. At the threshold, I turn back and see her under the bakery awning: slight in her black sporty raincoat, with damp red ringlets framing her face, looking into the depth of her puddle, nibbling the very edge of her airy cookie.

My cookie is the blue of a songbird's egg. I gobble it, there on the cathedral step, as the rain and blue food color stream down my hands. The sweet is so strong it curls my lips into something that must look like a smile. I step inside.

A priest sings the mass, and a mass of tourists pushes me to the apse. The domed ceiling is bluer than my cookie. A bearded figure in white looks down. He's wearing a gilt white nightgown, his arms spread wide, a stiff letter *T*, as if presenting a chorus line of sequined saints. The arms are straight until I am below him and see that they reach around the dome in a large arc. A hug around this roomful of chant. The priest's voice stops, but it bounces off of the stone walls, fills the basilica, a modal echo over the spoken drone of us lookers. I let my jaw fall, and I look up. The faces above are calm. I listen. I wait for the walls to let go of the chant.

Back outside, I wave to my sister, still parked next to her puddle, looking wistfully at a pit bull on the end of a stranger's leash. She is still eating her meringue.

We walk wordless to the Metro stop. On a blank cement wall, someone has spray-painted, in relaxed cursive:

regarde le ciel . . .

I want to mention it to her. Point to it. Ask her what she thinks it is about. But her head is bowed. She looks into the wet gutter. "Sare," she says. "Look." She points. "You can see that trash can reflected backward in the water."

The Artstars

At our hotel, there's no room in our room. Our kid beds were stacked, so our lives could spread onto the carpet. But here, it's twins. Side by skinny side, an easy reach over the gap, over the orange, stained shag. She pops Ambiens with a plastic cup of box wine. Her poisons are many, and they make her snore. I poke her in the shoulder with a knitting needle, and sometimes she quiets. I am up. I watch erotic chocolate commercials. I watch French people competing at ciphers. The French people turn strings of senseless characters into less senseless ones. I understand nothing.

I knit a row, and another. I look at the code in my pattern book: K1, P2, YO. It's a scarf. Maybe for Becky, if she will stop snoring. It is bright red. She hates the color anyway. It will go into the box, most likely, at the top of my closet, the stuff I knit for no reason.

A man on the television wins a cipher. He puts letters in order to make a word I don't recognize. He puts arithmetic operations in order to make a number I feel nothing for. A bell dings. The host smiles and congratulates. The studio audience smiles and congratulates. They love the number and how it was put into order. I love how they love the number.

I watch for hours. The scarf puts itself into order, until my eyelids fall.

We eat croissants and *pain au chocolat* in the breakfast room. Becky stares at raindrops trailing down the window and slowly emerges from last night's poisons. She gulps her strong coffee. I sip. I gobble my breads. She nibbles.

I page through my guidebook. "Where shall we go today? Left Bank? Right Bank?"

"Oh, something *sculpture-related*, no doubt," she says into her bowl of coffee. "Or *churchy*. We really need to *see more churches*."

"It doesn't have to be my thing. It can be your thing. It can be literary, if you want, no? Here," I say, and hand her the guide. "I think James Joyce's apartment is right around the corner."

"Oh *goody*! Let's have an *epiphany*! Maybe if we go to *James Joyce's apartment* and *Henry Miller's whorehouse* that will make me *a better writer*." She doesn't accept the guide.

"Well, then what? Anything you're dying to see?"

"You're not the free spirit you think you are," Becky says, looking out, or at, the window. "Free spirits don't need to plan every second of every day."

Stand firm. Hold your ground. Her bait is just that: bait. Don't be the fish. I close my eyes and try to picture Irving Bloom: his calm, calming face across the coffee table in his office, like the bearded saints of the blue basilica ceiling. I open my eyes. My sister is looking at me. "You don't need to control everything, Sare."

"You don't need to shit on everything, Beck."

"Yes. Yes, I think I do. I need to shit on everything. I think that's my job description." She takes the book from my hands, finally. She flips through, looking at pictures, not reading. Looking for things to shit on.

"I'm getting another pastry," I say, pushing back my chair, pushing down tears.

"Tell you what," she says. She closes her eyes, then fans the pages and pokes her finger in at random. "There. We'll go there. It better not be a church."

I used to have this fantasy about her death.

Go on.

She dies in her sleep. Nothing violent or intentional. She . . . slips away.

How does it feel when she "slips away"?

I can't describe it.

Try.

Free, I guess. And sad. Sad, but free. Wow, I suck.

It's just a fantasy, Sara. Your thoughts can't hurt anybody.

You sure about that, Irv?

Why does your sister's death make you feel free?

I've always felt like there's something I need to protect her from. It.

What is "It"? Death?

No. Not death. Something in life. I don't know. I never should have brought it up. I don't feel comfortable talking about this.

You came here to feel comfortable? To talk about the weather?

Yes. I came here to talk about the weather.

Is there weather in your fantasy? About Rebecca's death?

You don't quit, do you? Yes. Actually. Maybe it's raining. Easygoing rain. Cleansing. Like Paris during Lent.

Did it rain when you and she went to Paris?

It rained every goddamn day.

Do you think the rain had something to do with what happened in Paris?

I don't know. I don't know what to blame.

The cemetery is cobblestone lanes flanked by miniature chapels. In the wet air, moss turns a deep green between chunks of granite, and the lane recedes in mist.

Maybe today will be beautiful.

The place is peopled with the famous dead. We touch the shiny black marble over Édith Piaf. It is littered with wilting flowers. We say hello to Proust, and Céline, and Balzac. Becky is quiet in this magical place. The mist means tourists are few. Becky points to a bronze figure, a young female nude draped with a flowing metal sheet and dripping with green patina. "Look, Sare. It's like she's knocking on that headstone. Like she wants in."

"She's sublime."

"I know how she feels," Becky says.

"She must be a hundred years old," I say. "She'll be here for at least a hundred more."

"If no one bombs this place."

"Yes, if no one bombs this place."

Becky looks up at the sky. "Nope. No bombers," she says, with a contented undertone.

It feels like a window. She seems to like it here, for real. "Hey, you mind if I draw for a while? Just sit over here, while you roam and check the place out?"

"Sounds good." It's the warmest thing she's said all week.

It's something my friend Steve suggested I try, when I told him I was coming here: get over my fear of 2-D. *Draw for fun*, he suggested. *Draw sculptures. Paper and ink are just materials*, Steve says. *You know how to love your materials. Collaborate with them.*

At first, it is no collaboration. I sit on a low retaining wall facing the bronze figure. This overcast morning, I can't tell where the light is coming from. I keep thinking some judge is looking over my shoulder, like in drawing class. Every mark I make is going to ruin this drawing. I brought watercolor pencils, a gift from Steve. *They're very forgiving*, he said, as if he needs forgiveness. That dude never feared a blank page. He has hundreds of breathtaking sketchbooks. My first attempt here looks like a broken cartoon. With a spastic burst of my hand, I cross out the whole page, then turn to a new one, pause, and begin with a long, green line to indicate the curve of the figure's baroque hip.

The watercolor pencils mix with the misty air in a way I start to like. I push pigment across the rough page and watch the mist settle on the fiber in droplets. I stop for a while and scrutinize the figure. To me, she is not knocking on the gravestone. She is tired. She is leaning against the stone to feel the cool wet granite against her cheek. She is worn out, waiting for her beloved to come back. She's not yet ready to go in, to go down, into the mud.

I think of all those mornings, knocking on the bathroom door before school. Not just to go in, but to coax my kid sister out. *Becky, you done in there? Becky? We'll miss the bus. Your hair doesn't need to be straight. Everyone loves your hair the way it is.*

Easy for you to say, she would reply.

I draw the statue's curly locks. Not the frizzy mop that my sister has re-signed herself to, but the long, languorous curl she used to try to cultivate. A big drop of rain splashes in the middle of my drawing, pushing the green into the blue. I let it soak in, then blot it. My statue is unrecognizable. It looks like a calculated distortion. Cubist, flat, and gray-green, with the arm dripping over there and the hip up here. Now she looks more live than statue; her hair has a halo of frizz, like Becky's in sunlight. I decide I like it. I decide to quit while I still like drawing.

I close my sketchbook, pack up my pencils, put it all into my backpack, and tread up a knoll to look for my sister.

I find her near the crematory, supine on a marble slab, hand in hand with a granite figure, her eyes closed like his, in frozen repose.

"What the fuck, Becky?"

"Meet my new boyfriend."

Behind her, a Vietnamese family of ten exits the crematory, all dressed in black. A woman, my age, looks at Becky lying on top of the grave, then locks eyes with me. She is angry. Or maybe confused. Her eyes look bloodshot. She flips open her black umbrella.

"Becky. Get up. NOW."

"Jesus, Sare. Get a sense of humor," she says; then she sees the mourners and zips lip before joining me, walking briskly the other way.

We hide behind a wall of stacked graves, a weathered grid, a patchwork quilt of French names and birth dates and death dates. Behind the marble, I imagine, are rows and rows of feet. "Why were you *lying down* back there?" I ask.

"He looked lonely."

"No, I'm being serious. This place is not a joke."

She recoils, as if I slapped her. "Why are you so judgmental?"

I shut up. We walk, wordless, along the length of patchwork wall, then back into the misty, cobbled lane.

We encounter a tall art deco grave in boxy sandstone. It's a winged figure, ready for a headfirst leap. The stone is covered in lipstick kisses, sealed behind plexiglass. "If I kiss the grave of Oscar Wilde, will I become a wit?" Becky says. "Will I write inimitable quips?"

Some Americans approach us in the lane, talking too loud, fringy with pa-tchouli and moccasins, carrying guitar cases covered in Rasta decals. "Which way to Jim Morrison?" asks one, not even attempting French.

Becky points. I think she's pointing the wrong way. The Americans obey her directions. Becky watches them walk away, then shouts to their backs: "If we sing 'Redemption Song,' will we all be redeemed?" They don't reply.

"I think you pointed them the wrong way."

"I know."

"Why'd you do that?"

"I did them a favor. Look, it's Gertrude," Becky says, pointing down. The grave is low, simple, the opposite of Wilde's, ringed with young weeds. Atop the author's headstone are pebbles left by other pilgrims. My sister pokes her forefinger through the rocks and finally picks one; she clinks it into her coat pocket.

"Becky, c'mon. Someone left that there for her."

"A stone is a stone is a stone," Becky says. "You hungry yet? I could go for some Vietnamese."

"Beck. C'mon. Put the rock back."

"When did you get so bossy, huh? Were you always this way? I'm starving."

Irv, am I bossy?

Do you think you are bossy?

I don't know.

What does "bossy" mean to you?

It means Becky is talking. It's her favorite word.

She calls you bossy?

Only when she wants me to shut the fuck up.

Does it work?

Yeah. Yeah, it works all right.

"What are *nems*?" I ask Becky over the table in a Vietnamese diner, up a little side street in Belleville.

"Fuck if I know. What's in the picture?" She flips through her menu and lands on a page depicting fruity drinks in tall tumblers. "I think I'll try Cocktail Number Six." She points to a yellow concoction with mint leaves and pearly chunks.

"I can't even tell what's in that."

"I don't care, as long as it's vodka."

My mouth begins to object, but I swallow my comment back. *Judgmental. Bossy.* It's her body. What do I care how she lunches? The waiter stops, and I find myself pointing to the same picture, the mystery drink, and to the *nems*, whatever those are, and on the facing page, a translucent ravioli-looking dumpling and something that is probably a salad. Perhaps heartened by the low price tag, Becky points to several nonliquid items as well.

Soon, our table is covered in plastic plates. I feel conspicuously American— taller, hungrier—and try not to care about the stares from nearby tables, tables of

Parisians with normal food quantities. From the corner of the long, thin dining room, a yellow bird cheeps in his cage, approving of our gluttony: *Eat! Eat!* We obey.

"This is just right," says my sister into her next Cocktail Number Six. "You see? Isn't it great to just order from the picture sometimes? Doesn't it make you feel *free*?" True, the drink isn't bad—lychee or grapefruit or pear; honestly, I can't tell—and the *nems* are crispy and tasty, and Becky offers me a bite of her grilled pork chop, reaching her fork across the table to my mouth the way we used to when we were little. I don't want to leave this place, with its bamboo motif and encouraging bird; whatever magic put my sister in this generous mood, I don't want it to vanish.

"I liked the cemetery," Becky says. "Not just the famous people. I liked the *place*. If I lived here, I would go there all the time! The moss creeping through all the stones . . . the names, those crazy Froggy names! I could spend a day just reading the names. Jean-Bernard Dupont Lestrange? I want to know *that* guy. Forget all the famous artists."

"Did you happen to catch when he died?" I ask. "Lestrange?"

"Nineteen forty-five, was it? Something like that. But he was only in his thirties."

"Do you suppose he was in the resistance? Or a collaborator?"

"Oh, not my *boyfriend*. He couldn't have been a *collaborator*."

"Ah, yes. *Him*." I smile, my best nonjudgmental smile. I try not to picture my crazy sister lying on the stranger's gravestone, with the sad family looking on. I look at the table's caddy of condiments—hot pepper sauce, a bucket of forks and knives, napkins—find momentary comfort in their everydayness. "I liked the cemetery too. It felt so good to just *work* for a while, you know? Steve was right. It's good for a sculptor to draw. It felt great to just sit down all by myself and put ink on the page again."

"Hmmph," Becky says. She puts down her fork. I don't know exactly what I've said wrong, but something. She picks up her glass, sucks at the fat straw until the cold emptiness rattles in the bottom. Most of the food between us is gone, along with the fragile bonhomie. She tries to get the waiter's eye. "I need another one of these. I wish our man would come back."

This would make drink number four, for her anyway. It isn't yet two o'clock. "Maybe coffee this time?" I can't help myself. "To energize for this afternoon?"

"Hmmph," she repeats, louder now, and successfully gets the waiter's attention for her refill. He points to my empty glass with his pencil.

"*Non, merci*," I say to the young man. "*Et c'est tout.*" I make the little check motion with my pinched fingers. The bird in the corner objects. My sister exhales loudly. She looks out the window, then at the busy bamboo wallpaper, then at the birdcage in the corner, while the waiter retreats.

The Artstars

Finally, she faces me. "You can really be a cunt sometimes. You know that?" Her voice is quiet, calm, direct.

I feel a hot flush climbing my spine. I have nothing to say back.

The bill arrives. Becky snatches the plastic folder from my hand and pops in her American Express.

When we were in Paris, I dreamed my head was bleeding.
That sounds important. Were you injured?
No, that's the thing. Nothing hit me. It was coming from inside.
Like a parasite?
No. More like . . . a tumor. I parted my hair and looked in the mirror, and there
*   was all this blood and goop, and this place where my scalp was eroding,*
*   and this thing was poking out. This face.*
Whose face? Your face?
No. More like an animal. A cat. A big cat. Like a tiger.
Did it make noise? Was the tiger roaring?
It sounded like it was in distress.
Why was the tiger in distress?
Why do you think? It was trapped inside my skull. With my brain. Like a tiny
*   little hotel room with orange carpet.*
And that is an uncomfortable place for a tiger? Your skull? With its orange
*   carpet?*
It may as well be a jail.

Could be our five collective tumblers of Cocktail Number Six or the unnerving, lubricated lunch conversation, but we find ourselves on a street unindexed in my guidebook. We have walked right off the tourist map.

"Put that away," hisses my sister.

"What was the name of that artery back there?"

"We're having an adventure. Put the book away."

"Everyone says the *banlieue* is dangerous."

"That's like saying Brooklyn is dangerous. You're being a *worrywart*."

"Maybe I'll ask someone?"

"We're WALKING." She marches up to the next corner and turns. I have no choice but to follow.

We walk single file down narrow, dank passages, me trotting behind like a tired dog. The skinny sidewalk is crowded with shoppers, none of them tourists, none of them speaking English or possibly even French. In dark storefronts, men in caftans squat over giant bowls of vegetables I cannot name, and salted fish, and hills of spices, carrying on rapid commerce with their buyers. The walls are tagged with secret messages—not the bright, artful graffiti I love, but small, furtive territorial claims. Over there, a young man's head droops over a paper bag of some poison he has just inhaled. He can't be fourteen. People step over him, as if he does not exist. Becky does not linger to look or comment. She faces the sidewalk straight ahead of her, with a singular purpose and a long stride, deeper into this unmapped world.

I've given up asking her to slow down and check a sign. We are in it now. I follow. If we find ourselves in the heart of the *banlieue*, then that is where we will be.

> *I want to hear more about that afternoon in Paris. Are you ready to talk about that?*
> I guess.
> *Have you thought some more about what exactly set you off?*
> *Well, the walking, I think. She just started taking crazy turns. We were going in circles, down these stinky alleys, but we weren't actually getting anywhere.*
> *And you prefer to get somewhere?*
> *She wasn't even trying to help us. Even her stride was aggressive.*
> *You say she took crazy turns. Why, do you think, was this labyrinthine route her choice?*
> *Because she knew it wouldn't be my choice. Same shit as when we were kids, and she'd climb to the skinny top branches of a tree just to taunt me and call me scaredy-cat.*
> *OK, that's something. Interesting nickname.*
> *She didn't make that up. It's not hers.*
> *I mean vis-à-vis your dream. The tumor meowing to get outside your head?*
> *Oh, jeez. I didn't think of that.*
> *What if your "scaredy-cat" were actually a tiger?*
> *Then maybe the tiger needs lessons in being a tiger.*
> *Maybe. Good. It's good to see you laugh.*
> *Well, I wasn't laughing in Paris.*
> *Why not? Because you were lost?*
> *No. Because Becky wanted to be lost.*

Becky leads me on her angry bird walk for a half hour. I hurry after her but can't catch up. I keep one eye on the sidewalk to dodge puddles of pee, another on the back of her black raincoat. "Beck! Wait up!"

"Quit telling me what to do!"

In a doorway stands an elderly man in an embroidered ankle-length shirt and crocheted cap. He eyes us both, head flipping back and forth like a witness to ping-pong. He looks amused at first, at the drama of two lost foreign girls, until I am close enough for him to see I am crying; he reaches his hand out to catch my sleeve, a look of paternal concern on his face.

"*Mademoiselle? Tout va bien?*"

"*Oui,*" I reply, though we both see through my lie. "*Ma soeur,*" I say with a point to my receding leader, and the old man releases my sleeve. Becky turns at the next corner, and I trot ahead to keep her within eyesight.

At the turn, I behold a long street flanked by industrial buildings, nearly empty of pedestrians. My feet are starting to hurt, and my backpack is heavy, then heavier. Becky is blocks ahead of me now. It is useless keeping up. I slow to my normal pace, grateful she is at least in view, and catch my breath.

The long street opens onto a sunny waterway, a straight canal with a cobbled walk right along its edge. Becky stands on the cobbles, looking in the water. Waiting. I should thank her for waiting, but I don't feel grateful. I join her at the water's edge.

"Canal Saint-Martin," she says.

"I think you're right. That would be good. Let me check. I think if we follow it that way, it points to the Seine." I pull my backpack off and dig out my guidebook, then flip to the maps in the back, feeling a glimmer of orientation and relief.

A hand sweeps in and slaps the book from my relaxed grasp. The pages flip in the damp air, while the book arcs, then lands right in the gray water, out of reach. The book floats for a few seconds, then turns over on itself. I turn to my sister. She is looking right at me, finally, lips pinched.

"Becky," I say slowly, barely containing it. "Why the fuck would you do that?"

"Doing you a favor."

"Like you did those Jim Morrison people a favor?"

"Yes, like I did those Jim Morrison people a favor."

I look back in after my lost book, not at her; I could not possibly look at her. "I don't think I can take this anymore, Beck." My voice is measured and wavery. "You are wearing me down."

"THANK YOU," Becky says, much louder than me. "FINALLY. FINALLY you ADMIT IT." Her face is red from the exertion of her angry walk, from the exertion of planning how to tell me off. "You can't stand to be with me. You can't wait to be ALL ALONE so you can SIT and DRAW PICTURES by YOURSELF."

"You're right," I say quietly. "You're absolutely right. I can't wait."

"Well, FUCK YOU, and HAVE A NICE DAY."

I don't look up. I watch the book bob in the canal. Its bright cover, a picture of the ornate ironwork of the famous tower, my annotations bleeding in blue from the margins of the dog-eared pages—everything mixes with the reflections in the rippled water, reflections of the city itself: rain clouds, a tall footbridge, a green garbage truck on the side of the canal.

The book turns again, then sinks into the murk. I look up. Becky is gone.

You have a yelling sister on the street, and Parisians do look. They sit at their café tables, facing out, and don't even hide behind newspapers and menus. They stop sipping their *pastis* or *café crème*. Even their little dogs stare from beneath the tables. The sister walks away, and the Parisians continue to stare. I wait. I let them look at the spectacle that is an American fool crying. I wait for my sister to come back. To return, and act like nothing happened, like always.

Until something new boils in the back of my throat, and I decide to call her bluff. I spit into the canal after my dead book, and my feet begin to walk. I follow the quay. I don't see Becky ahead. I don't want to. I just want to walk. My heart hammers in a way that feels good. My head feels light. My heel has a blister, and something about the pain feels right. I pick up the pace, not to get somewhere, but just to feel the rush of blood, the heat of my own body working. I walk in the direction of my instinct, toward the city center.

Soon, I see packs of tourists again: rotund Americans with rotund cameras, young Midwestern women wearing large silk scarves, pretending to be French. The locals walk in pairs or alone. Like me.

And they meander, the locals. They think while they walk. They don't rush. I begin to wonder why I do. So I can get back to the orange hotel, the tinderbox, the sister? The uncivil war? The canal turns into a greenbelt. A couple sits on a bench near a fountain, kissing under a pink umbrella. They have nowhere better to be. Neither do I. And I want a coffee. I step into the nearest café and sit at the bar.

I sweeten my *café crème* with the paper tube of sugar. The espresso machine behind the bar is shiny and reflects the inverted bottles of booze hanging opposite it—the uppers versus the downers in a beverage face-off. I want to draw it. The bar is not crowded. I'm alone, and I feel like doing it. I pull out my notebook, watercolor pencils, and brush and pour a little water in my saucer, setting everything in front of me like a surgeon.

I open to the page I was working on at the cemetery. The green has dried and faded, in the way of watercolor; it's lost the vibrancy of this morning. I hate myself for not anticipating this. *Collaborate*, I say aloud, and the bartender looks up from her puzzle to see if I need more coffee. I shake my head and look back down at my drawing, realize it is a portrait of Becky. Of course it is. Isn't everything? The curlicued, drippy hair, knuckles poised to knock, brown as if bruised. The statue's eyes closed, resigned to a sorry fate. Becky all over.

I take a gulp of coffee and turn to a naked new page. I don't think. I barely look at the paper. I stare at the chrome machine, let my brush move on its own, smudging in the reflected colors of liqueur: Curaçao blue, Galliano yellow, Chambord pink. I feel the anger fade and begin to get lost in the colors. I order another coffee. I turn to a new page, try the drawing again—same subject, but with a better notion this time of how it all will go together.

I don't notice the man standing nearby at the bar, sipping his tiny beer, watching each swash of my brush. Not at first. Not until he says something to me in rapid, unintelligible French, and I look up with a blush. "*Désolée*," I say. "*Ne comprends pas.*"

"Oh, sorry," begins the man again, with a heavy accent. "I said, I am looking at this machine for more than ten years and did not *see* it until today."

I take it for a compliment. "Thank you. This isn't my regular work. I confess I am just learning to draw."

"Then what is your regular work?"

"I'm an art teacher. In New York."

"You are just learning to draw and you are an art teacher?" He locks eyes with me for a mock-serious moment, then we both break into smiles.

"Yes, that's how we do it in America," I say. "We teach before we know."

He smiles slightly and sips from his little goblet. Green eyes behind fancy glasses, Gallic nose, and the tan of someone who takes a month off every year. His hair is all-over silver and clipped very short.

"I'm a sculptor," I say. "I'm just learning how to make things flat."

"I hear if you drop an anvil on it, that will work."

The bartender laughs. She has been listening in all along.

"Are you seeing many flat things in Paris?" the man asks.

"No, can you recommend me some?" I'm emboldened by the brush in my hand, by the stranger's playful interrogation.

"*La Joconde* is very good," he says. "You know her?"

"The *Mona Lisa*?"

"Yes, that lady," he says, smiling in the style of that lady.

I cock my head. "What about something flat that isn't thick with Americans?"

"Let me think," he says. "Have you been to Notre Dame de Chartres? Not the Notre Dame over there. The other one. The old one. It has a beautiful stone floor. During Lent, they remove the chairs, so pilgrims can see the floor."

"Yes, *the floor.*" The bartender has now officially joined the conversation. She and the man are familiar, I notice. Maybe he loves her. Maybe he never saw the coffee machine for looking at the woman making coffee. She is chic and slim in her tight-wound, long cotton apron and high ponytail. "You can step on the floor," she says.

"Floors are good for that," I say, then realize my rudeness. She is kind enough to use my language. I should not make fun of her.

"She means the design," says the man, serious for real now. "It is a way for praying. To walk in the design."

"Oh," I say. "My sister will hate that. Pardon my ignorance, but is it Lent now?"

"Yes," says the bartender.

"You do not give something up?" says the man. "For Lent?"

"Maybe I need to start," I reply.

I eventually wind my way back to the hotel, following black arrow signs from landmark to landmark, stopping outside the Pompidou to watch a puppeteer, and again in the Marais for a falafel, and again at Place des Vosges to draw for a while, and again at Shakespeare and Company to replace my sunken guidebook. By the time I step into the hotel lobby, one of my feet has bled all over the heel of my sock. The street is dark. The night clerk smiles his brisk recognition and hands me the room key my sister has not yet returned to claim.

The room is neat. The housekeeper has pulled the bedspreads taut and replaced the towels. The thick curtains are shut, keeping out the streetlight. The water glasses are new.

Becky has not been by.

I sit on the edge of the little bathtub and wash my tired feet with the shower hose. I flop onto my twin bed and open a box of Bonne Maman cookies. I sip Becky's box wine, and watch television, and wait. I knit. I feel my shoulders knot up as time passes. The cipher program is on again. The numbers are blurry and not reassuring. The new rows in my scarf look more tightly knotted. I hear feet in the hallway, but they pass the door right by. Suitcases wheel along on the hallway tile: thump *thump*, thump *thump*. A woman scolds a child in what sounds like Italian.

The cipher program ends, and it dawns on me I should be worried. I flip through my new guidebook for the Practical Matters section. It shows photos of police uniforms. A list of emergency numbers: police, rape crisis, embassies, suicide hotline. I wouldn't even know how to dial a phone. I keep flipping through; it's complicated, making a call here, unless I purchased a cheap mobile, which I did not. The book recommends a phone card. I would have to find an open grocer. Everything was rolling up, when I was walking here, hours ago. My feet are raw. I'm in my pajamas. I have French cookies I need to eat. Fuck her.

I think I need to move back to California. New York is killing me.
I thought you really liked your job.
I do. I adore my job. The students are great. Steve has been good to me.
Steve is your boss?
Not exactly. He's the department chair. He's a friend. He put in the good word for me. We went to school together.
Do you have other friends in New York? I don't hear you talk much about them.
Do you mean, do I have a "support system"?
Yes, that's what I mean.
I do. Ben—I met him at an artist's colony; he's a poet—and his boyfriend, Virgil. And Steve will always take my calls. And I like his friends. They always include me.
Good. Good. What about Becky? Her friends?
Honestly, I've been here less than a year, and I get more social invitations than she ever did.
Why do you think this is?
She would say it is because I am more famous than her.
Are you?
Yes.
Is that why you get more invitations?
No. Of course not.
What if I told you that I think Becky has never been your responsibility?
I would laugh in your face.
Look at me. Can you look at me? I think Becky has never been your responsibility. OK. You're not laughing.
I thought it would be funny.

Even sleeping lightly, which is all I can manage, I barely register the wee-hours knock. My door. Not the neighbor's door. "Sara," says a man. I don't recognize the voice.

Then my sister, louder: "Open up already!"

"Sh," I say, clicking the many locks, and three people tumble into the tiny room. Becky has one arm looped around the neck of a young man with a beard and long, black, braided hair. Becky's other arm is draped around a peasant-skirted young woman with freckle-tanned bare arms and sun bleached, straight locks pulled around one shoulder.

"She's a bit drunk," whispers the woman in American English.

"I'd wager more than a bit," I say. I usher them into the narrow aisle between beds, and they drop Becky onto one of them. My bed, it happens. Becky's eyes survey what must be a spinning room, then close.

"Is there an ice bucket? Or a wastebasket?" says the man, also American. "In case she hurls?" He wanders into the bathroom. "Got any aspirin?" he calls.

The woman, petite, looks up into my face with deep blue concern and grips my bare forearm. "Can we have a word? Maybe in the hall?"

Her perfume reaches my nostrils: sandalwood, patchouli, maybe a little cannabis. "You look familiar to me," I say, and let her lead me through the door.

She leans against the flocked fleur-de-lis wallpaper in the narrow corridor. The lights are dimmed. All the rooms are quiet. "I think your sister is going through something," she says.

"Père Lachaise," I say. "That's it. I saw you there today."

"Something serious," the woman says. "She is going through something serious."

"Didn't you two have guitars earlier?"

"Yes," the woman says. "We left them with someone who I hope is trustworthy, and to be honest, we have to get back. Listen, your sister came and joined us in the cemetery, and she brought a box of wine, so the more, the merrier, right? She was singing along. She knew all the words. Next thing you know, the wine is gone and she's getting all weepy and shit. She keeps crying about some guy named Topper."

"That's her dog. Back in New York."

"OK. Now that makes sense. She says she wants to die, but she couldn't do that to Topper. And she feels bad because she is ruining your life. She kept talking about leaping off of something. We were pretty sure she was going to try something; that's why we brought her back here."

"It's how she gets attention. She's done that since we were this high."

"No, I'm serious," says the woman. She stands up straight and grips my shoulders, looking me right in the face. Her hands are strong. Her voice is feathery. "She is really suffering. She has such a dark aura. She is in real deep psychic pain."

"That's her shtick."

"Her what?" says the woman, backing off. "It was kind of scary."

"Look, I'm really grateful for you guys bringing her back. You really didn't have to do that. But I'm glad you did. Don't worry. We got this. We've seen all of this before."

The Artstars

"Oh." The look on the girl's face is one I do not expect: pity.

The hallway is not heated. I am shivering in my pajamas. The man exits the room. "Did you ask her about the money?" he says to his friend.

"No. Oh, yeah." The woman's demeanor turns childlike. "We don't have a lot of dough, you know? And we're trying to stay in Europe as long as possible, and we had to take a cab here. Is there any chance you could help out?"

I don't even know what to say. Better were they to just leave Becky, yelling and wasted in a cemetery in a foreign country? I go back into the room and find my wallet. Smallest I have is a fifty-euro note. "Thank you," I say to the woman, handing her the money through the doorway, like I'm tipping a takeout delivery guy. I don't have the balls to ask for change.

I lock the door and take Becky's box of wine into the bathroom. I open the little plastic tap and tilt my neck like a baby bird, then let the nectar flow straight from the box into my mouth, dribble down my chin onto my pajamas. It is too sweet, I decide. It is horrid. I empty the rest into the sink, watch the color swirl against the white porcelain. Better down the drain than inside my sister. I brush my teeth and return to claim the other twin bed.

She stirs, flips her body over onto her back. I wrench her back onto her side, so she faces the ready wastebasket. "Thanks, Sare," she slurs. "I forgot about that."

I stroke her forehead, move aside some curls. "Don't want you to end up like Hendrix."

She lets out a sigh. "Or Mama Cass," she says.

"Or fucking Jim Morrison," I say.

She laughs a little. I'm not ready to share a laugh yet. "You owe me fifty euro," I say, then turn off the reading light.

Sunlight leaks in around the edges of the thick hotel curtain. My sister snores. My pajamas are stained with cheap burgundy. The room smells like vomit. The vomit is in the wastebasket, thankfully, but I'm not cleaning it up. I shower quickly, put Band-Aids on my feet, load up my backpack, and leave.

I think of the housekeeper having to clean up that vomit. She shouldn't have to do it either. I have heard her, singing calypso in the hallway, making joy in her day of drudgery. I slip the little plastic sign around the doorknob: *SVP, NE PAS DÉRANGER*. Let the room funk up until Becky is ready to clean her own mess.

In the breakfast room I load up my plate with fruit instead of pastry. Maybe I feel like being healthy today. I sip my coffee and look through my new guide. As I slip the tube of sugar into the cup, I think of the café yesterday, the man's recommendation for something flat. Yes, maybe today I will get the heck out of Paris.

The Practical Matters section tells me all I need to know. It is easier than I expected to take the bus to Gare Montparnasse, and to find the train going to Chartres, and to buy the ticket from a nice lady with a British flag pinned to her lapel.

The car is nearly empty. It is brightly painted and new and smells spotless. I look out at the backyards, then the fields and the gray, gorgeous clouds. I take out my sketchbook. I draw. I don't even look down. I feel my way around the paper, putting in green, and darker green, and black.

I think of the woman at the hotel, singing while she works. If I exhale, and let my eyes go blurry, and just look, just look at that incredible sky, and forget who the fuck I am, I know how the woman feels.

The cathedral dwarfs the tiny town, a hamlet stolen from a storybook. Beside a river stands a row of cottages, brown timbers and whitewash set with small windows and boxes of new flowers. I should be leading a goat, tapping its butt with a stick to make it cross this little stone bridge.

I can't resist a wander. My feet don't complain too much. I step into a meat shop and butcher my order, but the old man just smiles and takes my money and gives me something edible. I take my lunch down a hill and up another and settle in a cemetery to eat, overlooking the cathedral. The sun is out. The rain has stopped. This ham is not what I thought I ordered. It's better.

I look at a row of boxwoods clipped into crisp pyramids. I want to draw them. I do, for at least an hour. I take out all my supplies and take it all down: the boxwood, the gravestones, the medieval cathedral beyond, changing with the moving sun. I think of Monet. He had the idea right. I let pools of watercolor make the basic shapes in green and gray and orange, then hatch in shadows.

After lunch, I mosey back down to the river, then up the opposite hill to the church.

The inside echoes, like a canyon. Feet and furniture strike the floor; whispers carry. I can only see a handful of visitors. I bend my neck and regard the ceiling, crisscrossed with vaults, lit by colorful, high windows. The columns are tall as redwoods and too fat to reach my arms around.

Halfway along the nave, the chairs have been pushed to the side and stacked to empty the floor. Inlaid, stone in stone, is the flat thing the stranger recommended: a big bull's-eye labyrinth, scalloped on the outer edge. A circle of winding pathways, ending in the center with a stylized flower, like the rose window beaming down onto it. A navel in the belly of the ancient church.

A woman, dressed entirely in white—white smock, white pants, white turban, white backpack—removes her sandals and sets them at the perimeter.

I lean against a column to watch. She steps, slowly, on the worn path of light gray stone between the dark outlines, into the labyrinth. Her step is deliberate: heel slowly rolling to toe. She extends her hands in front of her, palms skyward, waiting to receive something. The path turns back on itself, and now I see her face. She has an air of naked receptivity. Not faith. Not exactly. She is not doing this because she believes in anything—except, perhaps, the doing. Her eyes are on the path, a few steps ahead. At each turn, she pauses and looks up at the stained glass wherever she is facing.

I take out my supplies and open to an empty page. The woman is moving so slowly, I can't help drawing her: the fluid, open line of her arms; her face, open too; her spine, like a dancer's, straight, but not stiff.

When she reaches the center, she falls onto her knees and closes her eyes, palms still open. Maybe it's not right for me to draw her. Maybe this moment is hers, not mine to record. I turn to a new page and watch—not drawing, just watching—as the woman retraces her barefoot steps, exiting the labyrinth as slowly as she entered it.

She sits on the floor to put her shoes back on, then swiftly, surprisingly, walks right over to me. Her demeanor is friendly. She says something in French. I do not understand. I shrug my apology. "Have you tried to walk the labyrinth?" she asks.

I shake my head. "What is it like?"

She laughs. "It is right here," she says, without a trace of derision, "and you ask me?"

"I mean, what does it feel like for you? What does it give you?"

"Clarity. Sometimes just quiet. Sometimes an epiphany."

Epiphanies! Oh goody! says Becky in the back of my head, where she always is, looking for stuff to shit on, as per her job description.

"Hey," I say, and flip back to the page I was working on. I rip out the unfinished picture of the woman and hand it up to her.

She smiles. "For me?"

"Sure. I'm sorry if I was intruding."

"Thank you," she says, "but I am the one intruding. You pray like this, with your pencil, no?"

"Maybe so," I say. "I hadn't thought of it that way."

I wait for the woman to leave before I try it. To answer my own question: *What is it like?*

Hopscotch is what it is like. Not what I expect at all. It's like she's with me—not the nice lady in white, but Becky, my snarky sidekick, laughing at each turn, at my willingness to bend to superstition. Sidewalk chalk and don't-step-on-a-crack. An arbitrary complication. It's not a maze, not a labyrinth of walls—it's a system of black lines, a contract, my choice not to step on or over the black stones. I walk slowly, carefully, like the woman before me, giving it a good shot. Heel to toe. On the path. Arms open to epiphanies.

I don't want an epiphany, I realize. How's that for my epiphany? Each turn, like the crazy walk through the nineteenth arrondissement, is me following orders; me, in compliance. That's me. Taking care of shit. Reading the guidebook. Walking between the lines. That's me, ponying up fifty euros I can't afford to the drunken-sister delivery wagon. Here's what pilgrims do: obey. They obey even if it hurts. They buy their bus ticket and their train ticket, and they shut up and walk inside the lines.

I don't finish the labyrinth. I don't need to. I know how it ends. On your knees, on the hard, cold floor, waiting for luck, waiting for insight. I'm done with insight. I just want to draw.

Back outside, I circle the lopsided basilica. The towers, flanking the front door, don't even try to agree: one square, one pointy. Around back, buttresses fly and a hill slopes to a terraced garden. A pair of teenagers bicker on a bench. I keep circling, looking for my subject. The side doors of the cathedral capture me, surrounded by welcoming saints carved from ancient slabs.

I sit on the steps to draw a row of martyrs. They wear medieval robes and pointy slippers, have veiled heads and matter-of-fact faces. Each stands on top of something: an artichoke tree, a castle, a man pouring water, a goat, a pair of peacocks, a dog. The stone has yellowed, or maybe it is the angle of the sun, more oblique now as the day wears on. On a new page, I mix brown and yellow into the silhouette of three figures, then draw contours of drapery in felt-tip pen, letting the lines go fuzzy.

I feel myself going fuzzy too. I am drawn to the figure standing atop the dog. It's a female martyr, with virginal veil and hand resting over her heart. She is elongated, like all the figures—long fingers, long body, aquiline nose. Her slippers are soft, like stockinged feet, curled around the body of the dog.

The dog. The dog has floppy Labrador ears and crosses its front paws, lies on its side, and looks over its shoulder with that true doggy expression—*Do it some more! That's the spot!*—relishing the attention of human toes. How many times have I seen my sister's old guy Topper in precisely this pose? Becky in the wingback chair, digging her bare toes into his soft, huskyish fur; him looking up at her, vocalizing sometimes: *More, more.*

The sculpted dog wears a collar with a ring. He's the martyr's pet; they belong to each other. And I'm put in the mind of Bluey, my sister's first dog, before

Topper, before real dogs, before language, before bunk beds, back in our shared room. She had a crib, and I had a twin, with an arm's span in between. Some nights Becky went to bed inconsolable, face and pajama shirt soaked with tears and snot. *Let her cry it out,* Mom was fond of saying. *Don't let her manipulate you.*

Oh, did my sister wail. It tugged at something in my belly, tugged tears from my eyes too. She wasn't manipulating me. It wasn't a ploy. It was an expression, a bottomless well of it. I wanted to reach across the span and poke my fingers through the bars—*I'm here. Don't be scared. Don't worry*—but never did. I obeyed. I stayed in the lines. I obeyed my mother. I did not obey my heart. And the crying would go on and on and on, until it didn't, and I would finally go to sleep. When light came through our window the next day, Becky would be curled up, clutching her blue fuzzy dog, awake but wordless, still hiccupping from the night's jag, resigned to it, with her face red and puffy and her curly hair caked with dried saliva.

What do you do for a kid with such deep-rooted sorrow? Do you pray?

I draw. I retrace the lines of the dog, over and over, with the fuzzy felt tip. I think of the arm's span between us now. The sun is falling, and I wonder if Becky is still in bed, in a room stinking of sorrow.

I have drawn enough for today. It is time to get back to Paris.

The train from Chartres fills more at each stop, and my chest fills too, with something gray. The French really soak themselves in perfume. Becky would notice too, were she here. Perfume means you're hiding something stinky, we used to say to each other when gifted with Avon Christmas perfume from a kind auntie. What a stink my sister is in now. And I don't mean the vomit. I mean the real stink, the kind a housekeeper can't clean up, the kind you carry with you wherever you go. This train is way too slow. By Versailles, we're standing room only, and I clutch backpack to chest and lean against the window and try to still my heart. I can't bear to look up at the Eastery sky, full of puffy cookie clouds and innocent blue. I look at the gravel beside the tracks, let it blend into a gray-brown blur.

Back in Paris, I run to the bus, then from bus to hotel. The night clerk hands me the key with a clipped nod. I take the stairs, no patience for the little elevator.

The privacy sign is still on our door. All the air goes out of me. Oh, poor girl. Poor Becky girl. I turn the key in the lock.

Let's talk some more about why this urge to leave New York.
I feel guilty all the time.
Why do you feel guilty?

Proximity.
Why do you feel guilty?
Responsibility.
Why do you feel guilty?
I have everything, and she has nothing.
What is "everything"?
I don't hate the world. I'm capable of happiness.
How does that make you feel, that she is incapable of happiness?
It breaks me. It breaks my heart. I'm broken.

The room smells fresh. The vomit is long gone. The window is open. The beds are made. My pajamas are folded and tucked under my pillow, the way Becky used to long ago. The housekeeper didn't do that. Becky must have cleaned.

Her bags are gone from the closet. Her shampoo is missing from the bathroom. On the bedside table are the bright orange flame of a fifty-euro note and a small pile of stones: Becky's souvenirs. The stones weigh down a letter, scratched in Becky's hand:

Sorry for being such a mess.
Need to get home now.
Need to dry out.
Need to hold Topper.
Promise me you'll enjoy the rest of your vacation.
You are a free spirit, when I am not hanging around.
I love you.

I race down the stairs and ask the clerk if Becky checked out. "Yes, early this afternoon," he says. I go to the corner grocer and buy a phone card. I follow directions in the guidebook. I call the airline: Becky has departed. I call Becky's apartment, get the machine. I don't know who to call next. I dial Steve.

His voice is all it takes to set my tears rolling, until I'm hiccuping like a kid. "Sara, *breathe*," he says.

"She did this to punish me."

"I know," Steve says.

"I think I need to come home," I say.

"What would your shrink tell you to do?"

"He would tell me to stay."

"Then stay. You're in Paris, for Chrissake. I'll go over and check on Becky."

"You don't have to do that."

"Stay. I'll call your hotel tomorrow and let you know everything's OK."

I do what I'm told. I obey.

I will go back to Brooklyn. I will go back to Brooklyn and see Becky and try to talk about what happened. I will apologize for ditching her. She will apologize for ditching me. Nothing will change. Not really. Becky will go on the wagon, then off again, then on again, then off again. I will see more of my shrink. I will see less of my sister. I will miss her. Until I see her again, and my blood will run hot, and I will hear things I can't bear to hear, and I will say things I grow to regret.

But first, there are three days alone in Paris. What's a free spirit to do? I don't know. I am too unmoored to know. I can only fish for the answer. I put away my drawing materials. I put away my guidebook. I pick up the stones from the table, put them in my pocket, and return to every damn place Becky and I visited. I drop one stone in front of Sacré Cœur, and another in the Louvre courtyard, and another on Gertrude's headstone, and so on, until the last one lands between square-pruned trees in the shadow of the Tour Eiffel.

I walk back to the hotel, minus the rocks, feeling weightless. Along the way, I come upon a Japanese garden I read about in my sunken guide. It's open. I go in. I enter a cylindrical room, a meditation space, a chapel with nothing to bow to: no cross, no ark, no Buddha; just two chairs, facing each other, on each side of the room. I sit. I look up at the light squeezing through gaps around the circular ceiling. I look across at the empty steel chair, as cold and quiet and hard as the one I sit on. And I look down at the stone floor, beautifully, randomly patterned, carved by the blast of a nuclear bomb.

The Beginning of the End of the Beginning

1. In Which My True Head Makes an Appearance

When your best friend smashes fluorescent light tubes across your chest, because you asked him to, because you thought it might mean something, because you need to mean something, and you bleed into a water tank while smart people watch and analyze, and the smart people go home and you go to the emergency clinic with nothing but your mother's credit card, and your girlfriend says "We are not doing this again," your shit starts to come into question. Art: that's my shit. That's the shit that got me here. That's the shit that always gets me here.

Then the credit card declined itself, and my girl, Shell, had to shell out hers. And the doctor—or nurse, I didn't ask—who must have been a dozen years younger than me, tied off her last suture and looked up at me with the concern one reserves for crackpots. I was an uninsured crackpot with a master's degree and a score of stitches I would have to remove myself. Let me say that again. I was an uninsured crackpot with a master's degree and—Christ. You don't want to hear it. Nobody wants to hear it.

"Maybe I could get an office job," I said to Shell on our predawn walk back to her place. "Like a male secretary."

"With green hair, Clay? Seriously?" She squished her hand through my sticky, fried mop and gave me a closed-mouth grin in the light of a passing ambulance. Her lips were sun-weathered, blistered, firm, holding in the rest of a difficult speech. There was no missing her direct eyes, her hard smile. Then she closed those eyes, walked with those eyes closed rather than look at me, all bandaged and Frankensteined.

I'm not that dumb. Yes, I'm dumb, but I know a cue. Before we went to bed, I shaved my head bare. I could not stop rubbing my hands across it, the taut, pasty skin. My true head revealed.

2. Positive Thinking

When I first moved here, my cousin the Wall Street math geek took me for drinks downtown. Happy hour, and the outdoor bar was full, and it was one of those muggy summer nights when there isn't enough beer in the world. Around me, the drones shed ties, jettisoned suit jackets, rolled up starchy white sleeves. Women let their lipstick fade around the brown necks of bottles, and their glossy, staid hairdos turned tousled and ordinary, sexier for their true natures. I noticed a wealth of unexpected information peeking from necklines and shirtsleeves: Over there, a leather hippie necklace on a clean-cut man. The man beside him had arms covered in tattoos, bright images of playing cards and dice. Another guy, with a glass of seltzer in front of him, fiddled with an AA chip. "This is all theater, isn't it?" I asked my cousin.

"What do you mean?" he said. His suit looked glued on.

"This putting on a tie and going to work thing. It's theater, right? It's a costume."

"Except these people have worked hard to get where they are. *Years of school.*"

I didn't try to tell him that my people work hard too. My people go to school too. I let him go back to talking about his new favorite propaganda. "Dude, you're not listening to me. This method really works. You write your desire for money on a piece of paper. You write the amount of money. You read it aloud every day. Then your *faith* will create *vibrations* that *put your desire in motion.*"

"Tony, that's completely batshit."

His eyes had a green burn that I didn't like. "That kind of negative thinking will *manifest itself* too," he said, with that tough-love tone my mother gets when she's saying *no.* "It's the power of auto-suggestion, Clay. It's a *law.* It's a *fact.* When you think like that, you're only *creating your own failure.*"

"Tony, I have had my picture in *Paper* magazine. I don't consider myself a failure." As I said it, I felt the red rise to my face, the hot ick of saying something ridiculous, maybe even more ridiculous than Tony's attitudinal theories, more ridiculous for its naked vanity.

"I'm going to a *Think and Believe* workshop next Saturday," he said, "if you want to come with. You really could benefit. Look what it's done for me." He leaned back in his chair so I could get a finer look at what it had done for him.

He was full of born-again glow, in his clean blue shirt and Hamptons tan and gentleman's haircut and prim horn-rims.

I didn't answer. I would have said something negative.

3. Ready

The blue sharkskin suit waved to me across the thrift store, but I did not wave back. I bought what I was there to buy—a gray wool pinstripe, and starchy white button-down with minimal pit stains, and wing tips, and the most Republican tie I could find on the crowded rack: hemoglobin red with tiny elephants. If I were my dad, I would trust me in this tie. Plus, I dig elephants.

The jacket was slit all the way up the center back seam. Those were always the classiest suits—the undertaker specials, worn only once, and not to the dance hall either. Shell had shown me this old ragpicker trick. Just restitch that seam, and the suit comes back to life. It wasn't in Shell's nature to worry about wearing hand-me-downs of the dead. I didn't know what my nature was. Maybe I needed a new nature.

Black socks and mouthwash, and before too long I sat across from a spectacled young woman at a temp agency. "I have to be honest with you, Clayton. Your typing numbers aren't great."

I hadn't anticipated the skills test. All I did was dress. No research. It was pathetic; me hunting and pecking in my careful suit and tie, with a clamor of keystrokes all around me—people who knew what the Christ they were doing.

On the wall in the interview room was a poster, a cartoon of a hapless fly caught in a spiderweb. MILLENNIUM BUG STOPS HERE, said the caption. DYNOFFICE TEMPS. THE RIGHT Y2K SKILL SET.

I was no Dynoffice dynamo. The interview lady split her attention between her computer monitor and my flushed face. She peered at both of us over the top of her glasses. She looked like a librarian—maybe the sexy kind, or maybe the kind who shushes exuberant child readers. "Clayton, will you take my advice? Get yourself one of those typing teacher programs. Practice. Practice *a lot*. I like you, but I can't send you out with numbers like this."

You like me? said the tiny exuberant child in my head. "OK," said my grown-up mouth. More money to borrow from Shell, or my mother, or my supposed best friend, Marvelli, or some other half-willing helper. More hassle, the whole thing. As usual, all highways led back to money.

All the way home, I fiddled with my pocketknife, maybe freaking the G train populace, but did I care? It was a Swiss Army knife, a gift from Shell. I flipped out each gizmo and polished it with my shirtfront: the knife, the saw, the can opener, the scissors. The slim pair of tweezers tucked into a sleeve. The toothpick.

"You'll always have what you need, when you need it," Shell had said, with a devilish squint, when I opened the gift. "It's very manly of you to carry a knife like that."

"Are the Swiss known for being *manly*?" I asked her.

"They're known for their precision," she had said.

"Are you implying I need to be more precise?"

"I just think you ought to be *ready*," she had replied.

Ready for what? A typing-skills test? The knife hadn't saved me. No equipment would have saved me. But my Shell, she knew all about *ready*. Once, she showed me her old Girl Scout uniform—minty green with a sash covered in badges, some inscrutable, so she narrated: "Cooking. Baking—not the same as cooking. Archery. Fire building. First aid. Knot making. Sewing. Carpentry."

I loved her—the little version of her I imagined in the green getup, earning her carpentry credential, and the big version too, the one who pshawed and laughed at her youngster self: "I wasn't very good at baking. I burnt the ripples in my piecrust. I forgot to put on the foil."

I would have eaten her ripples. I would have given her a badge. I wanted to be like her. I wanted to be like the pocketknife, full of compartments and gizmos. *Ready.*

4. How to March

I sat in the dark in my studio, in the blue light of the flickery computer screen. The typing tutor had a clicker—a metronome—and my fingers jabbed the keys of the old computer in time with the beat:

ASDF ASDF ASDF ASDF

ASDF ASDF ASDF ASDF

JKL; JKL; JKL; JKL;

JKL; JKL; JKL; JKL;

It was a march. I was determined to do this, and I couldn't stand doing this, but I was determined to do this; and if I did this for the rest of my life, I would die, which would be a relief, because it means I would stop doing this.

It was like that exercise in college, the one where we marched around in a circle for four unbroken hours, seeing what surprises would come up. An act of faith, said the professor. A leap, the first three hours, waiting and waiting for something—anything—to rise from the deep whatever. The deep self. The deep collective self. The deep horror of what we were doing together.

I couldn't remember what rose up from the deep whatever. Only that we marched. And marched.

It used to be Shell's computer. She upgraded. She didn't look like the upgrading type, what with her holey thrift-store T-shirts and patched jeans, but she was. She was going to throw this computer away, until I grabbed it. The machine groaned and farted like an old man getting up out of a La-Z-Boy chair. I could feel the thing getting warm against my leg. The computer sat on the floor, under the table I set up in my studio—not even really a table, just a couple of cardboard boxes with a lauan door suspended between them—me on a kitchen stool. My butt was getting numb on the hard steel stool. I liked the numb. I straightened my spine. I felt my hands missing the keys the screen was telling me to type.

POPO POPO UPUP UPUP

POPO POPO UPUP UPUP

QWQW QWQW EQEQ EQEQ

QWQW QWQW EQEQ EQEQ

The metronome stopped. I clicked on the button to tally my score.

Ding ding dong. The tutor's cutesy mascot face popped up. *Nice try, Clay!* said the balloon over its head, *but your score could be better! Would you like to try this exercise again?*

"No," I told my tutor aloud, like it could fucking hear me. "But I will, since you asked so nicely."

Through the thin, homemade walls, I heard my subtenant, Maddie, laughing, talking on the phone next door. I wondered if she knew how to type twenty-five words a minute, like I barely could now. She was a photographer. She knew better. When it came time to pick an art school major, she picked something functional. She didn't miss rent. The month before, I used Maddie's rent to pay Shell back what she'd lent me the month before that to pay my mother back for what she'd lent me three months before for groceries. I was an idiot, back then, in the major-picking phase. *Performance art?* Right.

DODO DODO NONO NONO

DODO DODO NONO NONO

IDIOT IDIOT IDIOT IDIOT

IDIOT IDIOT IDIOT IDIOT

I didn't miss a tick of the metronome. I tallied my score. The tutor admonished me for improvising. It was 3:00 a.m. I heard Maddie, the workaholic, rinsing prints, finishing up, scrambling up into her bed loft. Enough marching in step for tonight. I zonked right onto the couch, next to my nondesk. I didn't take off my shoes.

5. The Lights Dim

Back in 1985, I sat in the dark in an undergrad lecture hall, looking at slides. It was winter, the end of the semester, and the Modernism and Postmodernism survey class was coming to a close, and the professor had promised *fun stuff* for the day. *We will not be bored today*, he kept saying, then showed photos from Fluxus performances and Happenings in grainy black and white. Steve Pak and I sat up in the second row, near the screen, with our coats and scarves pooled around us on the gummy floor, our feet up on the empty seats in front of us, our giant, hardbound sketchbooks in our laps.

I loved sitting next to the Pakman. He drew a little version of every slide. I spent half the lecture looking at the screen and the other half watching his sure, steady pen trace the major contours of a Matisse or Picasso. Sometimes he took up a whole page of his sketchbook, re-versioning the painting, especially if the professor left an image up for a lengthy commentary. Pak never wrote any notes. He just drew and seemed to think hard about what he was drawing, retracing lines as the professor pointed with his flashlight arrow to the same lines on the screen. Pak's renderings of sculpture were even more fun to watch come into being—his uncanniness with highlight and shadow, his experiments with hatch marks that rivaled Rembrandt.

Me, I was an idea guy. I floundered in studio classes but could not stop taking them. I could draw nothing. I was jealous as hell. Everyone around me had won high school prizes. I just had stray impulses. *I can never do this*, was always my thought. *I will never be able to do this.*

But that day, performance art day in History of Modernism and Postmodernism, Pak didn't draw a thing. He just sat there beside me, breathing through his mouth, while the reflected screen glow on his face changed with each picture. And up on the screen was a young, slight Taiwanese man with a shaved head, standing stiffly in front of a time clock, punching a card. On the next slide, the same man, the same pose, but his hair was longer. Next slide: same pose, longer hair still. He punched this clock, took this photo, every single hour for a year, the professor said. A whole year. My heart swelled up with something warm, there in the dark lecture hall, and Steve Pak whispered, "I could never do that."

"I could." That's what my swelling heart was saying. That's what I dared to whisper to Steve. "I could fucking do that."

6. A Really, Really Big Show

Shell and Marvelli came over around midnight, and I was at my desk with my cutesy tutor. My typing score had improved. Not that that meant anything, with improbable words like DODO and NONO. My butt was more numb. I feared standing up, for the stiff horror in my back and hamstrings. I heard Shell's key and her deep laugh, and Marvelli lumbered in ahead of her, huge and bat-like in a long, gray duster coat. His mustache was waxed into Victorian question marks, and his felt top hat was a little squished. "Claymation! What the fuck you doing? Why you dodging my calls?"

"Sorry, man," I said, attempting to keep my fingers moving, but it was not easy to talk one word and type another. "I'm on a mission."

"We needed you tonight at the meeting. This is going to be the biggest show *evar*." He plopped on the couch without removing his coat. I could smell his late-summer essence: cheap brew and sweat and reefer. He had an open tallboy in a paper bag, his road beer. Shell had one too. He never rode the subway without one, but it was a new thing for her. Also new: a long silk aviator scarf, à la Isadora Duncan, like she planned to fly somewhere, or dance somewhere, or both. She half skipped into the main part of my space—the part without stacks of junk—and twirled around, letting the scarf fly behind her. This was not my Shell. This was not the Shell of heavy construction boots and framing hammers. This was about more than a road beer. I tried to focus on my screen.

Marvelli hadn't stopped talking. "The biggest performance, the craziest fucking thing yet, Loisaida *or* Williamsburg. We got a *professional knife thrower*. From a real fucking *circus*. And that trapeze *chica* from downstairs."

"That's great, Marv," I said. I felt Shell slip behind me, into the gap between me and the wall. I stopped the typing, reached backward, and put my arms around her. She set her cold, naked beer can on the top of my bald head. It felt good. She sipped the beer and kissed the cool wet spot before sidestepping away from me.

"We need you for this one, Clayter," Marvelli said. "What's this fucking mission of yours?"

"Making a living. That's my mission. Right, Shell?" She drummed her fingers on the end of my dumb table, fake typing. She shrugged. I didn't get it. "Hey, huh? What about your emergency-clinic fatigue, Shelly? You're all, *we are not doing this again*?"

Marv didn't let her answer. "We need someone to get tied up to this giant rocket, see, and the circus dude will throw knives. Everyone's all, let's get Clay. You *own* that part."

"I still have stitches from what you did to me last time."

Shell, amnesiac, plunked down next to Marvelli on the couch. Her eyes were lit. "We're going to have three live goats," she said.

"Will the goats be live *after* the performance?" I asked.

"Of course," she said.

"They're rentals," said Marvelli. "From some halal butcher shop I wandered into down Flatbush. This dude really likes the theater. He thinks I'm a Broadway producer. You want a beer?"

"I can type thirty-five words a minute, as of tonight," I said.

"What the fuck is wrong with you?" Marv said. "Shellista, what the fuck is wrong with him?"

"I'm broke," I said.

"So what? Everyone's broke. That's what credit cards are for."

Shell wouldn't look at me. I didn't get it. "I'm BROKE broke," I said, and Shell, bless her, finally quietly nodded to back me up.

"You can get bread from Meisner's dumpster," Marv offered.

"Good. I'll use that to pay my rent."

"Seriously, you shouldn't ever have to pay for food. Did you know you can forage greens and berries in Prospect Park? And the dumpsters out back of C-Town are always throwing out expired Twinkies."

"Twinkies don't expire," I said.

"*Hunting* and *gathering*. Forget all this money bullshit. The LAND." He emptied his road beer down his gullet. "We can LIVE OFF IT. Here. Have a chill pill." He peeled a tallboy off the sweating six-pack on the floor between his plaster-splattered boots, handed it to me, then cracked a new one for himself.

I gulped back my begged nutrition. "Please tell me the goats are not principals in the knife-throwing or the trapeze act."

"Or the Weeble wobble," Shell said. She was leaning against Marv in a way I didn't love. That couch was too wide for her to be sitting like that.

"The Weeble wobble!" shouted Marv, shooting up from the couch. He strode into the middle of the room. His big duster coat flapped behind him. "We forgot the best part! Henry Bracken's Weeble wobble will be there. The bottom is concrete, so like, it's bottom heavy, get it?" He balanced his beer can on his hand, then swayed it back and forth with his other hand, like the inflatable clown kids used to punch—like I used to punch, when I was a kid. "Weebles wobble, but they don't fall down. Right? I think they have to pour the concrete on-site. Otherwise we will have to find a crane just to move the fucker. We may strap the rocket to the Weeble wobble."

"And me to the rocket?" I said.

"Yes!" Marv said. "Precisely. So you'll do it?"

"So I can have knives thrown at me, the wobbling target?"

"Exactly." Marv spread his arms wide, then clasped them in a goofy *namaste* and bowed. "Thank you, Clayton. I knew you would say yes."

"I'm saying no. I'm retired. No. I will not do it."

"It's a *professional knife thrower*," Shell said, from the couch.

"Exactly," Marv said. "It won't be little old me flinging shit this time. This guy doesn't even need glasses."

"Marv. Shell. Look. It takes no skill to bleed in a performance. It just takes balls. And my balls are feeling a little sore right now, and if you'll excuse me, I have to get back to my typing."

"But you're so good at it, Clay," Marv said. "You don't flinch."

That fucker. He knew my weak spot. *You're so good at it.* I didn't even answer. I relaunched the typing tutor. The ticking timer started. I typed along with the beat. I could feel Marvelli standing over me, behind me, watching my fingers miss, slurping his beverage. "Clayman, this is some Dada shit you're typing here," he said, then shut up and watched me practice.

7. At the Dance Hall

Marvelli stuck around for another couple of hours, first looming behind me and watching, shouting out the tutor's words—or nonwords—tapping my shoulders in time with the metronome, then drum-rolling in my score and announcing the result to Shell. "Thirty-nine! We lost ground! We need a cheer! Get out those pom-poms!"

Pom-poms were the antithesis of Shell. There was no cheerleading badge on her scouting sash. I watched her, across the room, in between rounds of typing exercise. She stood at the bookshelf, perusing titles, her head tilted sideways to read. Her neck was sunburned. Her blond-streaked hair was tied up into two braids, barely long enough, her hot weather standby. Bits of it stuck out and haloed her head in the light from the old lamp by the window. I watched her reflection in the glass. She looked at CDs now. She ignored Marvelli. She ignored me. She sucked her thumb, something she only did asleep. Never awake.

"Wait, whoa. Clayman," Marv shouted in my ear. "Don't you think you ought to try that round again? Like the typing *chica* says?" I typed ahead. I could ignore too. "I'm telling you, Clay, you're *made* for this knife-throwing thing. At least let me *introduce* you to the man."

"Marv, he said no," Shell shouted, suddenly, from across the room. "I told you he'd say no." That's my girl.

"He *said* no, but did he *mean* no?"

I typed. I kept on typing.

Shell put a disc in the player, then cranked up the dial. It wasn't neighborly, not at this hour, but I didn't stop her. It was a K-Tel disco compilation. I think someone gave it to me for laughs. She faced the window, and I couldn't tell if she was looking through the glass to the city outside or at its surface, at her own image. Her spine swayed, almost imperceptibly, a private roll of the hip along with the flare of funk guitar. She was too young to remember this song, to remember it the way Marvelli and I did—the stilted seventh-grade parties in suburban rec rooms, the California Hustle, the New York Hustle, all those hustles, the Hollywood of it all: Love Boats and Fantasy Islands and unfortunate shoes and Xanadus, the roller rink without a partner, the school gym without a partner, the bat mitzvah without a partner, before we had found our own, found our freaks.

I felt Marvelli's hands go still on my shoulders. I noticed I had stopped typing. I saw a look of something on Shell's face, in the glass—a look of something new, pensive, and faraway, and maybe a little sad. Marv saw it too. He strode over to her, gripped her waist in one hand and his tallboy in the other. The hustle, the old hustle—he wanted her to do it with him, and he beckoned me over too, beckoned with his beer hand. He was stepping forward three times, and she was picking it up quickly, and backward three times, and I couldn't. I could not stand this song. I needed to type. I must type.

I restarted my exercise. Marv gave up on me and gave in to the steps: the front, the back, the spin to the side, the clap. Type. I needed to. Shell was smiling now. She was laughing. Not a carefree laugh. Another kind. The inscrutable kind, the kind she had mastered, the kind I found irresistible, usually. Usually, but not now. Now, I typed.

"Clayman, you got any beer?" Marv shouted. He fluttered the useless plastic rings over his head, the spent sixer. "We're working up a thirst over here."

I didn't answer. I pressed *return* to tally my new score. From the corner of my eye, I saw him digging through my fridge.

8. A Dirty Name

After he drank my last beer, Marvelli left on a quest for the next. The K-Tel continued on disc two. Shell lifted my hands from the keyboard and pulled my arm around her as she flopped onto my lap. The metronome clicked. The nonsense words flashed on the screen. My butt hurt on the old stool. She rubbed her hands on my head, like everyone seemed to want to now, the fine fuzz of a new start. She kissed my ear and sank her body against my chest. The weight of her.

"Don't you think you've been at this long enough?" she wet-whispered in my ear. "C'mon, baby. This isn't you."

"I thought you wanted this. I thought you wanted me to get a real job."

"A day job, Clay. Not a round-the-clock job." She smelled like reefer and sweet sweat and floral perfume. It wasn't her usual smell.

"This is temporary. This is boot camp."

"I don't like what's happening to you," she said.

"Nothing's happening to me."

"Plenty has already happened to you."

"I thought you wanted this. I thought you were a pragmatist."

She snapped back, away from me. "Why would you say something like that?" She held herself at arm's length. There was something new in her eyes—a coolness, an unfamiliarity. A magnetic push where the pull used to be. I wondered which of us was actually undergoing a change.

"Pragmatist is not a dirty name, Shell. It's what I love about you."

"Yeah, right." She was across the room again. She turned off the disco. She shouldered her bag. Something had happened. What the hell had happened? "I think I need to get home. I forgot to feed Cherry."

"You never forget to feed Cherry. Cherry won't let you forget to feed Cherry. It's not in your nature."

"Well, this"—she pointed to the nondesk, to the very computer she had tossed to me on its way to the trash—"*this* is not in *your* nature."

"I think nature is mysterious," I said, to her back.

She turned—just her head—and gave me the pinched smile of a pragmatist. She stood for a moment, in the doorway, lit from the bright hallway behind her, her Isadora scarf aglow as she flipped it over her shoulder. "Something here doesn't smell right," she said. She did not slam the door.

I had a sick feeling. No way I could sleep now. I restarted the typing tutor but couldn't focus. What was that fucking scarf about? What was that sudden exit about? Did she think I was cheating on her?

Was I? With this animated character in the computer, voicing its encouragement at teacherly intervals? Pushing its four-letter Dada shit?

9. Trying On the Mask

First time I ever saw Shell, she was up a utility pole, in a homemade harness, with a big old crescent wrench, doing something very illegal. In the light of the streetlamp she had just scaled, she looked like a haloed character from a Fra

Angelico fresco—hair almost metallic, filling with luminosity where the braids discombobulated themselves. Her bare arms were muscled and sunburned and busy. She appeared, from my safe position on the street beneath her, to be rigging up a loudspeaker as large as herself. She shimmied down the pole, plugged something in at its exposed base, then shouted over her shoulder: "Try now."

Marvelli's voice came through the loudspeaker, booming from the sky like God. I looked at this braided newcomer standing before me, wiping the Brooklyn grime from her hands onto the ass of her denim overall shorts. Her legs were lean, and her boots were industrial weight, covered in spilled green paint. The wrench now hung from a worn leather tool belt slung low on her hips. I must have been staring like a fool, for the way she looked at me. "Hi," she said. "Are you OK?"

"I think I love you," I said.

"Thinking! Stop that!" She shook her head and walked away.

This was my beloved can-do girl, one of the talented many that Marvelli had a way of recruiting in his travels. That night, Marvelli spoke his master-of-ceremonies gobbledygook through Shell's new God-speaker, and I got to be the principal player, gliding down Berry Street on Big Ed, my neighbor's fiberglass prop horse. Behind me was a spirited, motley marching band, announcing my arrival. Big Ed wore stainless steel armor, made from industrial scrap gleaned from my other neighbor's metalwork business. I wore armor too—a pointy helmet, a face shield, a breastplate, gauntlets—and was so obscured I doubt Shell even recognized me as the love-blurting fool who had watched her steal the city's electricity. Not at first.

At the after-party, maybe thanks to the mask—which I did not remove—I convinced her to sit with me for a while, while Marvelli nodded his approval from across the room. She held my hand, and her stolen electricity shot straight through the steel gauntlet and up the nerves of my arm. I watched her heart-shaped mouth as she spoke, as she sipped through her straw, as she licked her lips. She looked through my eyeholes—looked hard, until recognition hit—but she didn't drop my hand. She asked to try on the mask.

Later, she tried on the entire suit of armor and sat astride the horse, posing for photos I took in my mind. Still clear, these mental photos; still easy to access, even now, no camera required: My messy studio. The lamp by my window. A woman way out of my league. The shine of armor and the shine of her muscular arms. One arm held high, the pose of victory. She flipped up the face mask and beamed at me, and maybe she wasn't just using me for my knighthood. And then a clatter of armor parts on the floor, and her delicious mouth, and Big Ed watched as I did what I had been dying to do all day.

Pragmatist. Not a dirty name. Wasn't it heroic? Wasn't she my pragmatic hero? Or was I supposed to be the one riding in on the horse? Wasn't that what all this get-a-job was about? Just another kind of horse?

What was I getting wrong?

10. The One Thing

My new desk was a real fucking desk. A big fat one, L-shaped, with a chirping, flashing phone, and oak drawers, and a computer that didn't groan. It was a real chair too, with padding and lumbar support and a lever on the side to shoot the seat up and down. I fiddled with the lever way too many times. High? Hard on the back. Low? Hard on the shoulders, all pushed up to my ears when I put elbows on the desk. Hard was relative. This hard was nothing. This hard wasn't the rusty steel stool at home, and ramen dinners, and rent due, and a girlfriend who didn't pick up the phone anymore.

Lisa, the secretary next to me, shot a look.

"Too noisy?" I asked, squeaking the chair once more on purpose. I smiled my best.

"You need help?"

"Not with this, but yes, I will later, no doubt. With something."

"No doubt." There was a wink of trouble in her eye, the good kind. She was my mother's age, but nothing like my mother. High Staten Island hair, rouged cheeks. She wore a tennis-ball-yellow suit and half glasses on a chain. She squinted through the lenses at the computer screen. I wondered if I was going to need glasses for this gig, like everyone else. I wondered what she majored in or if she had majored at all. "You look accident prone," she said.

"I assure you I am. You better stand back, if you don't want to get spattered. I'm covered in stitches. No joke." They were starting to itch. I had to remind myself not to scratch and risk bleeding on my pressed button-down.

"You need Tylenol? I got a pharmacy in here." Lisa opened her desk drawer. It was full of silver pill packets and white bottles of generic remedies. "It's quicker than going to the health center."

"There's a health center?"

"Third floor. He calls it the *dispensary*." She pointed to my new boss, who stood at my desk with an envelope in hand. "Rowan forgets we don't have National Health."

"We should have," Rowan said, and Lisa wrinkled her nose, like they had this conversation daily. "Clayton?"

"I prefer Clay. I came by to introduce myself earlier, but you were on the phone."

The Artstars

He shook my hand, and his hand was damp and reserved—not the firm business grip I expected—unlike all the other hands I grabbed that morning, including Lisa's. He was thin. Gaunt, even, in his heavy, brown tweed suit. His hair was long for a gig like this, gray on the sides, sparse at the top. His glasses— yes, of course glasses, the job requisite—were basic wire frames, didn't scream money. Nothing about him screamed money, like I'd expected. His tie was slightly bent in places, like it had been rolled up in a desk drawer.

"Clay. Welcome to Singer Martin. I'm afraid you'll find us rather a bore around here, in lonely old Compliance."

"I'm capable of being compliant," I said. "I don't mind boredom."

"Brilliant. If you could please hand deliver this to Bridget Yee on thirty-five, I would be obliged. Are you a notary, by chance?"

"Afraid not. But as of last week I can type sixty words a minute."

"I wish I had some typing for you, but I'm afraid we type our own these days."

"Unbelievable. The one thing."

"Excuse me?"

"Nothing."

"Filing, we'll have plenty of that. I hope you remember your alphabet." Rowan walked back down the corridor to his glass-walled office and shut the door, and the light on his phone line turned red again. I could see him, or part of him, twirling in his chair, winding and unwinding the phone cord around his index finger.

"Ready for that Tylenol?" Lisa said.

"No, I'm good."

"How about hot chocolate? Or Pop-Tarts? I got a pantry over here too." She opened the desk drawer below the pharmacy drawer. Boxes of crackers, cookies, instant soup. I wondered if mice were an issue. "It's easier than going to the cafeteria."

"There's a cafeteria?"

"Oh, honey. This whole place is designed to keep you from leaving. By the end of next week, you'll be bored out of your gourd."

Hard to be bored. My heart quickened at the thought of all the convenience. I hung my suit jacket over the back of my chair, adjusted my tie, and set off to find Bridget Yee.

11. The Walls

The search for Yee turned into a meander. First on my floor—took a bad turn in the maze of beige half walls, and something grabbed my eyeballs—a splash of crazy color—and I let myself get pulled in that direction. It was a silk screen. A hefty one, repeated faces of Chairman Mao, in a famous grid, just parked on the weight-bearing wall in the corridor of cubicles. No stanchions, no alarms. I could probably walk right out with the thing under my arm, if I were that kind of person.

"It's a Warhol," said a disembodied voice, a woman.

"Yes," I said to the air.

"I'm over here," said the voice. She was a woman my age in a cubicle seemingly designed for a child—pink cartoon characters standing on top of her computer monitor, and a Hello Kitty piggy bank waving at me from the bookshelf. "They just rotated the artwork," said the woman. "I was looking at a creepy David Salle for two years. And not good creepy. Creepy creepy. This is an improvement."

I felt my face relax. Maybe people in here were no different from people outside. "You big on art?" I said. She wore a plain beige pantsuit. Her hair was beige too. No jewelry; hardly any makeup. If it weren't for the kiddie menagerie all around her, she would get sucked right into the wall and disappear.

"I used to be big on art," she said. "Then I became a realist. Not like an artist realist, but like a realist realist."

"Understood." I felt a line of stitches on my rib cage itch but did not scratch.

"Singer Martin has an awesome collection," she said. "For them it's an investment, of course, but we can think it's for us. Sometimes I wonder if the artists have any clue their stuff ends up in a cubicle farm. They probably don't care. You seen the Rauschenberg down on three, by the cafeteria?"

"I haven't even seen the cafeteria."

"I get it. The food is not great. You gotta see the Rauschenberg. It's a huge triptych. A girl's face, some spaghetti, and an airplane, I think. Some of his later stuff. Oh!" She straightened. "And find a reason to go to thirty-five. There's an amazing Jennifer Bartlett up there. Right on the wall behind the elevator banks. I once went up there just to look at it. I didn't even make up an excuse."

"I'm going to thirty-five now, it so happens."

"Well, then you have to look for it. It's kismet."

12. A Girl's Drawing of Home

I did find the painting. Found it, then stood dumb before it and stared. Hello Kitty lady was right.

It was about seven-foot square, some kind of baked enamel on steel plates. From the end of the hall, you could see the faint shape of a red house in the middle of the painting, with a blue sky above and a green lawn below, like the schema from a little girl's drawing of home. But up close, it was a grid of taped squares, each busy with its own complex spatters and stories. That pointillist trick of near and far, and thick impasto, which I could not help touching, because it was right there, and no one was guarding it, and no one was even noticing it existed. I wanted to coo to the painting, like a lover or little kid: *Don't worry. I love you. The rest of those fools are fools.* I kept thinking about Steve Pak and his giant hardbound sketchbook, and watching him duplicate, quickly, a Jennifer Bartlett painting from the screen in the lecture hall. It was another pointillist house, a bit like this one. I remembered not liking it at all, thinking it was too soft, too regularized, too OCD in its faith to the grid. But the real thing was nothing like the thing on the screen or the thing in Pak's notebook. Up close, I knew the real deal now. I could not stop touching it. I was probably hurting it but I could not help myself. The enamel paint was cool and nubby against my fingertips, and I probably would have tried licking the painting, just to get a better sense of its essence, had a prim young woman in a slick black suit not tapped me between my shoulder blades. I jumped.

"Can I help you, sir?"

"I'm looking for—" Flustered. Forgot the lady's name. Looked down at my envelope, which was, thankfully, labeled, in the dramatic scrawl of my new boss. "Ms. Yee. I'm looking for Ms. Yee."

"I'm Bridget Yee." She sized me up quickly, then snatched the package from my hand. "Is this from Rowan?" She didn't wait for the answer. She clearly recognized his writing. "Just as well he didn't bring this by in person," she said. She ripped the thing open in front of me and shook the contents into her free hand. A lone gold key. A house key. Nothing else.

I wasn't sure what to say. I had a feeling it wasn't Compliance business.

"Anything to send in reply?" I suggested.

"No." She folded her arms over her chest. It was a look I'd seen before, on Mom, on bad days way back when, during the divorce. On Shell, more recently, more inexplicably, the night she visited with Marvelli and left me to cheat on her with my typing tutor. Bridget Yee looked firm, frozen, finished with something. A magnet that had flipped polarity. "Thank you, whatever your name is," she said. "We'll see how long you can put up with Little Lord Fauntleroy."

13. Tillions

Several themes emerged during my first week at Singer Martin. Most notable was the complete lack of typing. "I used to type ninety words a minute," said my secretarial comrade, Lisa. "I've probably lost all of that. I used to know shorthand too. Now they ask me to do charts and stuff in Excel. I don't know Excel from nothing."

I, too, did not know Excel from nothing. I wondered if there was a cutesy home tutor for that. I did not know how to fax. I did not know how to print labels. I did not know what a T and E report was. I had never heard of a purchase order. I did not even know how to answer the phone properly (hint: it's not "Hello."). I kept looking over at Lisa, and she would be shaking her head slowly, going *Mmmm, mmmm, mmmm.* She took pity on me at each impasse and showed me how to proceed. "We all got to start someplace," she kept saying, like I was a teenager. I just took it. I was grateful. I kept thinking about the paycheck on its way. I did not mention my terminal degree. It seemed it would be rude. Or foolish.

Another theme: a witch hunt was on for whoever was leaving half-finished bottles of orange juice and Gatorade in the pantry refrigerator. "Either drink it or toss it," said an angry computer-printed sign taped to the door. And underneath, scrawled in red Sharpie: "OTHER PEOPLE EXIST. IN CASE YOU FORGOT." I was at no risk of forgetting the existence of other people. Between my chipper phone-screening for Rowan and Lisa reminding me to close file drawers to prevent injury, there was hardly a moment to wander the halls by myself and touch paintings from the Singer Martin collection.

We received a memo midweek from central management that caused quite a bit of fuss: *Subject: Singer Martin Now Has One Tillion Dollars Under Management.* Through cubicle walls, behind the file cabinets, I heard one stranger after another talking about it on the telephone. "Tillion? What's a tillion? What's next, a gazillion?" A *tillion.* It was my new favorite word. I could not wait to tell Shell. If only she would take my phone call. But she did not pick up.

The cafeteria was a novelty at first. It was a carousel of food stations— sandwiches, omelets, design-your-own pasta—and a long salad bar with ten choices of dressing. Packs of worker bees buzzed from station to station with bright blue trays, no one wearing a suit jacket. Many flipped ties over the shoulder before digging in. Tables lined the bright south window overlooking a small harbor outside. Or, one could fill a cardboard box with lunch and return to the desk.

Designed to keep you from leaving.

Day one at the cafeteria, I piled a plastic clamshell dish with greens and tuna and garbanzos from the salad bar, only to have it weigh in at twelve dollars, more than I had in my pocket. The cashier took my ten and waved me through with a sneer, which made me afraid to get on her line the following day with my cheap cup of coffee and hard-boiled egg. By Friday, even the giant—and yes, beautiful—Rauschenberg spaghetti triptych was not enough to draw me to the cafeteria. I brought a baloney sandwich from home and ate outside, by the yachts, in the shadow of the Twin Towers.

The Artstars

And by Friday, I had had my fill of filing too. Very large steel drawers, jammed with inscrutable legal documents in hanging folders with little colored tabs. I easily spent six hours of every day sitting on a library step stool, dropping stacks of CONFIDENTIAL-stamped folders into other folders—sorting, labeling, quietly singing the ABC song to myself each time I forgot which letter came next. I dutifully locked the drawers at the end of the day, and Rowan came by to get the key. By Friday, my back was tired, my brain was tired, and I think the entire staff had noticed I wore the same two suits in rotation for the week. "Care to go bend an elbow with me, Clay?" Rowan asked, pocketing the file key for the weekend.

"He means drink beer," Lisa said.

"Aw, I was supposed to meet my cousin Tony Baloney for drinks, down in the plaza."

"Sounds like a party," Rowan said. "Mind if I join?"

Lisa caught my eye. Her brows were raised; her shoulders were shrugged. Her coat was already on. Her heels had transformed into sneakers, the Friday night anti-Cinderella. She wasn't joining the party, that was sure. I had a feeling she knew something I was about to find out.

But you don't say *no* to your new boss. "Come along. Why not," I said.

14. Infection

Rowan started in on me in the elevator: "Lose the noose, Clay. That right-wing, wing-nut necktie. Lose it." I complied. By the time we got to the bar, the only one with a tie was my wing-nut cousin.

I introduced them. The usual what's-your-line New York hello, after the pints arrived, because, after all, we are what we do. Tony described himself as an equity trader on the cash desk. Rowan seemed to know what that meant. I described myself as the resident expert on the English alphabet. Rowan laughed. Tony did not. Rowan said he was a compliance officer.

"Officer?" I said. "Like a *left*enant?"

"Like a cop," Rowan said. "We make sure the greed part of capitalism doesn't make people stupid. Keep those honest people honest."

Tony looked askance at Rowan's already half-spent beer and shook his coiffed head. "That sounds like negative thinking to me."

Rowan didn't pause. "Right. Because we all know that all investments just go up and up and up."

"You have to think positive," Tony said. "It works. It's a law. It works for me."

Hoo boy. I slouched behind my pint glass. Some of me wanted to change the subject, but more of me wanted to find out where this was heading.

Rowan parried. "We're in a bubble. Everything works for everybody. It's tulip bulbs. It won't stick. Wake up, Tony Baloney. Nineteen ninety-nine is a party we are all going to regret in the morning."

Tony flushed under his starchy collar. "That's a retired nickname."

Tony Baloney. I felt awful. "I'm sorry, Tony," I said. "I never should—"

"Clay," Tony said, his cool color coming back already, cool Tony all the way, "I thought you were *thinking positive.* I thought that's why you finally got a job. I don't like what I'm hearing. I don't want to be infected." He snapped a bill from his sterling money clip and weighted it down with his barely drunk beer. "Say hi to your mom."

Rowan and I stared at each other for a second, then at Tony's empty chair. "Sorry," I said. "I forgot to warn you he's a Thinker and Believer, or whatever the Christ they call themselves."

"No, I'm the one who should be sorry. I brought the infection. I'm a regular Typhoid Mary with my unmagical thinking. And look, I busted up *your* party." But he was already commandeering Tony's abandoned libation, offering—with a tilt of the head—to pour out half for me.

"Nah, I need to pace myself," I said.

"I need to *pick up* the pace. I've had a sorry week." He popped a complimentary nut into his mouth, then washed it down. "I was dumped."

Yes, Ms. Yee. "I kind of figured something like that. Only I thought maybe you dumped her."

"God, I wish," Rowan said, plopping his forehead on the table before sitting upright again and flipping his too-long hair from his face. "It's us against them. I swear. You married, Clay? Encumbered?"

"No. Yes. I'm not sure. She doesn't call back."

"I want to be rid of my telephone. It only reminds me of my own abject failure." I thought of his red phone light, aglow all week while he talked to who knows who behind the glass walls of his office.

He pulled a prescription bottle from his pocket, palmed the childproof cap, and knocked back a tiny white tablet. Then, he spun something on the table, something flat and gold—a key. I thought of the key for Yee, naked and lonely in its interoffice envelope. I wanted to say something comforting. "You're a long way from abject," I offered.

"Not as far as one might think," he replied.

The bar was getting crowded—mostly men, mostly in dress shirts, casual Friday khakis here and there. I watched eyes dart as they stood at the bar in packs. They didn't touch each other, didn't quite look at each other. They eyed the young waitresses, the suspended TV screens, eyed everything but one another's eyes. A clamor of talk reverberated and cluttered the concrete room. Rowan said something I couldn't quite hear. I looked back at him. "Huh?"

"I said my mortal beloved ex claims she saw you *caressing a painting* up on her floor. Really?"

I shrugged. "Am I fired?" I felt my heart go fast—stupid, stupid thing to say.

"Maybe so." He paused, then winked. "She called you an *oddball*. Does that offend you?"

"No, *oddball* I can accept."

"Do you like art in some kind of special, *intimate* way?"

"It's more of a love-hate relationship."

"Ah. Yes. It doesn't call you back." He signaled, barely, with his index finger, to the waitress for a refill. I was still on beer number one.

"No. It doesn't call me back."

"You are among the army of New York creatives who compromise themselves by donning business suits and wing-nut nooses and consorting with the likes of us and our *tillions* of dollars. Waiting for Art to love you back. Waiting for Art to telephone. We must be *rid* of the telephone. We must be rid of waiting."

"You like art?" I asked.

"I like excitement," he said. "I like people who don't work in a compliance department. Or a legal department, or any *kind* of department. I've had it with departments. We should be rid of them, along with telephones."

"And waiting."

"I like to be surprised. I have not been surprised since nineteen eighty-seven, I fear."

I had a thought. Maybe it was the wrong thought, but I had it. The poor thing looked so dejected, with the foam of beer number three on his frowning upper lip, and a cross furrow in his forehead, and a girlfriendless apartment to go home to. "You want to go to an underground performance? In Williamsburg?"

It took him a short heartbeat to slap his credit card on the table.

15. In Which We Encounter Trolls

They led with the three live goats, which was the smart choice, because I don't care who you are or how important your destination is—if you're walking down a Williamsburg street on a balmy fall evening and see *three fucking goats* standing on top of a small house, you just stop right there. You stop, because the bar can wait, the friend can wait, happy hour can wait, dinner can wait, your gotta-pee dog can wait, because you are dying to know *why* the goats are standing on top of the small house.

The goats were in no distress. They had on small business suits. They appeared to love the elevation, safe from the gathering crowd up on their slate roof, with their pile of straw and bowl of water.

The small house was at the edge of a fenced lot, near the gate. Maybe it was where the parking attendant once waited out a cold shift, or maybe its purpose was always to be a gingerbready perch for three nattily dressed gatekeeper goats. They didn't bleat. Maybe they had nothing to say. They stood in their spotlight, carelessly chewing.

"That one there seems to have a three-piece," observed Rowan.

"The eyeglasses are a nice touch," I said. "And that bowtie on the one on the left. He even tied it right."

"I wonder how one fits a goat for a three-piece suit," said Rowan. "I imagine the horns are a bit of a hindrance. Not just any goat can pull off the jacket *and* the vest."

The house had a single gable, like the idea of a house, like the schema of a little girl's drawing of home. A single Dutch door in the center of the front was flanked by curtained windows. People were reaching up, snapping fingers, whistling, trying to get the attention of the goats. But the goats, they did not care. They did not notice. They had their own business, up there in their goat roost.

Rowan, with a childlike eagerness, reached up too, but the goats paid no mind. "They are rather standoffish, no?" he said.

"Maybe you have to offer them something," I said.

"Swiss watches, perhaps?" Rowan said to me and a total stranger, a young man covered in silver rings and holey body parts, the grooviest of the Billyburg groovy. He didn't laugh.

"Now that is standoffish," I whispered in Rowan's ear. "Uncool is so uncool." Rowan laughed. He didn't care. He was becoming surrounded by the pierced and judgmental, and he didn't care at all. He was impervious, like the elevated goats in their tweed apparel—maybe if you're just high enough, you forget what falling feels like; you forget to judge first, lest ye be deemed a dweeb.

The silver-covered dude pushed me aside with his shoulder and shot me that same look. The same look he gave Rowan—the look reserved for narcs and millionaires. But I was not Rowan. I was not impervious. I felt my blood beginning to churn—I was invited to *be in* this show, after all, Mr. Pierceder-Than-Thou; hell, they *begged* me, so why are you looking at me like I have no right to be here? Just because I'm wearing my work disguise? I was about to say something to the little asshole, something to reclaim my place in front of the goat house, when the top of the Dutch door swung open and a familiar face poked out.

Marvelli was wearing a tall, metallic gold turban. His mustache was waxed into super-curly curlicues tonight and dyed a deep black. He wore an old caftan, the one his brother brought him back from Turkey, and large gold hoops in his ears. His face was powdered white, his eyebrows arched in black greasepaint, his lips a scary blood red. He lifted a golden bugle and blew to silence the crowd. One of the goats finally looked up from his supper to see where the note was coming from.

"LADIES AND GENTLEMEN AND ALL OF YOU IN-BETWEEN!" Marvelli shouted through a heavy-echo microphone. "POETS, KNOW-IT-ALLS, KNOW-NOTHINGS, SAYERS OF NO! SAYERS OF YES, YES-MEN, YES-WOMEN, AND YOUR REBELLIOUS, YES-REFUSING CHILDREN! DONKEYS, ELEPHANTS, GOATS, AND GO-GETTERS! LAZYBONES, BONE-CHEWERS, GLEANERS, DUMPSTER-LOVERS! BULLSHIT-TALKERS, BULLSHIT-MAKERS, BULLSHIT-EATERS, AND BELIEV-ERS OF BALONEY! CHILDREN. CHILDREN! CHILDREN ARE WE ALL. WELCOME! WELCOME TO OUR SHOW. MY NAME IS MARVE-LIOLIOLIO, AND I WILL BE YOUR HOST, YOUR TOUR GUIDE, YOUR NARRATOR, AND YOUR NIGHTMARE. FOLLOW ME, IF YOU PLEASE, IF YOU DARE, IF YOU KNOW WHAT'S GOOD FOR YOU, WHICH IS WHAT'S BAD FOR YOU."

"I like the way he thinks," said Rowan into my ear.

Marvelioliolio stepped through the Dutch door, revealing the rest of his full-length robe and curly-toed golden slippers. "CHILDREN." His voice boomed like God from speakers inside the lot. "CHILDREN, PLEASE FOLLOW ME INTO OUR TALE OF WOE."

With the crooked staff of a shepherd, he knocked three times on the steel gate: *clang, clang, clang.* Loud, rusty gears cranked, and the gate slid slowly on its tracks. A hot feeling rose, unexpected, from the pit of my gut.

On the walk over from the subway, I had enabled Rowan in the purchase of a round of forty-ouncers, old school Brooklyn malt liquor, with Tony Baloney's twenty. Turns out Rowan didn't carry cash, wasn't ready for the cardlessness of outer-borough commerce. I wasn't sure of the protocol—do you *help* your new boss to pickle himself silly, if that's what he wants to do?—but as the gate's gears creaked and the gap of stage light cracked wider, I was grateful for the bagged bottle myself. Because it struck me, stupid me, all of a sudden, that I was going to see Shell tonight.

I was going to see Shell, and Shell was going to see me. Shell was going to see me, and I was going to see Shell. *I should not be afraid. This woman—I have seen her sleep with a thumb in her mouth.* My stomach was full of lava. A cool gulp of Colt 45 was barely a tonic.

Marvelli unrolled a long parchment scroll and read in the voice of Marveli-oliolio:

ONCE UPON A TIME, THREE BILLY GOATS NIBBLED DRY, DISGUSTING CHAFF FROM THE SCRUBBY PASTURE OF A FORGOTTEN BOROUGH. OVER THE WATER, THE THREE BROTHER GOATS SAW THE LIGHTS OF SOMETHING PROMISING. THERE WERE OTHER GOATS OVER THERE— BEAUTIFUL GOATS, SMART GOATS—LIVING THE GOOD GOAT LIFE. THE THREE BILLY GOATS TOLD THEMSELVES, LOOK! THIS BOROUGH ACROSS THE WATER, IT MUST BE BETTER! LOOK AT THE SHINING HEIGHTS OF THE SKY-SCRAPERS! THE COLORED, WINKING LUMINATION! OH, THE POSH PENTHOUSES THEY MUST HAVE, WITH THEIR WORLD-CLASS PAINTINGS ON EVERY WALL! OH, THE HORS D'OEUVRES, THE ENTRÉES, THE SORBETS, THE SUCCU-LENT POOLS OF SAUCE! THE GOLD-RIMMED PLATES, THE GOLD-PLATED SPOONS! THE GOOSE LIVER! THE SERVICE! THE STAFF! THINK OF WHO WE COULD BECOME, OVER THERE, ACROSS THE WATER! WE WANT THAT LIFE, THE GOATS TOLD THEMSELVES. HOW CAN WE GET ONTO THAT PEARL OF AN ISLAND?

THEY NEEDED A BRIDGE. THEY WALKED AND THEY WALKED AND THEY WALKED AND FOUND A BRIDGE. A BRIDGE! THEY EXCLAIMED. WHAT TREMENDOUS GOOD FORTUNE!

NOW, MY BEST BELOVEDS, HOW WERE THEY TO KNOW, THESE YOUNG BILLY GOATS, WHAT WOULD BE THE EX-TREME TOLL OF THEIR CROSSING?

Beyond the gate, in the lot, was a scale replica of the Williamsburg Bridge, all girders and Christmas lights, made of scrap wood and cinder block, span-ning a waterway simulated with billowing blue fabric and scraps of mirror. Be-yond the bridge were the lights of an artificial city, a minicity, created inside the bounds of the lot. The bridge looked rickety and only about wide enough to walk two abreast, which people did without hesitation, following the man with the shepherd's crook. I stole a look at Rowan to make sure he was onboard. His eyes were full of fire, and his smile was wide as we stepped onto the footpath.

I wondered if Shell were behind the design of the bridge. I swigged and looked out at the rippling crepe of water, and up at the full moon, and then at the green-tinted lights of the city replica ahead of us—an Empire State, a Chrysler, a World Trade Center maybe as tall as me, all dumpster cardboard and gray paint and stolen electricity. Beyond the fake Manhattan twinkled the real one, over the real river, in the smogless, fogless, starless night.

There was a commotion up ahead, at the mouth of the bridge. Trolls emerged from underneath and milled about a roadblock with an air of boredom and menace. They wore green face paint and green fright wigs and pointy prosthetic ears and noses. And blue police uniforms. I saw one shine a flashlight in the face of the judgmental hipster from earlier. Hipster-boy laughed, dug through his pockets, showed his driver's license, and handed something over to the troll, something from his wallet. The troll finally waved him through, into the miniature city.

"Are we going to need money?" Rowan asked. "Do you suppose they take Amex?"

"Money—no," I said. "It's not like them. They don't really care for money. They love gleaning and the barter system."

An Asian guy in a gray flannel business suit was at the roadblock now, and a gaggle of troll-cops circled to debate his worthiness to enter. I could not get a close look at his face, but he had my cousin's haircut. I was heartened—could I be this callous?—to think that this dude looked—was!—way more Wall Street than Rowan, who was without tie, shaggy-headed, unstarched, and untucked. The troll-cops gathered around the suited Asian dude, shoulder to shoulder, all folded arms and citation books. One had a billy club. The trolls huddled, then appeared to concur on something; then one of the trolls pulled a large knife from a hip sheath and pointed it in the Asian dude's face before aiming it lower and hacking off half of the dude's necktie.

"Sharp knife," I could not help saying. "That troll must have sharpened it." I did not recognize the troll, but it was hard to recognize any of them under the dim light and greasepaint.

Did I really want to be here? Did I really want this troll scrutiny? What would I even say to Shell if I saw her? Was she among the trolls? There was no turning back. This was a one-way replica bridge. "I suppose we could leap over the rail, into the stage water," I suggested.

"What are you talking about?" Rowan said. "Why're you so jumpy? What's to be afraid of? They are not going to hurt us."

I felt the nagging itch of my stitches; the scaly, healing skin under my stiff shirt. I looked at Marvelli and his tall shepherd's crook. "They might. They might hurt us," I said.

We had reached the roadblock. It was our turn to speak to the trolls. "What toll will you pay to enter this kingdom?" said the tallest one. I recognized his voice; he was the trombone player from our regular marching band. "What flavor of blood can you offer?" I recognized him, but I don't think he recognized me—the suit jacket? the shaved head?—was I not the green-haired Frankenstein he had seen bleed and ride horses and wear homegrown armor?

The troll turned to Rowan but did not address him directly, instead speaking to the other trolls as if Rowan were not even there. "He looks like he's aiming for Wall Street. He aspires to usury."

"We'll take his tie!" said another.

"But he has no tie!"

"Well, what does he have that we want?"

One of them handled the hem of Rowan's jacket. "These clothes? Are they s'posed to make him look important?"

"Dorky. Exceptionally dorky. But he craves *cool*, don't you think?"

"What on earth *does* he value the most?"

Rowan was polite and did not break the troll discussion; he clutched his spare beer under his arm while stealing a sip of the first. "Sir, is that an open container?" said one of the troll-cops, gruff and authoritarian.

"It does look *frosty and delicious*," said another.

"And refreshing."

"I think that might be what he values most."

One troll wrenched the beer from Rowan's hand, while another troll tugged the underarm beer away too. Rowan looked bereft. Maybe even panicked. His hands were empty and naked. I felt the need to defend him. Why was this troll-cop's need for refreshment more worthy than Rowan's? "Now you are free to enter this kingdom," said the troll-cop, shoving my new boss into the miniature city. Rowan stood at the minicrossroads of Essex and Delancey, waiting for me to pay my toll, whatever it might be.

"You want my beer too?" I said. "Is that the going bribe?" The trombone-troll still did not recognize me. "How about my tie? You can have it. It's a wing-nut tie—your father might like it." Still no recognition. The tie had been draped over my shirt and under my jacket ever since I had untied it in the elevator. I snapped it out and handed it over. "Here. Here's my payment."

"NO."

It was Marvelioliolio, standing behind the troll-cops, and they froze at the sound of his voice. "This young goat has *already lost* the thing he values most." He looked me in the eye. No twinkle. Serious. Not angry-serious. Sad-serious. "He has *already paid* his heavy toll." I felt my heart quicken and my head go hot. "He may enter the kingdom. He is already *of* the kingdom." Marvelli walked away. The troll waved me through. I joined Rowan in fake Chinatown.

"What was that about?" he asked.

"I don't exactly know."

"They confiscated my supper."

"Here." I took a last sip and handed him mine. He looked instantly relieved, just to have it in his hand, just in case. The Asian businessman stepped around mini–City Hall and directly over to us. Did Rowan know him? But he looked right in my face with a colossal grin, then reached right over and rubbed my fuzzy head. "It *is* you! Clay!"

"Pak?" It was Steve, my old college friend, with much shorter hair, and grayer too; Steve, of the giant notebooks and crosshatches. "What the fuck, Steve? Jesus, I hardly recognized you. What's with the monkey suit?"

"I could ask you the same. Didn't you used to have hair? In bright colors?"

"I had to get a day job," I said. "This is my new boss. Rowan."

"Hey." Steve shook Rowan's hand.

"And you? You're an MBA now?" I asked, knowing already the answer. Steve had been in the Whitney Biennial already. Twice. I had been watching, covetously, from afar.

Steve laughed. "MBA. I like that. No, I had to go to court today."

Rowan pointed to the cardboard municipal court building a few steps away. "I see you just came from there."

Steve laughed. "You're funny." To me: "He's funny." He looked at the courthouse, as high as his knee. "Somehow this courthouse is a lot cuter than the other one."

"All courthouses should be cute," said Rowan, stepping downtown to check out the detail.

"You're not in trouble with the law, are you?" I said, more quietly. "The real cops? Not these yahoos?"

"Nah, I got divorced today." He puffed up his chest like a proud kid announcing his latest athletic achievement.

"I didn't even know you were married."

"Neither, apparently, did my wife." He seemed punchy, extra happy, or maybe drunk enough to fake it. "She used our home as a love nest while I was a visiting lecturer back in St. Louis."

"Dang."

He flapped his hacked half tie between his fingers. "We got a decent settlement. She can't get her hands on my intellectual property."

"Is that what you are now? An *intellectual?*"

He grabbed my neck in an arm lock. "Goddamn, Clayman. I can't believe it. I can't believe I ran into you *here*. Hey, what's his story?" He pointed to Rowan, who had wandered deeper into the replica city and was examining each building with a childlike quiet.

"I don't quite know yet."

"Hey, lads," Rowan shouted. "Check out the signage. *New York Cock Exchange.* Ha!"

"This little church is pretty cool," Steve said. "Look, they drew in all the gargoyle faces. I wish I had my camera."

"I'm sorry you got divorced," I said.

"Me too," he said quietly, letting the bravado fall from his face. "It was not my idea."

The fake streets of fake Manhattan were getting crowded. A steady stream of soul patches and ironic T-shirts spread from the epicenter of the roadblock. The three of us walked up little Park Avenue, past little Grand Central, then skirted little Central Park and braved the crowd forming around little Guggenheim. The chunks of rotunda were carefully scored cardboard. "Who built all this?" I asked no one in particular. Was this what Shell had been doing while not picking up her phone? And now that the little city was done, would her phone policy change? Or, was there a new troll in her bed, listening to my desperate messages, cackling his troll laughter?

Behind the hipster throng, the troll-cops locked arms and pushed, corralling the crowd. "This is an unlawful assembly." "Move it along." "You can't be here." "Please disperse." "This street is closed."

They jostled us northwest, into another bottleneck around little 125th Street, and I heard drumming at the open roller door of a big dirty building at the end of the lot. "Keep it moving, people," said the troll-cops. They shoved us away from mini-Manhattan, across where the Hudson would be, toward the building. Marvelioliolio stood at the doorway, flanked by two trolls on bass drum playing a steady, boring march beat, without flavor or syncopation.

"MY BEST BELOVEDS, LET US CONTINUE OUR TALE," said Marvelioliolio through the speakers overhead. "THE GOATS DID NOT KNOW THE TOLL WOULD TAKE ITS TOLL. THEY DID NOT KNOW THE TOLL WOULD BE ENDLESS. IT WOULD PULL THE GOATS IN. IT WOULD PULL THE GOATS DOWN. PLEASE COME IN, MY BEST BELOVEDS, AND LEARN THE BILLY GOATS' FATE."

We followed the horde, between the bass drummers, into a dark corridor. Along one wall was a row of very low desks with very low chairs. At each hunched a secretary in a prim vintage dress, pecking away rapidly at a manual typewriter. The typewriter sounds were amplified and echoed through the hallway, all rhythmic clicks and dings. They were typing along with the bass-drum beat, like a heavy metronome. Each secretary had a spotlight on the white page in her machine. I leaned down to see what they were typing, and my hunch was confirmed:

ASDF ASDF ASDF ASDF

JKL; JKL; JKL; JKL;

DADA DADA DADA DADA

NONO NONO NONO NONO

I looked around, hoping Shell was in the corridor. Surely she had something to do with this. Surely!

No sign of her. None of the secretaries had that freckled neck. She was not among the steady stream of audience members, who barely paid attention to the toiling typists. Ignoring! They were all focused on the end of the hall, where a strobe light flashed from what appeared to be an important room. Marvelli led with his tall crook, and the herd followed.

"Aren't they afraid of epileptic fits?" Steve asked. "From the strobe?"

"Oh, that's probably one of many hazards they have engineered for our excitement," I said. "You epileptic?"

"How well you know these guys?" Steve asked.

"Well, that one I know pretty good," I said, pointing to the curly crook. "This is gonna sound grandiose, but I think this *whole performance* might be directed at me."

"Like a song dedication?" Steve said.

"Well, yeah, actually. Yeah. Like a song dedication. Only more judgmental and prescriptive."

"You're right. That does sound grandiose," Steve said. The three of us stepped into the immense strobe-lit room.

It was impossible to tell what was in the room, other than ourselves. I was hypnotized and a little sickened by the strobe light, like I hadn't stood in the light of the exact same strobe before, like I hadn't ordered up a strobe light before, in other performances. Like I was just one of these Billyburgers, just one of these audience sheep being led by the crook. Was that what I had become? A spectator?

The strobe stopped.

Marvelli stood in the middle of the floor, in a circle of golden light. The room was tall and vast. "THIS KINGDOM ACROSS THE WATER HAD A UNIQUE TALENT," he said. "THIS KINGDOM KNEW HOW TO

PROMISE THINGS YOU NEVER DARED WANT. BACK IN THEIR OLD VILLAGE, THE BILLY GOATS HAD ONLY NEEDED FOOD AND SHELTER. THEY HAD ENOUGH TO GET BY AND WERE GRATEFUL FOR IT. BUT HERE, IN THE NEW KINGDOM, A NEW HUNGER AROSE—THE HUNGER FOR *IMPORTANCE*."

Above Marvelli's head, a twinkling began in the dark, and as my eyes adjusted, I could see the spokes of a pearlescent spiderweb. "HERE, IN THE NEW KINGDOM, DWELLED A SEDUCTRESS," Marvelli said. A figure descended, suspended on a rope, harnessed by her arched waist—Olga, my acrobatic neighbor, clad in a black unitard with a bright red dot on her abdomen. "THE SEDUCTRESS WOULD SPIN A WEB OF SILK AND PROMISES. SHE KNEW WHAT WORKED ON LITTLE BILLY GOATS. SHE KNEW WHAT THEIR STRONGEST WEAKNESS WAS—THE THING THAT DREW EACH BILLY GOAT AGAIN AND AGAIN TO THE MIRROR—DID YOU KNOW THE BILLY GOAT IS A CREATURE PLAGUED BY *VANITY*?"

Olga was just above Marvelli now, in the spotlight. He stepped back into shadow. "She's beautiful," Steve said in my ear. She spun, slowly, on the end of her sparkling filament, her limbs thick with muscle, but lithe.

"I think I know her," Rowan said in my other ear. A shimmery music surrounded us, a faint gamelan mixed with amplified typewriters and a high, whimsical fife.

"She's my neighbor," I said to no one in particular, as if it were meaningful. Olga reached her pale hands out, pointing to individuals, beckoning spectators with a curl of the finger and a wily smile.

Marvelli's voice continued. "DEAR BILLY GOAT, WHAT A HANDSOME SUIT YOU WEAR," he said, in the honeyed voice of a she-spider. "DEAR MISS GOATETTE, WHAT A LOVELY GREEN FROCK. DO COME CLOSER, SO I CAN SEE ITS FLATTERING CUT. COME CLOSER, MISS. LET ME SEE YOUR EXQUISITENESS." As he spoke, the Olga-spider reached to a woman standing at the edge of the spotlight. The woman reached back. She was a tiny, thin woman in a gauzy gown the color of currency. Olga grasped the woman's hand and pulled her into the light. "YOUR BEAUTY AND YOUR TASTE ARE A PLEASURE TO BEHOLD," Marvelli said, in the spider's voice, as the women gazed at each other in the circle of light. Olga grabbed the woman's second hand, pulling her closer in a pas de deux. "IN FACT, YOU LOOK DOWNRIGHT SCRUMPTIOUS."

At once, the gamelan turned into a loud jabber of drums, and the spider's silk shortened, lifting both women into the air. The gowned woman did not look panicked, but stared in hypnotized awe at the Olga-spider, who clutched the woman's forearms in the manner of a trapeze catcher. Together, the women rose to the center of the web overhead, and as the gamelan banged away, Olga rapidly wrapped her victim in layers of gauze, lashing her to the spokes of the web, rendering her immobile. The woman moaned, helpless.

The pounding stopped. "A SCRUMPTIOUS SNACK FOR LATER," Marvelli declared, in his own voice. "THIS IS THE FATE OF MANY A BILLY GOAT. THIS IS THE *IMPORTANCE* THE BILLY GOAT WINS—BECOMING A SCRUMPTIOUS SNACK, WRAPPED IN PRESERVATIVE FILM."

Steve looked up at the bound woman. "That is so fucking hot," he said in my ear.

"You are the best temp in the universe," said Rowan in my other ear.

I said nothing. A peculiar sadness was spreading through my chest. I feared opening my mouth, feared I might name what I was feeling. I looked up at the spider and her sack lunch, readied for her convenience. Olga descended again on her silky filament, ready to grab another scrumptious volunteer for her stockpile.

"CHILDREN," Marvelli said. "MY BEST BELOVEDS. WE ALL KNOW HOW THIS ENDS. PLEASE FOLLOW ME. COME SEE OUR FINE FINALE, OUR TRUMP OF TRUMPS." His crook led toward a door in the back and another courtyard. "COME, CHILDREN, AND SEE THE BILLY GOATS' GREATEST LOSS OF ALL."

16. My New Brother Is Revealed

The back courtyard was dark. Follow spots fox-trotted over the walls and the standing throng, then landed on their objects: two darkened doorways. Trolls beat drums, emerging in military formation from each end of the courtyard. Marvelli stood guard at one of the doors and shouted through the speakers, through the din of drums:

BEST BELOVEDS! WHY DO WE MAKE WHORES OF OURSELVES? WHY DO WE SELL OUR MINDS AND STEP BLITHELY INTO CAGES? DO WE FIND CAGES A COMFORT? DO THEIR WALLS HELP US FORGET THE VAST SILLINESS—THE SILLY VASTNESS—OF OUR DESIRES? BEST BELOVEDS, I WILL SPEAK TO YOU NO MORE THIS EVENING. I WILL ONLY SHOW. YOUR BILLY GOATS HAVE A VIEW NOW, FROM THEIR TOWER OFFICES. THEY CAN SEE THEIR FORGOTTEN KINGDOM ACROSS THE WATERS. THEY KNOW NOW WHAT THEY HAVE SACRIFICED FOR THEIR NEW COMFORTS. DANGER

WAS ONCE THE BILLY GOAT'S MUSE. NOW, HE HAS NO MUSE.
HE HAS A LIVELIHOOD BUT NO LIFE. HIS HEART HAS BEEN
COMPROMISED. HE HAS LOST THE FREEDOM OF FLIGHT!

The troll drum corps boomed a heavy samba, and Marvelli stepped aside.
A figure appeared in the doorway wearing a fat, white space suit, and the spotlight turned burnt umber, casting a Mars-canyon glow on the astronaut. The
figure stepped into the arena, in the moving pool of light, and I recognized
the stride. Gangly for one so petite, the firm march of the legs and hips, while
the arms flopped and swung. Her helmet was a hardened sphere, sealing her
in at the neck, and I couldn't see her face—I wasn't sure if I wanted to—and I
wished I had not given Rowan my beer. She stepped, in the high-gravity waddle
of our planet and her equipment, over to the massive concrete structure I only
now noticed had been in our midst all along.

The structure was a half sphere, flat on the top, round on the bottom, with a
surface cratered like our moon. The throng parted, stepping back to behold the
concrete form and the astronaut dwarfed beside it. Affixed to the flat topside
of the semisphere was a rocket about twice as tall as me, seemingly made of
steel and tissue paper and painted in red-and-white carnival stripes. The drums
boomed; the astronaut circled slowly, waving to her crowd. I did not wave back.
For a second, she faced me, and I could see her eyes through the plastic face
shield. She registered nothing. She was a stranger. I felt a hot rush in my compromised heart.

Someone leaned a ladder against the concrete half sphere, and the astronaut
climbed up it, then stood on the flat edge next to the rocket. She waved some
more, full of aeronautic bravado. I saw people around me put fingers to lips, to
whistle, but heard nothing but drumbeat. Drumbeat, and heartbeat, and the astronaut lifted off her helmet and tossed it out to the mass. Her little braids were
gone. Her hair was clipped short now, ready for flight. She unzipped her space
suit, slowly, down the front, and it fell from her shoulders to her feet. She kicked
the suit from the concrete platform.

She was naked. Bowed spine, lean hips, tightly strung legs, fluid arms.
Giant, defiant bush. Only her. Only her with a bush like that. I heard whoops
around me. I can't look. I can't see this.

It was the kind of show I used to tell Shell about. Complain to Shell about.
The fake authority of nakedness. The cheap and easy. Anyone can be naked. But
who has a suit of armor? Who has a space suit? Who has a mirrored loincloth? A
pair of lederhosen made of salami and cheese? A glittery grass skirt? A Turkish
caftan and crook?

Naked? *Really*? Wasn't my girl smarter than that?

"She's beautiful," Steve said in my ear.

"The beautifulest," I said back.

"Do you know her?" Rowan said in my other ear.

"I really don't know anymore," I said. "I have no idea."

Trolls pushed the crowd back into a wider circle as another figure ascended the ladder: Marvelli himself. He joined her on the platform and shook her hand in the manner of military heroes before kicking his curly slippers into the air and casting his caftan to the ground. He was naked now, too. He circled, too, and waved, a second superhero.

I had never seen Marv naked. It's hard to believe I'd never seen Marv naked. Never a skinny-dip, never a Turkish bath, never streaking through the streets of Williamsburg on a drunken afternoon. In addition to the leg full of inky filigree, which I knew well, he had a large golden eye—a stylized Egyptoid tattoo—on his upper abdomen, shiny with sweat, staring down the crowd. I stared back, until I could not stare anymore. Naked—naked, and *still* in costume. The fucker had me beat.

He and she, she and he. They faced each other, now, on opposite sides of the skyward-facing rocket and, on alternating drumbeats, crouched and pulled. The ladder had been removed. Crouch, pull, crouch, pull, and now the semisphere was rocking. Her butt flexed, her forearms went firm, and her face had the hot flush of exertion. She smiled at him, pure joy and ease. Push, pull. Shell and Marvelli. The hustles, all those hustles, in my home disco; the turns and claps, while I tutor-typed away. *We type our own. The one thing.* The hours, and the hard stool, and a hot feeling, and the rocket had a good sway on now. Both of them were grinning like pit bulls—the glee of naked sweating, the glee of pulling it off—and I knew all at once what I was seeing. All at once, what I had been seeing all along.

I couldn't see any more. I wanted my blindness back. My heart hammered louder than troll drums, and a hot sick welled up from my hips to my shoulders. Beside me, Rowan's eyes shone with wonder and anticipation. On the other side, Steve held both pinkies in his mouth for a whistle. "I need to go," I shouted, to be heard over the din. Steve gave a quizzical look, but I didn't stay to explain. "I'll meet you outside," I said, then turned and pushed my way between the amped-up onlookers, back from where I had come.

I jogged through Olga's empty spider chamber and entered the hall of typewriters. The secretaries were gone. Pikers. They typed for, what, ten minutes? Their scrolls of paper sat—inked on, lettered up, unread—unfurling from each typewriter spindle. I did not slow down to peruse their output.

A stocky man blocked my path in the narrow hall. I did not step aside to let the man by, this sasquatch in matador pants and a purple velvet coat buttoned up to his neck. He wore a satin headband and holsters slung crossways over his chest, a jagged X across his body—holsters filled with steak knives. He stopped short in front of me, took his gaze from the floor, and glared at me.

"Oh Jesus, I forgot about you," I said.

He looked startled—surprised, perhaps, that a guy in a business suit could speak. "Who the fuck are you?" he said.

"I fucking have no fucking idea," I said. "I'm nobody," I said. "I'm the guy who's leaving." I stepped aside, between the typewriters, to end the impasse.

I watched his back as he entered Olga's chamber, crossed it, and stepped into the loud outdoor arena. Then I trotted back, through papier-mâché Midtown, over Son of East River, through the gate, and straight into the real bodega across the street.

I had just enough change in my pocket, including pennies, to buy myself a single tallboy. I held the beer up to my hot cheek. I rolled the cold can across my forehead. The bodega man stared, then handed me a small paper bag, an invitation to leave his store. I popped the beer in the bag and walked, catching my breath, back to the little cottage.

The three goats still stood on the roof in their hot tweed suits. One of the goats had stretched taut his tether. He stood on the eave overhanging the sidewalk, seemed to need distance from his goat brothers, distance from something—from the drums? The whistles, the whoops? The trolls he feared lurked under the arch of the bridge? His eyes popped white at the corners. "Are you scared, little brother?" I asked him.

When I reached up to touch him, he did not shrink away. He did not shrink away when I scaled the adjacent fence and sat beside him, on the eave, soiling my dead-man's suit. He was young, and tame, and tucked into my armpit. I opened my beer and took a sip, then poured a bit into my hand for my new acquaintance.

He did not drink. "Are you old enough?" He did not answer. I had no idea what to say to calm a goat. I dipped my mouth into my palm and slurped up the goat's beer, then resumed work on the brown-bagged can.

From our eave, we had a view of fake Williamsburg Bridge and fake Manhattan. And behind it, distant: real Williamsburg Bridge, and behind that: real Manhattan, and behind that: a slim curl of moon, and behind that: space, darkness, space. The silly vastness. The goat and I looked down at the cardboard city. He bleated, finally, a timid vibration in my armpit.

"*Nice town*, know what I mean?" I said.

He bleated again and kept looking. From the courtyard full of folks, the drums turned into a roll and stopped with a raucous cheer. Another drumroll, another cheer, and another. I could not see the courtyard. I imagined my astronaut tied naked to something, arms splayed, not flinching, not flinching at all. Shell was never a flincher. Knives, she was not afraid of, nor a *professional knife thrower*, and the little goat burrowed deeper into my side each time the cheer erupted.

And then, a cannon sounded overhead, and a shimmer of sparks rained over yonder, over the courtyard. I held the poor goat with both arms, even covered his floppy ears at the squeal of rockets firing into the air. With each cannon boom, the kid jumped.

I was angry. This poor goat had had enough. *What kind of person* enlists young animals in the service of *naked performance art*, with timpani and fireworks? Is everything in service of our meaning? *Who was this person* I had been sharing my bed with, believing in, following advice of, borrowing money from? Was she the same girl who sucked her thumb in my bed, sound asleep and angelic? This cruel astronaut? This goat user? What the hell *kind of person*?

I was no professional knife thrower, but I had a knife all right—my old pocketknife; never left the house without it, not since a certain pragmatist invested in my readiness. I downed my beer, flung the bagged can into the street, flipped the knife open, and, with the goat tucked underarm, sawed through his tether one-handed, leaving a decent length of the cotton line. Goatherd style, I wrapped my new little brother around my neck like a stole, and he held still on my shoulders as I climbed back down the iron fence to the sidewalk.

17. Temporary Reprieve from Blindness

I crossed the street and stood in the dark of a strange doorway, with the weight of the kid on my back. His stupid suit itched my nape. The stupid nape of my stupid neck in my stupid bleached shirt that I bought for my stupid straight job so my stupid girlfriend wouldn't think I was so stupid.

"She's such a little shit," I said. "She's a shitty astronaut." I heard the lie right away. The goat probably heard it too. "OK, I don't know what kind of astronaut she is," I said. "I don't know anything at all." The goat repositioned his legs, stretched his hooves, wiggled to get comfortable on my shoulders. I felt air leave his chest in a sigh, and I sighed too. "I'm the shitty astronaut," I said. "I'm the shitty everything."

I backed further into the dark. I did not want to be seen as the thief I was. I backed further into the dark and stroked the bare foreleg of the goat. His fur was stiff. It only wanted to grow one way. I didn't try to fluff against the grain.

It calmed me a little, as quiet tears dropped onto my stupid lapel. "Was she even nice to you, little goat?" I said. "Did she ever rub your leg like this? Did she even talk to you?"

I felt the tip of the goat's winglike ear twitch against my fuzzy scalp. I scratched my head. I wanted to pick a hole in it. I wanted to pick a hole through my skull and scratch my thoughts right out in a heap of blood and goop. Thoughts chasing thoughts around in laps, torture of my own making; words spoken, now unforgettable: *Best beloveds, why do we step blithely into cages?* What about *him*—the curlicued, caftaned, God-mouthed, goat-using hustler—my used-to-be best friend? Who thought nothing of borrowing this creature—or worse, renting!—then returning him to the meat factory for a deposit? Monstervelli and his city circuits, his roundups, his recruiting for sidekickery, his army building, everybody seduced with the same line: *You're so good at it. You don't flinch. You're the only one. The only!* "Did he butter you up good?" I asked the goat, wanting to slap something. Instead I reached up to scratch the base of the twitching ear. The goat rested his head against my hand, and the soft weight of him in my palm—its tenderness—made me break into a sob.

One thing certain: I was not going to give back this goat. For the fate of a plate of curried stew? "You're with me now, little brother," I said, through a hiccup. I said it over and over—"You're with me. You're with me now"—as I worked to catch my breath.

The fireworks silenced. The troll band played something Souza. They got louder, closer, probably leading—if I knew them at all—their hipster army out over the homemade bridge, like the rats of Hamelin. I tucked against the dark wall and waited.

The troll band marched through the gate, in exuberant single file, up to Berry Street, then on to the targeted bar. The trolls did not see me. The rats of Hamelin did not see me. They were busy seeing themselves. I had no intention of joining them for the festive denouement. Back to the bar, always the same old, always backward, and besides, I had to get this goat home.

I scanned the hipster parade for my companions. My new boss—I could not just leave him in Billyburg. And my old friend: maybe I needed one now. Yes, maybe I needed one now, because maybe I was losing my shit.

The crowd thinned. The street grew quieter, just the usual Brooklyn ambience of honk and bark and *hey-you*. I thought I saw Rowan's indecisive hairdo disappearing into the bodega, then what looked like Steve waiting outside for him, looking spiritedly about—seemingly looking for me. "Psst!" I poked my head out of the shadow. "Psst! Pak!" His head turned. "Over here!"

I ducked back into the shadow as Steve strode up. "Claybird, what the fuck?" His suit jacket was off now, draped over his arm, exposing wet armpits and his chopped-off tie. "Why'd you run out of there so quick? Jesus, it was unbelievable! That big cement ride thingy, and that crazy man with the eyeball tattoo! Then those green guys started passing out flaming shots of some high-test rum—your boss, he's got a hollow leg, no?—oh! And the *knife thrower*. You missed the freaking *knife thrower*. One minute you're next to me, and the next, you were like a—hey, have you been *crying*? What happened? Are you all right, man? Clay, you—um . . . do you have a *goat* on your back?"

"Sh. Yeah. I kinda took him."

"I see that."

"I think I want to keep him."

Steve reached his hand up to the goat's nose, eyes wide, nodding the way my mother does when she's both afraid and amused. "Well, I'm glad to see you're still you."

I took a deep breath, shook out my head, and let go of the goat's leg long enough to smear snot and tears off my face with my sleeve. I felt my air coming back.

"What's Rowan doing?" I said. "I don't want to leave him here. This isn't exactly his—" I could not think of the word.

"Milieu?"

"Mil-fucking-*ieu*. I was going to say *comfort zone*, but that's just stupid."

"He's getting cash. We were talking about cabbing it downtown to my studio. I gotta get back to work, and he wants to see my new stuff. Wanna come?"

Did I want to come? *Did* I want to see the labors of my most successful friend, the work that for a decade made me pine with jealousy over his luck and skill and industriousness and crazy brain? *Did* I have it in me to keep from bawling in front of my new boss? Wasn't there some private wallowing to do? Hadn't there been enough art for one night?

"I have to figure out what to do with this guy," I said, and patted the goat's tweeded rump.

"Bring him along," said Rowan. He stepped into the shadow beside me. His arms were weighted down with bodega bags full of clinking bottles. He smiled at the goat's face. "He's a handsome fellow," Rowan said, like he encountered urban goats daily.

"I'm not sure I can get him in my studio," Steve said. "It's kind of a fortress down there. Ever since the bombing."

"Oh, we can get him in," Rowan said. "There are ways."

"Fortress?" I said. "Where the fuck is your studio?"

Rowan's eyebrows bounced, and he grinned. Steve pointed to the Manhattan skyline—the real one, over the river—and the twinkling pair of towers looming over everything, practically touching the moon.

"*There?*" I said. Steve nodded.

"You know, Clayton," Rowan said, "your new chum is predisposed to enjoy altitude." He gazed up at the creature growing heavy on my shoulders, addressed the kid directly. "Right, little fellow? Your ancestors made their homes on the tops of mountains."

18. The Troll at the Base of the Towers

We paused in the plaza between the towers to let the goat drink at the fountain. The place was quiet. It was just three men and a pet goat, and the big round drink, and the miniworld—the bronze globe—perched in the center of the fountain, like a cherry on a melting marble sundae.

"What say we nix his suit and tie?" Rowan suggested, petting his new goat friend. "It's natty, to be sure, but does it make him happy?"

Steve held the rope leash while Rowan and I tugged at the goat's garments. Rowan seemed to know how to handle the goat, could navigate the budding horns and sharp hooves.

On the ride over the Williamsburg Bridge, the kid had kicked me in the torso a couple times, not far from itchy sutures. The car-service dude had insisted on all windows down—his condition for transporting a farm animal. The wind had blown Rowan's hair into a decisive fright wig, Einsteinian wings framing a face filled with kid-like delight. "The art! The life!" he had exclaimed out the window, into the East River air. "Who needs a woman? I'm in love with my city!" And further, in the Bowery: "Just look how alive we are!" And in Chinatown: "I love this goat!" The cabbie had rolled his eyes at me in the rearview, and I realized, with my ungreen buzzed head and unchopped necktie, I really was the most normal-looking passenger in this man's car.

Me. I was not sure how to feel about that.

Rowan and I got the jacket off the goat pretty quick—it had come unbuttoned on the ride over—and the pants snapped right off, like toddler clothes. But the shirt and tie fought back. In unison, without planning it, Rowan and I both unpocketed Swiss Army knives, and Steve laughed. "Whose is bigger?" Steve said.

There wasn't time for a contest. Rowan sliced the tie under the back of the goat's collar, while I cut and ripped the pleat up the center back, like the undertaker special. Rowan flipped the scissors from his knife and snipped the last of the collar. The goat stepped out of his shirt, naked, into the plaza.

The Artstars

He wiggled his little tail bob and shook his head, ears flopping all over the place. "Will you look at this magnificent creature?" Rowan said. "What will you name him?"

The kid was brown and white and had a baby sheen to his fur. He had a wispy beard and wiggly ears and a tilt to his head that reminded me of Big Ed, the taxidermied horse. "Little Ed," I said.

"Yes, Little Ed," Rowan said. "Yes."

Little Ed's wide-set eyes were less frightened now. He seemed glad to be rid of the getup. He looked up at each of us, in turn, expectantly.

"You mind?" Rowan asked Steve, taking the rope lead. "I have an idea." The kid's back legs were springy as he walked beside Rowan to the tower's entrance.

I found a trash bin for the jettisoned suit. Steve brought up the rear with the bags full of bottles, muttering to himself, muttering to me: "There's no way those pigs in the lobby are going to let in a fucking goat."

A lone guard sat at the long security counter. He wore a navy-blue sport coat with a gold crest, more glee club than cop. "These are my guests," Steve said, placing a thick ID badge on the white marble counter.

The guard had the start of a troll beard and eyes ready for coffee break. I wondered if he had a cafeteria to turn to or a cache of NoDoz in his drawer. He picked up the card without looking up from his computer monitor. "I'll need state IDs from everybody," he said. Then Little Ed let out a squeal, and all hope of easy entry quit the room.

The guard craned to see over the counter, and his eyes bugged. "You can't bring that in here," he said.

Rowan ignored him and slapped his driver's license on the counter, holding the goat's tether with his other hand.

"Sir, you can't bring that animal in here."

"Oh, you mean my service dog?"

I bit my tongue. I dug through my wallet for my ID. I dared not look up at my new boss and his wacky wig and Little Ed not exactly barking.

"Sir, that is not a dog."

"Sir, that is most certainly a dog. Just look at him. Have you not seen the highland shepherd? It is a rare breed indeed, but quite suited to this kind of work."

"Are you *blind*?" the man asked.

"I don't think you should be asking me that question, sir," Rowan said. "It's actually *unlawful* for you to ask me that question, sir," he continued, causing the stranger's already-ruddy face to grow even ruddier. "As per the Americans with Disabilities Act, I am under no obligation to disclose my condition, only to identify my dog as a service animal."

Compliance Department in the house.

"I meant, sir," the man continued, "are you *unable to see* that your *dog* is *not a dog*?" He seemed unsure how to get this right.

Rowan's calm seemed only to unnerve the guard further. Rowan threw his shoulders back and rested his palm on the counter, with an air of serene civil disobedience. "I advise you to consult your supervisor as to my rights in this matter," he said.

They stood in a silent eye-lock for a full minute or so, until the goat emitted another barnyard remark. The man walked to a phone, out of earshot at the other end of the counter, and glared at Rowan, nodding and listening. Then he returned and wordlessly printed both of us a hard plastic pass, like a credit card with a portrait on it. My photo was brand new, shot on the spot, puffy post-crying eyes and mouth barely containing a guffaw. Rowan's was an older picture, with short-clipped hair and a professional, undrunk expression, recycled from a prior business visit to the building.

The guard waved us to the elevator bank. The goat skipped behind Rowan like he'd seen an elevator bank before.

We did not speak until the elevator doors sealed shut. I let out the belly laugh I'd been sucking in. We had the large car to ourselves. Steve set down his bags and, with a face-splitting grin, pointed both fingers at Rowan. "YOU. You are one *freaky* motherfucker."

"I suppose I am," Rowan said, calmly, flatly, then let a sly smile spread at the corners of his mouth.

19. Sky

The elevator car shook as it rose rapidly, with a rush of air and audible turn of gears. The cable hummed overhead like an outsized, plucked guitar string, and some floors emitted construction noise as we passed—a crescendo, then fade, then quiet. By the time we transferred elevators halfway up, I was woozy from the ascent. Rowan and Steve weren't rattled a bit, and Little Ed looked nervous but ripe for adventure, bouncing with my boss into the new compartment.

By floor ninety-six I had to yawn to pop my ears. "You're all the way fricking up here?" I asked Pak.

He shrugged. "I'm lucky. I won't front. I'm lucky."

The doors opened onto a rough-hewn hall with Masonite laid on the floor and stark fluorescent light. The drop-ceiling tiles were intermittent, exposing the guts of the tower's business: brightly colored telephonic wires, bendy electrical conduit like a mess of small intestine, steel girders coated with fireproofing.

The Artstars

"They are between tenants," Steve explained, leading us past unpainted new Sheetrock. "It's expensive, this kind of vacancy. So they donate the space to arts organizations. It's a tax write-off for them, a studio space for me."

He keyed a padlock and released a hinged wall, opening it onto a roomful of Pak. It could only be Pak. I had forgotten how it looked, the work space of a diligent sculptor, a sculptor of natural materials, whose use of the materials was as singular as a thumbprint. I took a deep drag of the aroma of his work: cedar, oak, wool fiber, straw, ferrous and earthy mud, leaves, ashes.

"Welcome to my aerie," Steve said, closing the wall behind us. Rowan and I stood in the entryway, drop-jawed, and stared all around. "This is my new series," Steve said. "Nests."

They were, quite literally, nests. Nests of numerous sizes.

Laid out in a spiral near our feet were a dozen donut-shaped ones, made of different substances, sizes ranging from soup bowl to truck tire, biggest in the center. "Those are full of themselves," Steve said, and it took me a second to figure what he meant. The largest nest was carved of some kind of knotty red wood, and it contained curled-up shavings, with bark and sawdust. It must have all come from the same log. Another nest, also wood, looked to have been carved with fire instead of a chisel, and in the charred center was a pool of ashes. Another, made of a veiny hunk of granite, had pebbles in its center, polished smooth like eggs. A white nest, smaller, made of what looked like Ivory soap, was filled with a bubbly liquid. Over here was a ring of chocolate, with fragrant chocolate shavings in the middle.

"I like that one," I said, pointing to the chocolate, then noticed another made of woven straw, with grass tufting up from the center. Little Ed had noticed it too and was having it for a snack. I gasped. Rowan and I both reached for the leash, which had fallen to the floor. "I'm so sorry," I said, horrified.

Steve just laughed. "Maybe he's hungry?" he said. "What do goats eat?" He set the beer bags down on a crate next to the north wall of windows and disappeared into a footlocker for a minute, before emerging with a plastic sack of dried corn husks. "Can he eat this? I'm not going to use it. I decided I'm not a Midwestern boy anymore." He struck a scarecrow pose, a bouquet of corn in each hand, head flopped to the side in mock sleep. "They're goofy, right? Corn-cobs? Better for Ed."

I didn't know what to feed the goat. Or if. I didn't know a single thing about goats, except cartoon goats eating jagged tin cans.

"Corn husks would be delightful," Rowan said, with full goat authority.

"You know something about goats?" I asked.

"A little. My granny raised goats. In Scotland. They'll eat anything."

"That's where you're from?" Steve said, handing over the package of corn.

"Heavens no. I wish," said Rowan. "It's breathtaking there. I'm from Manchester. Not a country boy."

We set a pile of goat snack on the floor and tethered Little Ed to a table leg. He ate with a noisy grind of the teeth. Now, I could resume looking around.

Several larger nests dominated the room; they were big enough for human-sized birds. Most striking to me was one made of woven twigs, nearly floor to ceiling. The nest was a canopied shelter for whoever might occupy it. I stuck my head inside and found three large eggs made of blue, bubbly, handblown glass. Up close, I could see the detail of the woven twigs—it was an intricate, deliberate pattern, with strips of cotton fabric woven in, giving density and insulation. The fabric was visible from the inside of the nest, but not the outside. "You just want to touch it," I said, what I always found myself saying about Steve's work. He had a way of rendering his materials lush. The fabric inside was a cushion for the fragile eggs.

"I made that one out of these fucking linens we got for a wedding gift. I couldn't bring myself to sleep on those sheets anymore."

"The eggs look so safe in there," I said. Steve shrugged, the way he always used to shrug when anybody talked about his work. He had removed his sweaty dress shirt and slacks and was now clad in the Pak work uniform: black jeans, black T-shirt, black steel-toed boots, which he sat on a crate to lace and tighten.

"What are these made of?" Rowan asked, pointing to a set of eggs in another large nest. The nest was about waist-high and was shaped like a mixing bowl, made of jute rope and the dissected guts of books. The pages had been woven through the rope with a jazzy improvisation—sometimes tight and patterned, other times loose and free-form.

"Beeswax and thread," said Steve. The shells had a lacy, wrapped-dipped look, dark yellow and translucent. Each contained a yolk—a ball within a ball, the inner one made of something heavy-looking and black. "Graphite, in the middle. The egg yolk is cast graphite," he said.

"How the hell did you do that?" I said. "The hollow ball, with the other ball clean inside?"

He didn't answer. He just smiled to himself. Pure Pak.

Little Ed had finished his snack and climbed atop the table he was tethered to, to look out the window. We all stopped our art meander to watch the goat. A calm overtook him, as he looked out at the rest of the island. His head cocked, reflected in the glass.

"You suppose he's thirsty?" Steve said.

"I can tell you, *I* am thirsty," Rowan said, and helped himself to a beer from his bagfuls.

"Hey, maybe you-all will celebrate my divorce with me?" Steve said. "I got some Jäger."

"You still drink that shit?" I said.

"C'mon. It's a special occasion," Steve said, with a determined cheeriness.

I wandered over to the table and stood next to Little Ed, looking out the window. We had to get up close to see more than our own reflection. The sky was dark and cloudless. The other skyscrapers were tiny as toys. All three bridges to Brooklyn were lit like Christmas garlands. I looked for my building across the East River, but it was hidden by others.

Steve and Rowan joined me, and someone handed me a glass.

"The kids in my town used to hang out and get drunk on top of a water tower," I said. "We felt like royalty up there, in the highest spot in town, looking down on everything."

"You feel like royalty now?" asked Rowan.

"No. But shit, this is a view. I can see why Little Ed likes it."

"I like it for the quiet," Steve said. "There is zero street noise. Just wind. Sometimes I'm looking down at clouds. Just me and my stuff, and the sky. I don't even play music."

"I'm jealous," I said, looking out into the clear night.

Steve pointed through the window. "See the lot over there? Right next to the Willy B? Where they had the performance?"

"Is that it?" I said. "That spot with the yellow light?"

Rowan stood shoulder to shoulder with the goat and knocked back his Jägermeister, then resumed his gaze out the window. His reflection in the glass looked melancholy. Eyes cast on something specific. He looked straight down, not over at Brooklyn.

"Hey, Pak," I said. "How'd you hear about it? The performance?"

"One of my students. She was one of those typing ladies. The beautiful one. I shouldn't stalk her. She's nineteen. I'm trying not to think about what I'm trying not to think about. Know what I mean?"

I didn't know, not precisely. Steve's woman problems were always the opposite of mine. He had choices. Babes of all ages preening in front of him. Tests of integrity and propriety.

"Wha'd you think of it?" Steve said. "The performance? I half expected to see you *in* it."

"Wanna know what I really think?" I said, forming my critique more in my mouth than my brain—swirling it, like the pungent stuff in my glass. "I kinda resented that naive goat story. Look at him." I pointed to Little Ed. "Does he look naive? Maybe the goats just got hungry and were sick of mooching off the other goats. That's what I think. Maybe they were *realistic* goats."

"I think they got it spot-on," Rowan said, still looking wistfully down. He was looking, I realized, at the roof of the very edifice where he sat and spent his days on the telephone, winding the cord around his pinky, turning and turning in his swivel chair. "Those are all cages," he said. "Those towers we are so proud of." He placed his hand against the window, spread his fingers wide, just thin glass between him and the sky. "Containers for our vanity. We pay a heavy toll indeed, for entrance into the club; then we're admitted, and we find no one in the club is happy at all, we're just talking it all up to convince ourselves we've made the right choice. And I'm not convinced anymore. Of anything. And I've quite forgotten where the door is." He looked ready to weep. I felt the need to do something but didn't know what. We stood quiet. Little Ed lowered himself to his knees.

"To my divorce," Steve said, finally, raising his glass in one hand and the Jägermeister bottle in the other. He refilled Rowan's, and we clinked, then drank. It was bitter.

"To your freedom," I said.

"Whether I want it or not," said Steve.

Rowan pulled that prescription bottle from his pocket and knocked back another pill with a gulp of beer. "Let's toast my ouster too. I've been banished by womankind again this week."

"Me too," I said. "I think. I think but I don't know for sure. I don't even know what I supposedly did wrong."

"I do," said Rowan. "I know exactly what I did wrong. What I *cannot stop doing* wrong."

I feared it was about to be more information than I wanted. Steve locked eyes with me for a second. Rowan kept his gaze out the window.

"It's this, gents," he said, holding up his empty glass in one hand and his beer bottle in the other. "I've been given an explicit ultimatum, and I chose my undoing. It comes in liquid form, and I require it, and I am henceforth married to it."

He looked about to drop his highball glass, and I rushed forward and took it from him. I thought of Lisa, back at the office, deferring, with a weary look, Rowan's offer to *bend an elbow*. She knew something I had a better inkling of now. My new boss had a reputation. His reputation might edge him right out of his swivel chair and window office. That cage was not as permanent as he thought it was.

"I think I need to sit down," Rowan said, looking around. "No chairs?"

The turn of his body seemed to make his legs unsteady, and before either of us could stop him, Rowan flopped into one of Steve's large nests, this one made of wheatgrass and colorful rags, woven tight. The sculpture gave in only slightly against Rowan's half-inert weight. He spread-eagled his limbs and shut his eyes. The beer bottle started to slip from his relaxing hand. I lunged forward and caught it, just before it hit the floor.

"Shit. Oh, shit. I'm sorry, Steve. I had no idea—" I said. Rowan looked asleep. He was breathing, but not listening, not anymore. "I didn't know he is like this. Oh, man. Steve. You grab his other hand, eh? We'll get him over to that spot on the floor?"

Steve stared at the man sprawled inside his sculpture. Rowan's shirt, long ago untucked, sported a big Little Ed stain, a muddy hoofprint. His mouth splayed open, and his beard was coming in. He looked emaciated, with his giant Adam's apple and exposed neck; a baby bird begging for a morsel.

"Steve? What should we do?"

"It's actually holding up pretty good," he said, pointing to the nest. "Hot damn. Should I get my camera? Maybe I've been waiting for something like this. Seriously. I was wondering how much weight . . . there's no armature in there."

"You should be *mad*, Steve. You should be mad. *At me.*"

"Huh?" He was already pulling an old Polaroid off a bookshelf, flipping it open. Then he stopped, stared straight at me, and lowered the camera. "Clayman, why you keep *scratching* like that? You been doing that all night. Do you have *chiggers*? Did you bring *chiggers* into my studio?"

"No. That is the one thing I did not bring," I said. I unbuttoned the top of my shirt and pulled it aside to show him the line of sutures next to my collarbone. "Stitches. They're driving me bonkers. I need to get them out of me. I have them all over my fucking chest."

"What happened?"

"Hey, maybe you can help me take them out. It's overdue. They are seriously making me cranky."

"Can I photograph them?"

"Shouldn't we deal with *him* first?"

"He's just passed out. He'll be fine." Steve pointed the Polaroid at me.

"What the hell," I said, and removed my shirt the rest of the way, then used the opportunity to scratch at my bare skin like I'd been dying to do since breakfast.

"Get over here, in the light." He sat me on a crate under one of the bare fluorescent bulbs and stood back to get my whole chest in the picture. "Jesus, Clay. Who did that to you? Say *cheese*."

The flash popped, and Steve flapped the wet print in the air, watching the image make itself before handing it over to me. My skin was pale and pasty. The black and blue was nearly gone. The stitches looked like insects, surrounded by red welts. My face was not in the picture.

He took a handful more Polaroids: a close-up of my biggest gash, under my pectoral muscle; then several shots of Rowan, now snoring quietly, and the nest holding its own underneath him; then a shot of Little Ed, kneeling on his table, looking down at his kingdom.

Steve lined the Polaroids up on a bookshelf, facing out, and looked at them for a quiet minute, thinking, scratching that new gray hair of his, before turning back to me. "I'm glad I ran into you tonight," he said finally. "I'm embarrassed to say how afraid I was of going home by myself. Even if I did 'win' in court today. I don't feel like I won anything at all. So I get to keep my artwork. Big deal. I can always make more work."

"Yeah."

"How'd you hear about that performance, Clay?"

"I used to be one of them. I almost didn't go. My girlfriend was in it. Or whatever she is now. I wasn't sure if she wanted me there."

"Which one was she?"

"The one in the space suit."

"Oh." He paused. "*Oh.*"

"Plus, I was supposed to spend the evening with my crazy cousin Tony, but Rowan came along and seemed like he needed some adventure."

"Looks like he got it."

"Yup. Looks like we all got it."

"You really want to get those stitches out? I can't guarantee I won't hurt you again. I got some scissors that are sharp, but you really need tweezers or something like that, no?"

"Oh, hey!" I dug through my pocket and pulled out the Army knife. The tweezers were in the little sleeve, right where they belonged. "Never used these before." For once, I was ready.

Steve smiled. "All right then. You want to lie down or what?"

We used a crate for the operating table. Steve made quick work of it. At first, I looked away, but then couldn't resist watching his technique: pulling each stitch away from my skin with the tweezers, then snipping, then tugging it free with a quick yank. I barely felt it. "You could be a surgeon if you wanted to," I said.

"I was supposed to," he said. "I come from a family of surgeons. I am a great disappointment to certain parties." I couldn't imagine this person a disappointment to anybody. *The Whitney Biennial*, seriously? I didn't say it. "Did she do this to you? The naked girl?"

"No. It was him. My best friend. The dude with the eye on his stomach."

"Oh." He paused. "*Oh.* Hmm. Maybe I see what you mean about the whole thing being a song dedication."

"Yeah."

"Lucky for them you showed up to hear it."

"Yeah. For them." I thought about Tony. Would I rather have spent the evening mooching off him, having a fancy steak and creamed spinach and hearing about *Think and Believe*? "Hey, Steve," I said. "Do you suppose there's anything you can make true, just by believing in it?"

"It sure as hell doesn't work with love."

"Yeah," I said. "I think maybe the person I've loved for a year is a *persona*. I've been faithful to a damn *persona*."

"Faithful. I'm fucking sick of faith," said Steve, pointing into the air with the tweezers. "Everyone says faith is a good thing to have. But where does it leave you? A chump?"

"You know what chaps my hide?" I said. "This no-nonsense crap. No-bullshit, I-can-do-anything woman who isn't afraid of telling the truth? She won't even *talk* to me. Kind of cowardly, hiding behind a *performance*. You know?"

"Chump, I'm telling you. Fucking chump, I am. Faith is overrated. Where does it leave you?"

"You're not a chump, Steve. There's plenty worthy of faith. There must be. How about art? You can believe art means something. Maybe that makes it true."

"I guess so. But then, what happens if you stop believing and you have a studio full of crap?"

"Then the crap stops meaning anything. See, that's what I'm afraid of."

"I think that's the last one. You want to save them?" He swept the twisted sutures from the top of the crate into his cupped hand and held them up.

"Maybe it's enough just to *want* it to mean something? Art, I mean?"

"You want this?" He held the handful of stitches lower so I could see them. I shook my head. He cast them like seeds onto the dusty floor, then brushed his hands together.

I sat up. He folded my knife back up and handed it to me. I waved him off. "Nah. You keep it," I said. "For your surgical career."

"Really? Wow. Thanks," he said. "I will use this." He looked quickly around, taking stock, then back at me. "Hey, you mind if I work? I really feel like working. I have two weeks to get everything finished and crated. We can talk. It's OK."

"How you going to get it all out of here?"

"Clay, what are you, a pragmatist?"

"I can't believe you just said that. No, I'm not a pragmatist. I'm a realist. Not an artist realist, but a realist realist."

"Bullshit. You're a SURrealist. Deep down. You are. This whole thing—the shaved head, the jobby job? *Surrealist.*"

"Maybe. I have no idea what to call myself anymore."

He shrugged. "*Names.* Anyway, I'll have help," he said. "Getting this crap out. Freight elevator. Handlers."

Of course. He was that far along. Things were different now than they were back in the days of hardbound sketchbooks in the dark lecture hall. He went over to a table in the center of the space, next to a half-finished nest. This one was made of telephone wire and yellow legal paper. It was a departure. Nothing looked natural at all. Artificial colors. Factory products. He was gluing the sheets of paper end to end, then twisting them into a long, tight rope.

"How long we been friends, Steve?"

"I don't know. Fifteen years? I haven't seen you in, like, I don't know, ten, though, right?"

"You know, maybe *time* is the secret," I said. "Maybe *time* is what makes meaning. Not belief. Right? Like maybe someday years from now, I'll call you up and say, 'Remember the night that dude from Manchester passed out on one of your nest sculptures, up in your mile-high studio in the towers, and I stole Little Ed, and you took my stitches out with a Swiss Army knife?' And we'll both go *yeah, yeah*, and we'll just *know* what it means. Right?"

"You crack me up," Steve said, without looking up from his hands. "*Meaning.* Don't worry about it."

"You really don't? Worry? About meaning something?"

Steve smiled to himself. "*Naw.* I just love my materials."

I shut up. I shut up and watched him love his materials. I watched the cant of his head, his whole face focused on his hands, a distant expression as he thought about the paper he was gluing and twisting, weaving and tying into the nest, as he thought about what he thought about and tried not to think about what he tried not to think about. Then a step back, an arm fold, a slow walk around the piece to check the changing effect. There was a sweet connivance in his expression; he was a coconspirator with his paper and wood and wire. I wasn't jealous anymore. *Lucky*, Steve had called himself. I felt lucky too. To be here. To see this work before the museum would, here, in the room of its genesis.

Then I stepped back too. I took a slow walk too, looked at Steve's space. I looked at the lineup of Polaroids on the shelf. I looked at Rowan snoozing, heartbroken and baby-like in the giant nest. I looked at Little Ed, wide awake, kneeling on his table, still as a sculpture, staring out the window, entranced by his new promontory. And the window itself, and the boroughs beyond it, the nice town of steel girders and glass and cardboard replicas, and all its citizens: its depressed, its pragmatic, its manic, its curlicued, its drunken, its mystical, its diligent, its freaky motherfuckers—together with the stuff of their lives—their materials.

This was my material. I knew it now. This had always been my material, this messy human stew. Hope and heartbreak and hope again, wanting to make it matter, the *story* of taking the old wood in your hands and carving something new. I didn't know what it meant. I still don't.

But that night, in Steve Pak's studio, in the high quiet of a waning century, I was certain of one thing: I loved my material. I loved it hard.

Even when it did not love me back.

Anne Elliott has been a sculptor, English teacher, performance poet, waitress, Wall Street analyst, ukulelist, costume stitcher, database programmer, and publisher of tiny books. She now lives in Portland, Maine, with her husband and many pets. For more information, visit www.anneelliottstories.com.